S0-BCZ-730

NECESSARY
EVIL

DAVID A. VAN METER

St. Martin's Paperbacks

The characters and events in this book are fictitious. Any similarity
to real persons, living or dead, is coincidental and not intended by
the author.

Published by arrangement with Little, Brown

NECESSARY EVIL

Library of Congress Catalog Card Number: 93-10787

ISBN: 0-312-95924-9

Printed in the United States of America

Little, Brown hardcover edition published 1994
St. Martin's Paperbacks edition/January 1997

St. Martin's Paperbacks are published by St. Martin's Press, 175
Fifth Avenue, New York, NY 10010.

10   9   8   7   6   5   4   3   2   1

PRAISE FOR DAVID A. VAN METER'S *NECESSARY EVIL*

"Compelling."

—*Kirkus Reviews*

"With an obvious gift for storytelling and plotting, Van Meter makes a notable debut with this dark, fast-moving thriller about obsession and violence . . . A solid and disturbing piece of work."

—*Publishers Weekly*

"Unique and chilling."

—*Denver Post*

"In David Van Meter's new work, we watch, mesmerized, the creation of a killer from an ordinary boy. In direct, believable incidents, we see cynicism and bitterness born and flower in a once-loving soul. It's a trip lived from the inside, and it means we will never watch the evening news in quite the same way again."

—Joanne Greenberg, author of
I Never Promised You a Rose Garden

"Wrenching . . . Powerful and compelling."

—*Library Journal*

"Keep the lights on and stand back for this thriller. It will disturb sleep and keep the nightmares near."

—*Ocala Star-Banner*

"A horrifying journey through the mind of a psychopathic killer. David Van Meter has created one of the most demonic—yet believable—villain/protagonists in recent fiction. A book to be read in one sitting—preferably not late at night!"

—Sandra Scoppetone, author of the
Lauren Lorano series

For Anna and Madeleine

one

It was Grandma's birthday, a golden day in October. We'd gone to the beach for a cookout. I was fishing the little waves with a driftwood stick I'd rigged with string and a marshmallow for bait. I'd promised to catch fish for the grown-ups' lunch, but the aroma of roasting hot dogs had me rethinking the menu. Grandad was the chef, tending the meat as it cooked slowly over the fire he'd built in a pit above the high-water mark. Nearby, Grandma was busy setting out our picnic on a big, green blanket. My parents were there, too, sloshing in the knee-deep and tossing a Frisbee. They looked happy. I took things at face value back then.

The early afternoon sun was warm, but the air was cool. We wore sweaters over our bathing suits. After lunch and a walk on the beach, we'd go swimming. Long past the time school started and the air turned cool, the Atlantic Ocean stayed warm enough for swimming. In those days, we stayed as close to the ocean as we could.

At dusk, we'd all pile into the family car and head home, sunburned and satisfied. Before we were halfway there, I'd fall asleep in my mother's lap, clutching a bag of shells for my collection.

I treasure the memory of that day. At five, I thought life would go on like that forever.

two

I woke at the sound of my name. It was the twelfth of September. I was seventeen. The moon lit up the inside of the dorm bright as a lightning flash. Five of my "classmates" in the juvenile detention facility stood in a ring around my bed. Their skin shone blue in the cold light. I didn't know their names. They had kids' faces, like me, and men's dicks. I knew what they wanted. I knew it would be worse later if I yelled. I struggled to get away. Four of them grabbed and held me while the first one took his turn. I didn't cry until all five of them were through and gone. The next morning, I saw the huge bloodstain on my sheet, a red circle like the Japanese flag. As I walked to the shower, I felt their eyes. I felt their pride. Water from the shower swirled more blood around my feet and into the drain. The species had collected another payment for what I'd done.

three

For my sixth birthday, Grandad took me and a gang of my Westfield classmates downtown for lunch at the Philadelphia Club. I couldn't have put it into words, but even at six, I think I understood that it took big bucks and an impressive pedigree to be a member. There was a huge crystal chandelier in the middle of the main dining room. The walls were paneled with dark wood and hung with grand portraits of stuffy old men. I sat next to Grandad, all puffed up with pride in my Westfield Academy blazer. Our table was wide and round and covered with a white linen table cover. Each place was set with delicate, gold-trimmed china, sparkling glassware, and confusing arrangements of silver. The black waiters called everyone "Sir," even little "Mucus Face," Norris West. I looked around the table and relished the awe in my classmates' faces. I felt like royalty when they brought out a fancy cake fizzing with sparklers, and everyone sang. After lunch, we saw *In Like Flint* at a big, downtown movie theater and ate outrageous amounts of popcorn and candy.

After the movie, Grandad took us on a private tour of his bank, the Franklin National. We saw the vault; the boardroom, with its gigantic marble table; the panoramic view of Society Hill from the executive dining room; and finally, Grandad's office, with its dark red carpet, thick as bedding.

Grandad's huge desk sat in front of two arched windows that framed a postcard view of Independence Hall. In the sitting area, there was a fireplace and a hidden bar. We argued about who would be the first to sit in the high-backed swivel chair. It was like a throne, all black leather and padding. I took the last turn and waited until I was sure they were all looking at me. Then, at the right moment, I sat back proudly with my hands pressed together pretentiously under my chin. "Gentlemen," I said, "meet the real Billy McIlvain, Creator of Heaven and Earth."

four

I was very close to my mother when I was growing up. I remember her sobbing when I started first grade. I begged her not to make me go. I think she would have let me stay home with her if she thought she could get away with it.

She and my grandmother and I went everywhere together. At the end of the day, when I was tired, they let me hang between them like a monkey. That Christmas, when I was six, the three of us rode the train into Philadelphia and went to Wanamaker's department store. I stood in line for almost an hour waiting to see Santa; then we went into this huge dining room and ate lunch. Chicken à la king and sundaes. My mother loved Grandma. They were always laughing and gossiping. They loved to fuss over each other's clothes and decorations. They were more like girlfriends than mother and daughter.

Grandma died suddenly the following spring, not too

long before I turned seven. I was never sure exactly what killed her. I do know it was Grandma's death that started my mother downhill. After that, it kept getting tougher to be her kid.

five

I was in prison thirteen years. I was a teenager when I went in and past thirty when I got out. It wasn't the same place all those years, of course. But it was prison.

When you're a kid, they don't want you getting raped by the big bad men in the real prisons. There's plenty of time for that when you're older. In the adolescent treatment facilities, it's just the other kids and the guards and teachers and the shrinks and the volunteers with their pockets stuffed full of dirty pictures who rape you. That is, if you're pretty, which I was at seventeen, when I went in.

I don't know how much of the change in my appearance was just getting older and how much of it was being inside. I got my nose broken twice and they didn't fix it right either time. It's not mashed or anything, it's just not the nose I was born with. I guess the biggest change I see is in my eyes. I have hard eyes. The lights have burned out. I was still pretty innocent when I went in, but it's hard for me to think of anything cruel one human being can do to another that I haven't seen or experienced by now.

You learn to survive, or you don't. One of my rules was "If it isn't happening to me, it isn't happening." That saved me a lot of grief. Over time, I developed an instinct I call "critical awareness." It means watching your ass when you're not aware you're doing it. Every sensory input passes though a subconscious screening system. Anything's not right, it gets flagged. The alarms go off. If you had to depend on conscious thought, you'd go nuts. A lot of guys do.

By my early twenties, I was pretty well settled in at Graterford. Everyone who wanted to mess with me had done it. They knew I could handle myself. I'd been lifting before I went in. On the inside, I learned to box. Boxing is encouraged. It's good mental hygiene for the inmates to beat the shit out of one another; it keeps them from doing it to the guards.

I knew prison was going to wreck my life even more than it was already wrecked, but I made up my mind early that I wasn't going to trash my mind with drugs and start saying "fuck" every other word like so many of the dumb, messed-up guys on the inside.

Reading helped me to survive. There was the prison library, also books and old magazines donated by bleeding hearts. Of course, security had to make sure the stuff was suitable, which meant they confiscated everything they wanted for themselves. The leftovers usually fell into one of two categories: complete trash, like outdated catalogs, and anything that took an IQ over 80 to comprehend.

In the category of complete trash was this three-year-old alumnae magazine from Sarah Lawrence College. Think about it: Some daffy debutante donates her Sarah Lawrence alumnae mag to the state pen. Anyway, I'm very grateful to her, whoever she is. (They tear off the address labels.) Her cast-off magazine saved my life.

six

These days, I work as a security guard at the Legacy Mint. I'm on the graveyard shift, 7:00 PM to 3:00 AM. It pays $7.50 an hour; no background check. Maybe it's a corporate guilt complex. They make millions contaminating our culture with treasures like the Angel Elvis Figurine and simulated-bronze busts of guys like Schwarzkopf and Ralph Kramden. "Collectibles," they call them. Being the security system for Legacy's assorted treasures appeals to my sense of irony. It's overpriced crap for gullible people with no taste. I guess anyone who'd buy a set of china decorated with scenes from their favorite soap opera deserves to get ripped off.

Just to complete the résumé, I also work sometimes as a sub delivering the *Philadelphia Inquirer*. Those nights, I go right from the mint to the paper drop. The timing is perfect.

I'm thirty-three. Jesus was thirty-three when he was crucified. I look like Mr. Joe Average. You might see me on a street corner and pay as much attention as you would to a trash can or a hydrant. I wear glasses now and my hair isn't as thick as it used to be. But I'm not exaggerating when I say I was a good-looking kid, a real all-American boy: Curly brown hair, streaked with blond. Clear green eyes. Freckles. A nice build, tall and wiry. When I got arrested and there were all those pictures of me in the paper, girls I'd never met sent me love notes and pictures of themselves with no clothes on. Like Warhol said, I was famous for fifteen minutes. I was a hero.

I have no heroes myself. I did once, but I learned what happens when you care too much about one person. I do have a purpose, not that you'd know it from the work I do. My purpose is to close the circle.

I live in Delaware County, near Philadelphia. It's a studio apartment in a cardboard building right off West Chester Pike, not far from where I grew up, at least in miles. Four hundred and twenty-five dollars a month, if you can believe it, and it's not much bigger than my last cell.

I guess it's prison decor. Nothing on the walls. No extra possessions. I like it that way. I'm a minimalist, I suppose. I like order. Inside, I got off on the order, the routine. The predictability was reassuring.

I keep it very clean. I bought a manual carpet sweeper, a broom, and a sponge mop as soon as I moved in. I have a thing about cleanliness and order. I don't mind admitting it. I blame it on Grace, my mother, the way our house was such a shit heap when she was drinking. I could never live that way again. The shrinks inside tried to make me think excessive concern for order and cleanliness had something to do with guilt or shame or hiding from who I really am. I told them it was bullshit. I told them I couldn't stand the filth in our house when my mother was drinking. I told them I couldn't stand to be reminded of it.

seven

My parents were away the weekend I turned eight. It was odd for them to go away together. They broke the news one morning while I was getting ready for school. Grace babbled anxious apologies while my father paralyzed me with his trademark grin.

Grandad stayed with me that weekend. He never missed one of my birthdays.

On Friday night, we had a fancy dinner at the Merion Cricket Club. I wore my school blazer and gray flannel pants. Grandad drank a toast to me with champagne. We had shrimp cocktail, artichokes, and prime rib. The club's little combo played "Happy Birthday" while the waitress presented us with enormous servings of baked alaska. While we ate dessert, I opened the presents Grandad had brought. One was a compass that lights up. I still have it.

When we got home, Grandad went to the kitchen to make a call. I was supposed to go upstairs and get ready for bed, but I stood on the steps and eavesdropped as I often did when my parents were talking secretively or having a fight. Grandad was talking to a woman. It was hard for me to think of him having girlfriends but I knew he did. Grandma had been dead over a year.

Grandad told the lady what a great time he and I had had at dinner. I felt so proud. It sounded like they'd canceled plans so Grandad could stay with me. He didn't complain; he just thanked her for being nice about it. She must have said something about my being his favorite grandchild. He didn't deny it. He said he couldn't help the way he felt.

I had no chance to savor those precious words. Without warning, I threw up all over myself and everything else within a three-foot radius. It splattered the wall and even dripped from the little spindles under the banister. I was overwhelmed by the awful thing I'd done and immediately burst into tears.

Grandad was there in seconds. I was terrified that he'd be furious the way my father always was when I spilled something or got sick. I couldn't stand to think of Grandad being mad at me. I shouldn't have worried. The only thing he cared about was me. He picked me up and carried me to the second-floor bathroom where Grace kept the thermometer. I had a temperature of 103.

Grandad never said a word about the mess. While I showered and got into my pajamas, he got busy cleaning it up. I can still see him on those steps, swabbing up my vomit: The chairman of the Franklin National Bank. My grandad. When he saw me watching, he looked up with a face full of love and asked if I felt better after my shower. That's what he cared about: whether I felt better.

While he was reading me a story, I got chills and a

stomachache. He was supposed to sleep in my parents' bedroom, but he got a pillow and blanket and slept on the bare floor next to me. I woke up a lot that night. Whether because I was sick or just to see if he was still there, I'm not sure. But he never left me.

I can still see him curled up on the floor of my room. I will never forget.

eight

The numbing monotony of prison life could really get to me if I let it. There was no future, only a present that extended to infinity. I concentrated on the little events like meals and security checks that broke up the days. When I had identified enough of them, it helped to create an impression that time was passing. Still, I have to admit that there were times when I wondered if it was. At other times, as the number of birthdays behind the walls started to add up and my hair started to thin and I became conscious of being closer to thirty than to twenty and I began to appreciate what it meant that I would have the first decade of my adult life and part of the second literally stolen, at those times, I couldn't bear to think that time was passing. I would have cut off both my legs to get out of there.

I found the Sarah Lawrence alumnae mag one April morning when a bunch of us intellectual types who helped out in the library were going through a pile of donated books and periodicals. I laughed out loud. None of the others could understand what I thought was funny.

It was in the back, with the class notes, where I saw him, in a little picture about the size of two postage stamps: Deidre Thayer Cummings, Class of '76, and her new husband. The notes said the lovebirds were on their honeymoon in St. Bart's. Oh joy, oh joy! They looked oh so pleased with themselves. Venus and Adonis were standing next to a little outdoor bar with a thatched roof, and holding up these drinks that had tiny parasols sticking out of them. They looked so smug, they must have been toasting the good luck of the solar system for having them in it. I suppose she was in her midthirties then, a blond, buck-toothed socialite type. I figured it was her second marriage. He looked older, around fifty, but perfectly fit. The hatred erupted the instant I saw his face.

I thought about it for a while, the hate, and decided I liked it, especially the feeling of connectedness that went with it. It might have been healthier to dismiss the whole business, but before long, I realized that finding Mr. Howe had given me a reason to go on living.

Almost immediately, I enlisted my friend Stan Mink, a swindler of some distinction, in the venture. Stan began his working life writing computer programs for the IRS, but he was a born con man, and while he swears he had never considered committing criminal acts as an adult, even after years of teenage escapades, it wasn't long before the potential for illegal profit that resulted from having access to intimate financial information about millions of people proved to be more than his true nature could resist. After working a variety of scams for several years, however, Stan screwed up and landed in the pokey. He took it very well, though. He had a short sentence and the pleasure of knowing that he had nearly two million dollars stashed away, earning compound interest, tax free, while he did his time.

Stan, of course, worked with the prison's computers. To his credit, he completely redesigned the internal system and was unfailingly generous with his expertise, teaching training courses for inmates as well as the prison staff. But Stan's mind is one that, without even thinking about it, finds the weaknesses in any system, computer or otherwise; and by a perverse quirk of DNA, instead of wanting to correct those weaknesses, he is driven to exploit them. The prison computer system was no exception. Within weeks, he was making mischief. He trusted only a few of us well enough to let on what he was up to. I considered myself lucky to be among them, and though I would love to proclaim Stan's genius to the world, I could never betray him.

I think Stan was actually flattered when I approached him about Mr. Howe. Within days, he was generating confidential information about the man: traffic tickets, medical data, credit reports. I've been able to track practically every aspect of Howe's life. When Stan got out, a few months after I did, the flow of information turned into a tide. Fat envelopes of printouts began to arrive at my home, sometimes two a month. Eventually, Stan started to complain because all the information he'd generated wasn't being put to use. I could see what was happening and I warned him to lay off: Howe belonged exclusively to me.

I respected the fact that Stan's pragmatic nature had

been offended, and I was more grateful to him than I could say, but not long after this exchange, I cut off all communication between us. For reasons of security, I could not even assure Stan that his work would eventually pay off. But it will.

Very soon.

nine

TARGET/SUBJECT: *Charles Spencer Howe. Married. Wife: Deidre. Children: Andrew, age 5; Elizabeth, age 7. Occupation: Trustee, The Eli Gentry Foundation, Boulder, CO. Initial Contact: alumnae magazine, Sarah Lawrence College.*

William C. McIlvain, age thirty-three.
Excerpt from my Private Computer Journal.
File Name: *Nemesis*

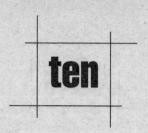

ten

At Graterford, there was this Polish guy, Milos Pizak. He cleared his throat. Always the same, three times in a row. "Unnngghh . . . Unnngghh . . . Unnngghh." He would do it every couple of minutes for hours at a time. All night sometimes, when people wanted to sleep. The acoustics on the block were so hot, you could hear a guy at the far end cut cheese. Pizak sounded loud as a diesel. Guys would yell and scream at him to stop. "Unnngghh . . . Unnngghh . . . Unnngghh." Night after night. "Unnngghh . . . Unnngghh . . . Unnngghh." Thirty times an hour. Pizak claimed he couldn't help it. No one believed him.

One day after Pizak had been on the block almost a year, someone with a homemade butcher knife cleared his throat permanently, all the way to his spine.

That first night without Pizak, the block cheered ten minutes for whoever did it. There is such a thing as showing consideration for your neighbors, even on the inside; especially on the inside.

Now I don't think of myself as a violent person, but I cheered as hard as the rest. The solution was extreme, but the greater good of the community had been served. Pizak had plenty of chances to change his behavior. His mode of violence was to put himself above everyone else. As the cheering showed, his killer had merely acted out the will of the community, and therefore should not have been judged violent; that is, if "violence" defines a behavior that conflicts with the common good.

I believe violence is a tool. If I use a hammer or a saw, that doesn't mean I'm a carpenter. If I fantasize about screwing Madonna, that doesn't prove I'm a rapist.

My father, Ned, was truly violent. He may never have used a gun or knife on a person, but he had ways of hurting that were much worse. Without raising a hand, he could make you feel lower than whale shit.

Some of my earliest memories of Ned involve his fights with my mother. Some nights, a few drinks was all it took, and they were off. I don't know how often they fought. My mind has erased some of those memories. Maybe two or three times a week when things were really bad, but I can't be sure. I would lie in my bed on the third floor and try not to listen. Sometimes I turned on my little radio or even sang to block the sound of their hate. When I heard crashing, I got afraid he would kill her. I couldn't stand to think of anything happening to Grace. When the fights were really bad and I couldn't stand it anymore, I would start down the stairs one at a time, hoping with each new step that the fighting would stop. As terrible as it was, as much as I wanted to run away, something made me go closer instead. A few times, I got as far as the kitchen door. I remember stand-

ing there one night and listening to her sob. I could tell
he was hurting her. I didn't know what to do. A panicky
feeling came over me. I cracked open the door. He was
shaking her by the shoulders and cursing her. Her dress
and bra were pulled down on one side so her left breast
was partly uncovered. The kitchen chairs were turned
over and there were a couple of broken dishes on the
floor. She was trying to hit him, but as close as he was
holding her, her punches had no effect. Without thinking, I yelled at him to stop. He turned toward me. His
face was all hot and twisted. He shouted at me to get
out, like I was an animal. He didn't care what I saw; he
just didn't want me to interfere. She tried to break free,
but he started shaking her again. Her head whipped
back and forth. She called my name; her knees buckled.
I ran to her and wedged myself between them. Their
waists were at eye level. I tried to push him away from
her but he was too big. He grabbed me by the collar of
my pajamas and tried to fling me aside but I held on to
my mother's dress with one hand and punched at him
with the other. I was crying and very scared. The pajama
collar felt like it would strangle me. I was afraid he
would kill us. I don't remember what happened. I guess
the fight stopped. I don't even remember exactly what
they fought about. I can guess: his affairs, her drinking
and spending. But, it's funny, I really can't remember
words in connection with those fights, just the noise and
the tears.

eleven

The Fourth of July, the year of my tenth birthday. I woke up sweating. It wasn't an omen. I always woke up sweating in the summer. My bedroom was the hottest place in the house. Somebody had put a partition across the west end of the attic and finished the walls and ceiling. It wasn't meant to be a bedroom at all.

Down on the second floor, the air was fifteen degrees cooler. I heard my father counting off sit-ups in their bedroom. There was another bedroom next to theirs, but Ned claimed that was his "study."

On the first floor, I saw signs that one of them had spent the night on the chair-bed in the living room. Grace was in the kitchen; I knew it even though the door was closed. I put my hand on the door to push it aside, but for a second, I couldn't. I didn't want to have to deal with her. I just wanted it to be two-thirty, when Grandad was due to take me fishing. I pushed open the kitchen door and forced a smile.

"Good morning, Mom."

She sat in a slouch at the kitchen table. Sunlight reflected from the neighbor's white siding came through the little window above the sink and gave the room an eerie glow. The odd light made Grace look even paler than usual. The droopy white robe didn't help. I could tell she was struggling to clear her brain. For a second, I wasn't sure she recognized me.

"Good morning, darling," she said. "Did you have a good night?"

"Okay, I guess." I started to organize a bowl of cereal for myself. I knew I had to keep my distance from Grace's moods. She was like a swamp when she got like that, and if you made the wrong move, you got sucked down into the same dark, unhappy place where she was. "Couldn't I sleep on the back porch, Mom?"

"Oh, Billy . . ."

"Nobody would see me."

"Billy . . ." She was shaking her head.

"I know," I said. " 'It's bad enough living with the trash without acting like them.' "

"You shouldn't mock your father." She fished the last Benson and Hedges out of a crumpled pack.

All I could find was an ancient box of Grape-Nuts that had been wasted by the humidity. I considered complaining but realized it might give Grace the idea she ought to cook for me. I stood on a chair and began rummaging through the freezer.

"What are you looking for?" she asked.

"French-bread pizzas."

"For breakfast?"

"They're really nutritious, Mom."

"I suppose they are." She sighed. I heard the movement of her chair behind me. "I should have gone shopping," she said. I found the pizzas. Grace was closing in. I knew she'd want a hug and kiss. I would have climbed all the way into the freezer and closed the door if I could, but I was trapped. My skin went tight as her fingertips touched my shoulders. She smelled of cigarette smoke and stale perfume.

"Do you love me, Billy?" she asked in a tiny voice.

"Of course I do, Mom." I said the words to a pint of strawberry ice cream, but I meant them. I tossed the frozen pizzas on the counter and gave her a big hug. Soon I felt the trembling that came with her tears.

As Grace stood there holding on to me, I heard my father bounce down the stairs. "I'm off," he yelled. The screen door slammed sharply behind him. Grace squeezed me tighter. I felt sick.

When Grace finished crying, she let go and shuffled off to get dressed. The frozen pizza was in my stomach a minute later. I'm sure it would have tasted better if I'd cooked it, but I couldn't wait to get out of there.

I took a walk to kill some of the time before Grandad was due to come for me. I took lots of walks in those days. Being out was always better than being home.

We lived at 929 Ammons Street in Llanfair, "the Asshole of the Main Line." Everybody knew the expression. The Main Line is a wealthy area outside of Philadelphia that runs along the railroad tracks. Llanfair is this funky little town near the east end. Somebody told me it was where the railroad workers used to live sixty or seventy years ago. Main Liners have always made jokes about

Llanfair being where the poor people live, so the town has an inferiority complex.

Our family moved to Llanfair a couple of years after I was born. Grace came from an old Philadelphia family. According to her, Ned thought he was marrying money. To everyone's regret, he was wrong. My parents weren't thrilled about moving from the apartment in Bryn Mawr to Llanfair, but with me in the terrible twos, Grace said they needed more room.

Most of the houses in Llanfair are old and small. But they're nearly all well kept, and most have wide front porches and big shade trees. Some of the bigger places even have cupolas and catwalk balconies.

Llanfair was a wonderful town for walks when I lived there. With the houses so close together and a high-grade assortment of kooks and characters scattered among the everyday folks, it was like a zoo, with the exhibits constantly changing. Really, the only thing wrong with Llanfair is that it's surrounded by rich people.

twelve

Llanfair always had a carnival on the Fourth of July. I hung out there and at the train station until it was past the time when my mother had said she was going out. There was a note waiting for me when I got home.

> Billy—
> Please don't let Grandaddy bring in a lot of smelly fish!! We have absolutely nowhere to put them!! If you want to save a few fillets, that would be fine. Have fun!!
>
> > Love, Mummy
>
> P.S. Your bag is in your room.

The crack about "a few fillets" annoyed me. Ever since Grandad chartered the boat for our fishing trip, I'd imagined myself coming home like a hero with a record-breaking catch of gleaming game fish so huge, so impressive, it would have Grace gushing, and wring the rare smile or word of praise from my father.

Ned was English. According to him, the Main Line snobs at the club where he was tennis pro tried to affect English speech and mannerisms. That made him feel superior. He always said that if he'd stayed in England, he would have been a champion tennis player. According to him, it was too much for a young man to adjust to the ways of a new country and play his best. He blamed "the Jew businessman" who brought him over. "He was so busy pretending to be gentile," Ned said, "that he never learned a goddamned thing about tennis. . . ." It was the same crap every time Ned had a few scotches. "Two matches I lost and he dropped me. Two bloody matches. He went off with some whore from the movies who'd had her nose done so she could pretend to be gentile, too. . . ."

I checked out the bag Grace had packed: a change of clothes; toothbrush, no paste; suntan lotion; no comb; and a roll of toilet paper. Grace always thought places wouldn't have toilet paper.

I heard thunder. At the carnival, I'd noticed a band of dark clouds in the west. I worried that the weather would spoil our trip. I put the toilet paper back in the hall closet and got some toothpaste and a comb. Out of respect for Grace, I guess, I kept the suntan lotion. It had probably slipped her mind that we'd be fishing at night.

Downstairs in the sideboard was our heirloom sterling-silver carving knife. It came out once a year, at Thanksgiving. Grandad did the carving. With that knife in his hand, paper-thin slices of turkey seemed to fall from the bird. I couldn't think of a better tool to clean our catch, but as I admired the intricate monogram on its handle, I realized that Grandad might think there was

something disrespectful about using his greatgrand-
mother's wedding gift to gut bluefish. In the kitchen, I
found a hollow-ground chef's knife with a plastic handle
and put that in my bag instead. Then I remembered the
compass Grandad had given me for my eighth birthday
and ran to get it from the top drawer of the chest in my
room. I was ready. I decided to lock up and wait on the
front porch.

I'd barely sat down when I spotted Grandad's car at
the end of the block. A minute later, he was waiting for
his hug. "Hello there, Billy, old man!" he said grandly.
"How the heck are you?" As always, the smile was a
foot wide and full of delight. I held back with almost
everybody, but not with this man. I jumped into his
arms.

"I'm great, Grandad! How are you?"

"Outstanding! Got everything you'll need?"

"Yes, sir. I even brought my compass. See?"

"Thatta boy! Is your mother home?"

"She's at the club," I said. Grandad dropped my little
plastic flight bag into the trunk. It made me feel good to
see it next to his handsome leather overnighter.

"Okay, then let's shove off."

Grandad had wanted to see Grace. Frequently, Ned
arranged things so she had to choose between him and
Grandad. Grandad knew why Grace stayed away from
him, and tried to pretend he wasn't hurt.

If Grandad hadn't had money, a fancy pedigree, and
been chairman of one of Philadelphia's oldest banks, he
might have made a living on his looks. When there was
a family party of some sort, usually at Great-aunt Edith's, he always attracted a crowd of women. His hair

was silver-white, combed straight back, and parted just left of center. He told me he first grew his pencil mustache when he was at Princeton. It was black then, but it had turned gray. He was sixty-two, but his pale blue eyes were still bright and lively as a kid's. He had a body better than most guys do in their twenties. I guess fifty years of tennis and swimming the surf will do that.

We were crossing the Delaware River on the Walt Whitman Bridge when Grandad broke a brief silence by saying, "You know, Billy, you're just like me!" I couldn't imagine a greater compliment. "I even looked like you do when I was ten. Do you find it hard to believe that your grandad was ever ten years old?"

"No, sir. I've looked at Grandma's old albums quite a lot. They're full of pictures of you." I was glowing.

"I have vivid memories of the year I was ten. The family lived in Chestnut Hill, not far from your great-aunt Edith's."

"Mom drove by the house once. It's huge."

"It was during the Depression, when I was ten. Our family was very lucky compared to so many others. Some people lost everything. That big old house was filled with less fortunate friends. Father was a kind-hearted man. . . ."

"Did you have fun, Grandad, when you were ten?"

"Oh, my yes. With all those people around, there were children everywhere. We made some wonderful mischief. In fact, as happy as the parents were to get back on their feet as the economic situation improved, we kids hated to break it up. Freddy Stolbert's family stayed at the house almost a year. He works at the bank. I had lunch with him just last week. Every time I see Fred, it seems he reminds me of the time we loaded up his older sister's bedclothes with mice. I can still hear her screaming," Grandad laughed, "and do you know, Billy, she still gives me the deep freeze after fifty-three years?"

"I don't blame her," I chuckled.

Grandad turned off the main highway onto a country road someone had recommended to him as a shortcut years earlier, when the family still owned a house in Ocean City.

"Where did you get all the mice?" I asked after a mile or two of gazing at the fields and tidy houses along the road.

"We trapped them, my boy! Actually, that's how it all started. . . ." I got the feeling Grandad had been waiting for an excuse to tell me more. "I designed a trap using a cigar box. Ethel, our housekeeper, had complained there were mice in her room and in the pantry as well. We had rather good luck with the trap and before long had gathered seven or eight. We kept them in an enormous jar with screen over the top. Fred and I agreed we couldn't part with our little collection without putting them to some good use. His sister was our principal adversary so we hit on a plot to breed the mice until we had enough to launch a campaign of harassment that would force old Marjorie to beg us for mercy.

"The morning after we booby-trapped the poor girl's bed . . . and her reaction didn't disappoint us; no sir, not a bit—she was wild, hysterical! Well, the next morning, we stuffed all but a half dozen of the mice we had left into her schoolbag and lunch pail." Tears of laughter

streamed down Grandad's face. And mine, too. "Th-they
sent her home from school at ten! Poor Marjorie, the rest
of the time her family was with us, she wouldn't go near
that bed. I think Fred and I would have gotten off scot-
free if we hadn't packed the mice in her school things.
That may have been the last spanking I ever got. Father's
face was like a beet.

"Marjorie didn't speak to me for thirty years. She finally broke the silence when our trust department began
administering her mother's estate. She knew I was the
real culprit. Fred simply wasn't clever enough."

The two lanes of blacktop cut through patches of pinewoods and swamp. In between, where the flat, open
countryside hadn't been bulldozed for somebody's subdivision, there were little farms where they grew fruits
and vegetables. Grandad said we'd stop on the way back
and buy tomatoes to eat with our fish.

The clouds were thinner over southern New Jersey.
Despite the air-conditioning and smoke-colored glass,
the sun's heat reached deep inside the car. I moved into
the shady spot next to Grandad. "Grandad," I said,
"what did you mean, really, when you said I'm just like
you?"

He smiled. "You were sitting there, just a little boy to
most, but I knew you weren't thinking little-boy
thoughts. You're brighter than the rest and more re-
sourceful. You have a lot of things on your mind. You
think thoughts beyond the grasp of most adults, and
you're more sophisticated. I was like that; at least I think
I was. It isn't easy. A good family can make all the difference. . . ." His voice trailed off. "I looked at you and
I saw myself."

"Want to know what I was thinking, when you said I looked like you?"

"You bet."

"I was thinking, 'I wish we didn't have to go back. I wish we could go on fishing forever, just you and me.'"

"I do, too, Billy," Grandad said. "I do, too."

thirteen

The parking lot of the Cape Fair Marina was paved in broken clamshells. Grandad's car made a crunching sound as it rolled over them. My heart was pounding like a jackhammer. I tried not to let on how excited I was, but the sight of a pair of sunburned fishermen dragging a big gunnysack bursting with bluefish was too much.

"Wow, Grandad, did you see *that*? Those fish must weigh a ton!" I climbed around in my seat to get a better look.

"You don't think we're going to catch that many fish, do you, young man?"

"Gee, I hope so. Almost as much anyway."

"Well, I expect us to fill *two* gunnysacks, with some left over to give away when we get in!"

When we got out of the car, Grandad pulled a scrap of paper from the pocket of his dark blue short-sleeved shirt. "Let's see, slip eight-D. I guess it's over that way." After we got a few things from the trunk, he reached for my hand and we started walking. It was torture for me not to run. Our load was light: just windbreakers, a camera bag, and a picnic basket. The charter included everything but food.

It was a little after five-thirty. The sun was making long shadows; a brisk breeze was blowing from the sea. I sucked in the rich salt air. If there weren't so much else to feel good about, I'd have been happy just being cool. We passed by row after row of handsome boats: sailboats, fishing boats, yachts fit for presidents and kings, speedboats, even houseboats—snug and tidy. I looked everywhere for slip eight-D. A cloud of gulls, shrieking for their supper, circled over the wake of a trawler passing in the channel beyond the marina. The boardwalk widened out as Grandad and I entered an area reserved for the big party boats that charge by the head for deep-sea fishing; just beyond were the charter boats. It didn't take me long to spot the *Ebony Witch*.

She was every bit as beautiful as I had dreamed. Her hull was as black as her name implied. The cabin, flying bridge, and gunwales were pure white. She had the look of a panther, sleek and cunning. Her tall bow stabbed the water like a knife and fanned out suddenly at her deck. I could visualize the sea yielding to her. The *Witch* was not made to be tied up. On the broad, teak deck behind the cabin were four fighting chairs, each upholstered in waterproof red fabric and mounted on a shiny chrome pedestal base.

"Oh, Grandad, is that boat really going to be *ours?*"

"Only the best, my boy!" Grandad squatted on the pier behind the *Witch* and squinted into the glare. "Maybe we're a little early," he said. "Captain Buch, are you on board?" I felt a knot of worry. They should have been there, but the boat couldn't have looked emptier or more closed up. "Hey, cheer up, Bill," Grandad said, rising. "They wouldn't dare miss a chance to take *us* fishing!" Grandad scanned the dock, his hands on his hips. I hung my feet over the edge of the boardwalk and sat uneasily. Below me, the salty bay water lapped lazily against the *Witch*'s hull.

Soon, I was aware of a thumping in the boards beneath me. A stocky man of fifty with weathered skin the color of strong tea was walking briskly toward us along the pier. Three paces behind him was a redheaded boy about seventeen, wearing cutoffs and a sleeveless sweatshirt that said "Tampa" in flowing script over a palm tree background. "I think we've got our crew, Billy, old man!" Grandad said happily. I got up quickly and took my place at Grandad's side.

"Chesterton?" the man asked. His voice was strong and friendly. He was all in khaki. His sweat-stained captain's hat was pushed back so its brow was away from his face.

"Captain Buch, sir, I'm glad to see you!" Grandad greeted the captain with a hearty handshake as he joined us. "This is my grandson, Billy McIlvain. I don't know which of us is more excited about the trip!"

"Hello there, Billy," the captain said as he shook my hand. His palm reminded me of pine bark. "I'd say you fellas picked a real good day for it. They've been practically jumping in the boat! Meet my nephew, Lance. He's gonna mate for me."

"Hi ya," Lance mumbled self-consciously. As he spoke, he took a half step backward and waved awkwardly with his forearm. "How's it goin'?"

After we stowed the picnic, the captain started the engines and Lance cast off. My weeks of anticipation were finally over. We were under way. As the *Witch* proceeded slowly through the back waterways toward the inlet, Lance joined Captain Buch on the flying bridge. Grandad took the solitary post at the bow, and I sat in the fighting chair I'd picked out for myself. If I had been any happier, it might actually have hurt.

Burbling along in the narrow channel, we passed a huge seafood restaurant decorated with neon sailfish and martinis. The line of people waiting to get in stretched from the front door to a miniature golf course halfway around the block. It amazed me that anyone would stand in line to eat fish.

Wind and current moving swiftly in opposite directions created a nice chop of fizzing whitecaps that met us at the inlet and made things bumpy. Outside the channel, foaming breakers rushed by and crashed in the shallows. On the down side of every swell, the brisk breeze whipped up the *Witch*'s bow wave and sent a drenching splash across the deck. Ahead was the Atlantic, calm but majestic, blue on blue.

The first good spraying drove Grandad to a drier vantage point. Shielded by the bridge, he took a new post by the starboard gunwale as far forward as the flying spray allowed. I remembered seeing him like that before, on his sailboat the *Eastern Star*. It seemed so long ago. Grandma was there. Her death had taken everyone by surprise. She wasn't even old; not really. Grace cried about it for weeks. Grandad didn't say much; he stayed away from us for a while. Grace said he'd be lonely, but he didn't act like it. It was hard to imagine Grandad being lonely or getting old, like Grace said he was.

Despite the wind and the motion of the boat, Grandad stayed strangely still, as if he were a part of it all. His eyes saw what no one else could see. Watching him, I was suddenly overcome with a sad, empty feeling. Without thinking, I went to his side and hugged him around the waist as tight as I could. He reached down with one of his huge hands and rubbed my back, as if he knew what I was thinking. The hollowness in my throat and the scared feeling inside me went away. I looked up and lost myself in his smile.

The sun was hanging crimson above a bed of purple clouds when we reached the Montauk Bore, a deep hole at the bottom of the ocean that was almost synonymous with good bluefishing. Earlier in the day, according to Captain Buch, there had been a crowd of boats around the bore representing almost every Jersey town with an anchorage. For company, the *Ebony Witch* now had only the *Big Bob*, a ninety-foot head boat, half loaded, from Townshend's Inlet.

"Slack tide," the captain grumbled as he climbed down from the bridge. "Nothing doing anywhere 'cording to the radio chatter. Should pick up in a bit. We'll have a strong incoming tide most of the night; moon's almost full. You could hardly write a recipe for better fishin'. If it weren't the Fourth, they'd be thick as bees at a honeypot out here."

As we began trolling in wide circles around the bore, Lance released enough line from my reel so that my lure was skipping and diving along the surface about a hundred feet behind the boat. The drag on the reel was set loose enough that I wouldn't lose the rod if a big one struck without warning. I gripped the rod and reel with enough force to squeeze the blood from my hands. My eyes were locked on the lure. Just below it, I was sure, dozens of scaly monsters were competing for the right to try me first.

The breeze slacked off as the sun settled into the bed of clouds along the horizon. At nearly twelve miles, the coastline was barely visible. The tiny silhouetted buildings reminded me of the broken teeth of an old zipper. The fuzz on my forearms was damp with evening dew. Underneath was a fresh crop of goose bumps. I became aware for the first time of the sorrowful clanging of the buoy that marked the bore. It was topped with a light that blinked on at irregular intervals. I stood rigid with tension. Grandad leaned casually against the stern, holding his rod as if it were part of him.

We'd been fishing about fifteen minutes when the *Big Bob* came to life with a huge roar. Seconds later, a cloud of diesel smoke passed over the *Witch*. Captain Buch's cigarette hit the water with a hiss. "Tide oughta start runnin' pretty quick now," he said. I checked myself; I didn't want to get caught with my guard down.

"I didn't see anyone on the *Big Bob* catch anything," Grandad said. The *Bob* circled away from the *Witch* a courteous distance, then plowed, full throttle, toward home.

"No better spot on the coast for three weeks," Buch said defensively.

Suddenly, my rod snapped against the stern with a sharp crack. *"I got one!"* I yelled. Line rushed freely from my reel.

"Go get 'em, tiger!" Grandad roared. He stepped away to give me room. Almost at once, Lance was there, arms around me, tightening the drag on my reel.

"Let me do it!" I said. "I want to do my own!" I cranked the reel furiously as line continued to unspool.

"Just tryina help, Bill," Lance assured me. "Let me tighten up on him a little. See? Keep your rod up. Don't leave no slack in it. Stay with him." Lance looked to Grandad for his approval. Grandad smiled broadly, and just then, his rod bent, shaking, toward the water.

"Hey! We're partners, Bill! I've got one, too!" He horsed it back to set the hook and began to reel in.

"Guess them people on the other boat just don't know how to fish," Buch laughed.

"Wow! He's strong!" I moaned. "Must be a whale."

"Stay with him, Bill," Grandad urged.

"Keep the tip of your rod up, son. Up! Put your back in it. Don't try to do it all with your arms. That's better." Buch must have seen tens of thousands of fish landed over the years. Still, I could tell he hated to see one get away.

"Guess you've got a better fighter than I do, Billy," Grandad said cheerfully.

"I can see him, Grandad!" I said. "I see your fish right there." The black-silver shape at the end of Grandad's line was now less than a foot beneath the surface; the feathered lure hung foolishly from its mouth.

"Gaff, Lance!" the captain ordered.

"No need," Grandad said as he lifted the fish over the stern with his rod.

"Nice one," I said, admiring Grandad's fish as it wriggled furiously on the deck. "I'll never get mine in."

"Keep fighting, Billy. I'd be happy to spell you."

"No thanks," I said. "I wanna do it."

Lance freed the hook from Grandad's catch, a three-pound blue, and tossed the unhappy fish into the big, built-in icebox at the stern. I pressed against the gunwale for support. My shoulders hurt. Everything hurt. I reeled line away from the stubborn fish a foot at a time, pausing as it dived for the bottom, holding, leaning, straining against it with my rod and back. Sometimes the fish took more line in a dive than I'd just won with the reel. My forearms were pure pain from elbow to wrist.

Suddenly, the fish took off toward the bow and bent the tip of my rod practically to the water. "Where's he going?" I cried.

"Go *with* him!" the captain ordered. "Walk! Move! Reel him in!" I think it had dawned on Captain Buch that he was watching something more than a battle between a pocket-sized bluefish and a wimpy ten-year-old. I shot forward, taking every inch of slack from the fish. The captain throttled the *Witch* to a near standstill.

"We're all with you, Billy," Grandad assured me. "Relax as much as you can. Fight him with your weight, not your strength. Save yourself."

"Hey look!" Sixty feet from the port side, my fish, gleaming in the deck lights like stainless steel, danced on its tail above the water. "Wow! Look how *big* it is!"

"Hold on!" Buch ordered. He jammed the throttles forward. "Reel him, Billy! Reel him just as hard as you can!" The *Witch* rose up and charged through the water toward the fish. I reeled frantically. "*No slack! No slack!*" the captain bellowed above the engines' roar. Nearly losing his balance, Grandad grabbed his camera. My line went limp.

"I've lost him! I've lost him," I moaned.

"Keep reeling!" Grandad yelled. "*Reel him!*" The *Witch* slowed suddenly and settled back into the water.

"No!" I yelled. "He's *here!*" Fifteen feet of monofilament separated us. The rod doubled over. I held on with everything I had left. Tears streamed down my face. For a second, my eyes clamped shut against the pain. Blood ran from a gash in my left thumb where the line had ripped through it. "Nobody help me! *Goddammit!* I can do it! I can do it!" Grandad and Lance hovered, afraid to touch me. The fish yielded more line. I reeled urgently, ignoring my pain. Lance stood by with the gaff.

"Don't screw up!" the captain roared at him. Grandad aimed his camera. Lance lunged with the gaff and missed. I howled as the spooked fish took off. I couldn't breathe.

"Hold him, Billy. Just hold him," Grandad urged, as he gently rubbed my back. "He'll come around again. You'll see. . . . Mind if I handle that?" he said, taking the gaff from Lance. "This time, Billy. This time . . ." He was practically whispering. I felt my lungs working again. "He's leveling, Bill. Look at your rod. See? The tip is straightening. Now bring him in. Nice and easy. I'm very proud of you. Stay with him. That's it. Perfect. When he reaches the surface, just keep your rod up. Don't reel, I'll pull him in. You've done wonderfully. Don't think about it, just keep r e e l i n g. Thatta boy."

For three minutes, there was no sound except the rush of my breath, the squeak of wet line, the purr of resting engines, and the gentle lap of water against the hull. The

captain, Grandad, and Lance stood practically motion-
less. I was working on raw nerves, but inch by inch, I
took freedom from a powerful, bulletlike fish. "I see him,
Billy!" Grandad exclaimed after what seemed like a
year's labor. "You're almost home now. I'm going to
lean over the side with the gaff. You just keep his nose
up."

"Oh, Grandad," I begged, "don't let him go. . . ." With
a powerful, certain stroke, Grandad hooked the fish
through the thickest section of its body and pulled it
hand over hand from the sea. Like a toy wound too
tight, it hit the deck flipping in a frenzy that seemed to
keep its middle fully three inches in the air. From a courteous distance, we watched it scoot from port to starboard and back again, desperately searching for the sea.

Finally, the captain announced, "Blackfin."

"It's a tuna, Billy!" Grandad exclaimed.

"A *tuna!*" I cried in amazement. "Cool!"

Lance, as if he'd been waiting to know the name of
the thing, began to chase it clumsily around the deck.
When he had the fish cornered between the engine hous-
ing and a tackle box, Grandad wrapped an arm around
my shoulder, and we moved in for a closer look.

"We better do something for that thumb of yours . . . ,"
Grandad said.

"Just look at it, Grandad. I can't believe it. *I* caught
it."

"Pound for pound, one of the fightingest fish you'll
see out here," the captain assured us. "Mighty good eating fish, too. I like 'em baked with plenty of lemon. Just
like eating steak. Nothing like that junk they sell in a
can."

"Wow. I just can't *believe* it." While my thumb was cleaned, Mercurochromed, and bandaged, my eyes never left the fish.

"Uh—eighteen pounds, two ounces," Lance announced, straining to read the scale. Grandad double-checked over his shoulder.

After a round of pictures, Grandad dropped his lure back over the stern, and I decided to examine the black-fin on my own. To the east, a milky circle of moon had risen above the horizon. Before it, a flashing light path caught the tops of massive swells passing silently through the sea. In the west, a million bulbs, on everything from Ferris wheels to fishing piers, sparkled like a diamond necklace between sea and sky.

"Thank you for your cooperation," I said solemnly to the captain. "I'm not sure I could have caught the black-fin if you hadn't steered the *Witch* the way you did."

"It's all in the job." The captain laughed. "You done real well."

"I've never caught a fish like that before."

"Gee, I figured you were an old hand." Buch chuckled. "How's he doin' back there, anyway? I seen you wiping him off. Did he break out in a sweat?"

"He died."

"Well, go back there an' catch one twice as big!"

"Okay," I said.

"Want me to have Lance put the tuna on ice, Bill?" the captain asked as I turned away.

"I guess so. He kind of stinks."

"We'll take good care of him."

"Thanks. . . . He seemed so much bigger in the water."

"You want a *bigger* one?"

"In pictures, you see them taller than my grandad."

"Not a blackfin, Bill," the captain assured me. "Biggest one ever caught wasn't much over forty pound. You're halfway there!"

"Really?"

"You bet! They stuff and mount 'em smaller than yours."

"On a board? Really?"

"Tell the truth, Bill," the captain said confidentially, squatting by his wheel to protect our privacy, "I only seen one bigger than yours in fifty years' fishin', an' that one got clean away."

With the tuna on ice and the deck swabbed clean of its blood, Grandad and I held our positions at the stern, silently admiring the show of moon and stars above us, and enjoying our good fortune: just being together on the sea. Within minutes, I felt the first sharp pull that signaled a new fight. A second later, Grandad snagged one of his own.

"It's a school!" the captain yelled from his bridge. "I see them on the finder. Echoes look like a seven-forty-seven! Lance, get them outriggers flyin'!" Lance jumped to release the lures from the tall outriggers on either side of the boat as Grandad pulled his catch over the side.

"Looks like about two pounds, Captain!" Grandad shouted, ripping his hook from the fish's mouth.

In almost the same instant as the lure from the starboard outrigger hit the water, Lance yelled, "Fish on!"

Like Grandad, I flipped a two-pounder onto the deck. "These fish are more my size," I laughed. Lance was reeling in the outrigger line as Grandad released his lure.

Right away, he hooked another. As I was trying to grab my fish, it fell free of the hook, and I threw my line overboard again.

We shadowed the huge school as it traveled up the coast with the tide. From Cape May to Atlantic City, fireworks displays dappled the horizon with color, but I didn't stop fishing to admire them. I was high on the action, and it didn't matter what else there was to see or how tired I got; I vowed not to quit before the fish did. When they stopped biting finally, I could barely stand.

After a candy bar and a soda, I counted our catch: 117 blues, ranging from one-and-a-half to almost six pounds. And one blackfin tuna, which Captain Buch had reported on his radio was a "twenty-pounder." Almost as soon as I announced the total, I realized I should have kept it to myself. The captain and Grandad put their heads together and decided it was time to go in.

"I'm sorry, Billy," Grandad explained. "But I'm about done in and it's difficult for me to imagine what we'll do with all we've caught already." I didn't have to say anything. Grandad knew how I felt about ending our adventure. "Would you like to make it an annual event, Billy?" he asked. "Go fishing with me next year on the Fourth of July?" He read the answer in my face. "I want you to know," he went on, "I never enjoyed this holiday more in my life than I did today, spending it with you. That's the truth."

I edged closer to Grandad, until we were touching. A huge hand gently cupped my shoulder. Its welcome warmth made me realize I'd been cold. We stood together in silence, surveying the wake of the *Ebony Witch*. "I love you, Grandaddy," I said at last, self-consciously.

My voice sounded odd to me. I wasn't used to saying "I love you," unless it was a response.

"And I love you, Billy."

"I'd like to go fishing with you every year, anytime you say."

"As often as we can."

"Let's shake on it," I said. I was glad to have hit on a manly way to seal our bargain. Grandad stepped back and extended his hand, stooping very discreetly to compensate for the nearly two-foot difference in our heights.

"Best friends?" Grandad proposed.

"Best friends forever!"

"All right, then. Let's eat!"

fourteen

While Grandad gave Lance instructions about cleaning and packaging our fish, I went below to investigate the contents of our picnic basket.

Captain Buch's standard of housekeeping deteriorated abruptly at the cabin door. The built-in table and benches were cluttered with rods, reels, and miscellaneous engine parts. I shoved aside the case and entrails of a small winch to make a place for our picnic. I soon had all the food neatly arrayed in the glow of the light that hung over the table. There were a dozen or more little tubs, cartons, and foil packages. I had no idea what any of it was.

"Oh, brother," Grandad sighed as he joined me, "this is just like Louise. I wondered how she'd managed to spend sixty-seven fifty on a picnic for two." Grandad rearranged a pile of grimy life preservers and slowly lowered himself onto one of the padded benches. "The whole time we were driving down, I had a feeling we should stop to buy chicken."

"I think she sent instructions." I handed Grandad the pink envelope I'd found in the basket. He grimaced as he took it from me, then put on his "readers," taking more time to do so than usual. The monogrammed envelope flap popped open as Grandad slipped his thumb under it. The inside was lined with foil. As Grandad removed his friend's note from the envelope and discovered that it went on for several pages, his face slumped into a frown.

"Here, Billy," he said, "why don't you read it? The stench of that perfume turns my stomach." Grandad cleared away a pile of tackle boxes and stretched out. As I began to read, he closed his eyes.

"*Dear Boys,*" the note began. I read aloud although Grandad's periodic groans made me wonder if that's what he'd had in mind. "*I'm sure you're* starved! *Zigfried at Rittenhouse Gourmet assures me that he's packed simply oodles of goodies for a scrumpsh supper. In case all of this is just too confusing, a few words of explanation . . .*" Grandad's Louise had the most extraordinary handwriting I'd ever seen. The bottom stroke of each letter in her spidery, upright script was perfectly aligned, as if she'd written every line against a ruler. "*Votre paté is in the yellow tin. . . .*" I welcomed the opportunity to show off my French. "*It's the same one we had at Irene's, George. Remember?? You said it was* divine! *I had them do an oyster mousse with capers en gelée (the blue plastic tub). Simply Yummy! The little foil things are smoked squab. Do watch out for bones! They're absolutely minute!!*" Not only was I unsure how to pronounce some of the words, I had no idea what she was talking about. "*In the white plastic, the most marvelous deviled eggs ever! The avocado cream filling is out of this world!—Almost too pretty to eat, don't you think? (I just love the pimento rosettes.)"* I felt a sudden urge to laugh, but I stopped reading and pretended to cough until I could go on.

"Zigfried was sure you'd want simply mountains of things to munch so I ordered two boxes of those marvelous Norwegian cheese toasts with anchovy. The tiny things in gold foil are chocolate bottles with cherry heering in, a special treat for your darling Billy. Audrey's grandchildren adore them." When I saw what I had to read next, I stopped again to "cough." Grandad was still lying on the bench with his eyes clamped shut. I was surprised he hadn't said anything. *"Yes, sweetness,"* the note continued, *"there is one for you!—Sorry, Grandad."* I giggled. "I can't help it." I bit my tongue and went on. *"I thought the petite rum baba would make a perf dessert. Rum is so nautical! Sorry there's no whipped cream! Oh yes, the thermoses!! Gazpacho done with clam juice—lovely. We'll have some with Smirnoff's when you get home!!*

"Have gobs of fun and don't forget to 'phone the minute you return. (Yes, I shall try not to worry, dearest, but Maude Finch's nephew drowned on a fishing trip with some of the Kennedy Klan two weeks ago and I've been sick ever since.)

"All my love and lots of kisses for you and darling Billy . . . Toujours, Louise.

"P.S. Be sure to use this cute basket to bring home all those fish! XXX L.

"Gee, Grandad . . ." I said after a brief silence. It was the only thing that came to mind. I slipped the note onto the table.

"God!" Grandad roared at last as he sat up. The sudden sound and movement startled me. He leaned for-

ward, groaning, and cradled his head in his hands. I wondered if he was seasick. "The woman's an ass, Billy, an absolute ass! Excuse me, I should never speak that way." He looked up. "I told her I wanted to put together a few things for our supper and before I could object, she'd taken over. A simple picnic supper becomes a state occasion, and as far as I can tell," he said as he took the lid off the avocado cream-filled eggs, "there isn't a god-damned thing here fit to eat. Look at this crap will you?" The cream filling beneath the pimento rosettes had turned a fecal color. "I'm sorry," Grandad said as he leaned back against the hull. "I guess I'm just tired."

"It's okay, Grandad. These little chicken things don't look too bad."

"You go ahead. I'll have something when we get in."

"They're the tiniest chickens I ever saw, but they taste pretty good."

"It's a squab, Billy, a baby pigeon. Barbecued chicken would have been ideal, but it would never do for Louise Calder-Biddle to be found in the company of a chicken, not when there's an obscenely priced, greasy, hard-to-eat substitute available. You see, a woman like Louise is uncomfortable with the commonplace, however superior it might be. She has no taste for reality."

"Mom says you like her," I said slyly as I sniffed and immediately re-covered the oyster mousse, a foul-smelling, watery goo the color of cigarette ash.

"She's presentable. Listen to me, talking to you like this. Do you mind? I don't get many opportunities."

"No, it's interesting. I like it."

"Very well. Not a word to your mother, though. This is strictly between us."

"Gentlemen's secret, right?"

"That's the spirit. You see, Billy, a man in my position must attend an horrendous number of social occasions. It's been awkward since your grandmother died. Having Louise has made it a great deal easier to move about in company."

"You mean she keeps all the other ladies away."

"Exactly!" Grandad laughed. "At my age, the number of prospecting widows and divorcées seems to increase geometrically every year. The best defense is to have one who'll run interference for you."

"Will you marry her?"

"Lord, no. Although I think she's beginning to expect it, which presents something of a problem: She tends to hysteria. For instance, if I were to tell her what I thought of this ludicrous supper she and her friend Ziggy whipped up at my expense, I expect she'd take to her bed for a week and her friends would begin calling me with dire confidences regarding her health. It would take hundreds of dollars in flowers and baubles to convince her of my affection. Much simpler to tell her we loved the supper and have the good sense never to let her do this to us again."

"I'll say!" I agreed, the voice of vast experience.

"Would you like to try some of the paté?"

"Ah—no thanks. I had it once. I hate it."

"Frankly, so do I. You might like one of those little guys in the gold foil. They're chocolate," Grandad said as he discreetly unwrapped one of the squab.

"What will you do if she asks you to marry her?"

"Well, luckily for me, equality of the sexes is a terrifying concept to Louise. She'd never ask. She'll merely

continue applying pressure. Oh, she has many virtues
. . . knows everybody, reads ravenously, comes from a
distinguished family, all that sort of thing, but, frankly,
she is not remarkably attractive. I think she waited a
good many years for a new man to come along after her
divorce. She'd never jeopardize our relationship over the
question of marriage, of that I'm quite confident."

"You sure know a lot, Grandad," I said, yawning.

"Your grandad has made a lot of mistakes, Billy. I'm
going to try very hard to share what I've learned with
you as you get older. The choices we make when we're
young are so important. Schools, career, women, friends
. . . all of it. It's difficult. In some things, you'll have to
learn by making your own mistakes, but there are ways
I can help you. There are certain things about . . . life in
our society that your father, as a foreigner, simply cannot understand. I hope you'll allow me to pass on what
I can as time goes by. I care very much about your happiness."

"I'm glad, Grandad. Dad never talks to me like this."

"Now you've got me doing it," Grandad said, stifling
a yawn. "Tell me, Billy, do you think your parents are
happy together?"

The question threw me. I knew my parents kept Grandad in the dark about our family, but it was hard for me
to believe he didn't know how bad things were between
them. "Gee," I said, "I don't know. Sometimes they
don't act very happy. They have fights. Mom says everybody does. I get scared listening to them sometimes."

"Of course you do," he said. He put his big hand over
mine and patted it. "Do they fight about money?"

"Sometimes it's about money. Mom thinks Dad stays at the club too much. She gets lonely."

"Do they fight about that?"

"Not exactly. I mean, that's not how it starts out."

"Does your father ever hit your mother? I know it's a painful subject. I've worried about her."

"I—I think so. One time, late at night, I heard a lot of crashing and banging downstairs. I turned up my radio real loud so I couldn't hear it. The next day, Mom didn't come out of her room all day, except once. I saw her in the hall. One side of her face was bright red and there were bruises all over her arms. When she saw me, she ran into her room crying and locked the door."

"What about your father? What did he say about all that?"

"I didn't see him that day. He must have gone out real early."

"Does this sort of thing happen often, bad fights between your parents?"

"Not too often, not every day or anything like that. More lately than before."

Grandad sighed. He seemed saddened but not surprised by what I'd told him. "I'm very sorry that you have to be troubled by all this, Billy. I think your father is very . . . dissatisfied with his life. Thing's haven't gone as he'd hoped. He's bitter. I'm afraid he blames me to some extent, and your mother. He takes his feelings out on her. I fear for her but she won't let me help. Everything's always 'fine' when I ask. I know she's not well. I see the anguish in her face. . . . I've worried you. Don't. Things will work out. We won't let anything happen to your mother."

"I hope not." the *Witch* was jostled suddenly by a large wave. Grandad and I braced ourselves against the table.

"She's a grown woman, Billy," Grandad said as the rocking subsided. "They're both civilized human beings. Marriage can be full of stress and sometimes people do and say things under stress that can be very hurtful, yet I'm not at all concerned that your father will do any real physical harm to your mother. If I were, I assure you, I'd intercede at once. Have no doubt of that."

"I get pretty scared," I admitted in a low voice. My shame was so great that I couldn't look Grandad in the eye. I stared into a little pile of needle-thin bones from the squab. "I don't know what's going to happen, and Mom, she's been acting so strange, forgetting all kinds of simple stuff and saying things that don't make sense."

"I know, Billy," Grandad said. He extended his sun-burned arms across the table and took each of my small hands in his. "I know."

I looked up. I had never seen such sadness in Grandad's eyes. He *did* know, and I could see that in his own grown-up way, he was worried, too. All of a sudden I wanted to cry, but I didn't let myself. I got strength from knowing that Grandad understood about the trouble in our family. In my heart, I knew he would never let anything bad happen to me.

Grandad said he needed some air and excused himself to go up on deck. The cabin seemed sad and lonely without him, but I didn't follow. I knew he wanted to be alone. I could tell he was really worried about my mother, much more so than he'd let on.

I watched as two flies excitedly checked over the remains of Louise's picnic banquet. The noise of the *Witch*'s engines seemed louder than before, her motion more pronounced. I curled up in the padded triangular space where the benches met at the bow and stuffed a musty rain jacket under my head. Within seconds, I'd made a free fall into sleep.

fifteen

I think what woke me was the gentle thud as the *Witch* nudged into her berth. Through sleepy eyes, I could see that all traces of our picnic had been removed from the cabin. The time had come to leave. I thanked the *Witch* and said good-bye. Grandad called for me. The trip was over.

The night air was still and damp, smelling of fresh-caught fish and the sea. Clouds had taken over where there had been stars. Captain Buch seemed smaller and less friendly than he had on open water. There was a round of quick handshakes and goodnights. Lance helped carry our fish to the car. The crushed clamshells had an eerie, luminous appearance in the cold blue light bathing the parking lot. Grandad's silence and slight stoop told me how tired he was. He fumbled momentarily with the keys before the trunk lid popped open. The Mercedes glistened in a gritty coat of dew. In the trunk, three nested coolers awaited the catch. Lance separated and stuffed them with packages of fillets. In the bottom of the trunk, Grandad spread an orange-and-black blanket he had bought to remind him of the fortieth reunion of his Princeton class. Lance loaded the coolers into the car, then lingered, lighting a cigarette, as Grandad made a place for the bag that held the blackfin.

"There an ice machine nearby, Lance?" Grandad asked.

"Down the end of the lot, by the Exxon. You can't miss it."

"Well, here. Thank you for all your help. It would have taken me all night, cleaning those fish by myself."

"Uh, thanks. You take care now. 'Night." Lance shoved the tip deep into the right pocket of his cutoffs and ambled off.

"Grandad," I said, "do you want the blackfin?"

He looked surprised. "That's a generous offer, but I have no way to keep it at my club. Tell your folks to have a big barbecue. Tell them the captain suggested it."

"Will you come?"

"If I'm invited."

Driving through the cozy back-bay neighborhoods near the marina, everything was strangely quiet, though it was not yet midnight on the biggest seashore holiday of the year. The jagged leaves of the sycamore trees that grew along the sidewalks hung dead still in the streetlights' glow, casting bizarre, menacing shadows on the pavement. To the west, I caught glimpses between buildings of the vast bay. Like a black hole, it projected nothing of itself, no merry twinkling of reflected light, only blackness. To the east, the bright lights on the boardwalk lit up the sky. There was still plenty of life over there.

"*There's* our road," Grandad said gladly, breaking a

sleepy silence that had carried us across the causeway
to the mainland. "I haven't covered this ground in some
years. Everything's so different, I was beginning to wonder if I'd gotten us lost."

The change of roads turned us northwest through
marshland and pinewoods toward the Delaware Bay.
Soon, we came to a tattered billboard that showed two
people who looked like Elvis and Tuesday Weld walking
hip to hip on an unspoiled beach. Below the couple, in
bold, red letters, it said, "Delcrest . . . a Dream for Lovers
only. . . ." It was punctuated with a big, red heart.

"Do you think it's air-conditioned?" I asked hopefully.

"I'm sure it is," Grandad said. "But I'm so tired I
could sleep on hot rocks. Anyway, if you believe my
secretary, she performed a miracle by finding us a place
to stay." Grandad swung the Mercedes west-northwest
onto a county road pointed to by a stubby red arrow on
the bottom of the billboard.

"Do you think you'll ever have your own boat again,
Grandad?"

"How I wish I could say yes to that. Boats are fright-
fully expensive, and so much work. . . . Yet when you
own one, there's a feeling that goes with it. You could
go anywhere in the world." He let go a huge yawn. "Excuse me. When we were getting off the *Ebony Witch*, I
was terribly aware of the difference it makes when
you've merely hired another man's boat and him to skip-
per it." He yawned again. "Listen to me rambling. I'm
sorry, what was it you asked?"

"Just that, do you think—" It was in that instant I saw
the other car. A sickening feeling of panic and helpless-
ness cut through me. It was too late. We were going

sixty. In the blinding flare of oncoming headlights, Grandad jammed the brakes. I braced. The old heap was skid-
ding straight at us, dead on my side of the Mercedes.
"Damn!" Grandad shouted. *"Jesus!"* The screech of tires
consumed his words. The rear end of the other car was
flying forward. I froze. The collision would be terrible,
side to side. Across the disappearing space between the
two cars, I saw the face of a woman. Our eyes met. She
looked as scared as I felt. Everything was motion. We
were out of control. . . .

We missed. As the Mercedes skidded across the intersection, the other car, a beat-up Pontiac, went into a full
spin inches to our rear, flew off the road, and finally
came to rest in a drainage ditch at the edge of a cornfield.

We stopped sixty feet past the intersection, on the
wrong side of the road. For a long moment, neither of
us spoke. Finally, Grandad leaned over the wheel and
gasped for breath. I thought he was having a heart attack.

"My God," he moaned.

"Are you okay, Grandad?"

"Yes. Are you?" His voice was thin. He hadn't looked
at me. I sensed his shame.

"Yeah, I guess." It was a lie. I was terrified. Grandad
opened his door and began to get out, but his legs were
shaking too badly to support him. He slumped back into
the seat. Through the rear window of the Mercedes, I
could see the other car. Its nose and white roof were
visible above the ditch. I saw moonlight reflected in the
windshield. . . .

"We should see if they're all right." There was no life
at all in Grandad's voice. More seconds went by. I

switched my attention from Grandad to the Pontiac and back again. Then, out of the corner of my eye, I thought I saw something move behind us, a shadow, a person crossing the road toward the other car. I couldn't tell. Suddenly, the Pontiac slipped back into the ditch as if someone had released the brakes; as it did so, my fear turned to something worse.

"I think we should get out of here, Grandad," I said. "They're okay. The car just moved. They didn't even hit anything."

"I'm glad," Grandad said with false good humor. Someone tried to start the other car. Grandad turned in the direction of the noise with a blank stare. A chill ran through me. It wouldn't start. They tried again and again. I thought I heard someone curse. Grandad suddenly sucked in some air and said, "We should probably see if we can help them."

"What if they're real mad, Grandad? Don't you think we should leave them alone?" Grandad just smiled and closed his door. He turned the starter key. There was a high-pitched, mechanical shriek. The motor of the Mercedes was still running. He backed around very carefully to get us headed in the proper direction. The smell of burnt rubber soured the air.

Grandad made a hard and prolonged stop well short of the intersection. On the far side, I could plainly see the silvery back of the stop sign neither of us had noticed before. The Pontiac had had the right of way. Grandad's legs were still shaking. I made sure my car door was locked. The Pontiac sat low in the ditch. I couldn't see anyone inside. Grandad turned to the right, intending to pull onto the shoulder and cross over to the other car on foot. Just then, there was a huge roar. The Pontiac climbed suddenly from the ditch, heading straight at us. Grandad tromped his accelerator. "Good God!" he shouted, "are they *insane?*"

We sped into the night. With a squeal of tires, the Pontiac backed around and was after us. "Do they think I *meant* to harm them?" I had never seen Grandad scared. The high beams of the Pontiac filled the inside of the Mercedes with light. I held on for dear life. "Fasten your seat belt, Billy!" Grandad ordered. The Pontiac swerved suddenly into the far lane and pulled alongside us. I could see two figures in front. An arm shot into the moonlight. Grandad accelerated. They matched our speed. Something hit the window by Grandad's head. The glass shattered in a thousand pieces. Grandad lost control momentarily, trying to duck as tiny bits of glass stung us in the face and arms.

"What can we do?" I wailed. "What can we do?"

Our car swerved wildly back and forth. I held on tight and tried not to panic. The Pontiac gave way. *"Goddamn you idiots!"* Grandad bellowed. *"Leave us alone!"* He got the car under control. The Pontiac was tailgating. It seemed to sag in the back. "We've got to get to the police," Grandad said desperately. "They must be mad. . . . I don't know this road at all. It might go to the bay, some little village . . . no police. At this speed, maybe a cop . . ." Grandad's voice faded. He began sounding the horn. It was all I could do not to cry, I was so scared. I tried to pray. The Pontiac was so close behind us I couldn't see its front bumper. Then, incredibly, it began dropping back. I prayed harder. A yellow sign whizzed by warning of a stop. Grandad eased off the horn. Tiger-striped reflectors appeared at twenty-foot intervals on both sides of the road. Grandad moaned, "What now?" I pulled my seat belt as tight as I could. With my right hand, I squeezed the handhold in the door. My left hand gripped the flared edge of my seat. The Pontiac was four car-lengths to the rear. The Mercedes skidded across a dusting of sand and gravel on the pavement as we passed a final flash of reflectors and the road ended. To our right, a hundred-foot path ended abruptly at a white-sand beach where tiny, moonlit waves spilled from the glassy expanse of Delaware Bay. To our left, a gravel road disappeared into thick pinewoods. To the rear, an old Pontiac waited.

"They'll never let us go back that way," I said anxiously, craning my neck. Grandad was rocking slowly in his seat, clutching the wheel. His face had a sheen of cold sweat. I looked back again at the waiting car. Its paint had no shine. Below the white vinyl top, it might have been blue, green, or gray. I couldn't tell. Suddenly, Grandad swung the Mercedes, spraying gravel, into the woods.

"This couldn't be worse than just sitting there," he hoped aloud.

"I don't *see* them, Grandad!" I said excitedly as we tore along.

"I pray it stays that way." As if answering our prayers, the road continued, wide and well graded. Our confidence grew. On both sides, surveyor's stakes tipped with plastic streamers marked the blocks of some new development. Then, suddenly, the road ended. In a tiny clearing littered with charred firewood, smashed cans, and plastic wrappers, we ran out of luck. "Damn," Grandad said sadly, "I was afraid of this." We slowed to a stop. "They must have known." The words chilled me. I swung around. There was still no sign of them.

"We can run, Grandad! They'll never find us!"

"We could . . ." He hesitated. His breathing was labored. He looked back. "They probably got bored and turned toward the nearest bar." He was trying to make himself believe it. It was all I could do to sit still. "Perhaps we should just turn around." His hand went to the gearshift.

"No, Grandad!" I yelled. "What if they didn't? What if they're out there?" Too much time was passing. Grandad was too tired. He sighed and sat back.

"All right," he agreed. "Why take a chance? The car's insured. We'll lock up and take off through the woods." I climbed out quickly. As soon as the night air hit my nostrils, I knew it was all wrong. A sound, a smell, something . . . It all happened too fast. The familiar sound of the electric doorlocks . . . A roar . . . Headlights winked on through the trees. The Pontiac pounced from fifty feet of darkness. Grandad and I ran in opposite directions to get clear. Brakes locked, the old car smashed into a corner of the Mercedes. The impact knocked it across four feet of gravel and crushed the right rear fender like a can. I heard laughter from the Pontiac. As a cloud of dust drifted through the brightness of its headlights, Grandad and I stared helplessly at each other across forty feet of trash and crumpled car, each wanting to run; neither willing to leave without the other. The engine of the Pontiac was silent.

"Billy," Grandad yelled, "get away!" I took three quick steps toward him. He waved me off and started to say something else, but it was too late. Doors on each side of the Pontiac swung open. Two men got out. My heart went still and cold. Grandad moved toward the men. I gave up the idea of running. I couldn't leave Grandad alone.

The driver appeared to be in his thirties. He was fat. The black, Jack Daniels T-shirt didn't reach his waist. His navel and the saddle of blubber that bulged over his belt were in full view. The two men swaggered toward Grandad. I moved closer.

"Fucked up pretty good, din't ya, sweetheart?" the driver sneered. His dirty-blond, jowl-length hair bushed out beneath a baseball cap with the emblem CAT. "You think drivin' a fuckin' Mercedes gives you the right to run a stop?" His eyes were small and mocking, like raisins beside his bulging nose.

"I'm very sorry," Grandad said uneasily. "I'm thankful no one was hurt." The other one, the skinny one, stroked his flat chin and smirked at us. He looked younger than the driver, but his thin blond hair had already receded half the distance from his low forehead to the back of his small skull. A wispy mustache bracketed the slit of his mouth. He took a swig of beer.

"Hey, Willie," he chuckled, as beer ran from the corners of his mouth down his chin, "don't he look like that faggy minister from Sea Isle? You know, the one married Ceil and Walt whatever-the-fuck-his-name-is. Hey, asshole, are you a minister?"

"Look," Grandad said, "we want no trouble with you. I apologize for missing the sign. It was my fault. We were coming back to see if we could help you when you came at us with your car. I'd be grateful if you'd accept my apology and let us go." The fat one, Willie, was checking the Mercedes' smashed fender.

"You gonna answer my question?" he asked. The cleft of his ass appeared above his belt as he squatted for a closer look.

"What was that?" Grandad asked. I prayed they would get on with whatever they were going to do and go away.

"You think driving this piece of German shit gives you the right to run a stop?"

"Certainly not. I'm tired and unfamiliar with the roads." It was an effort for Willie to stand up.

"You know, Bud," Willie said, inspecting Grandad like he was spoiled meat, "you got a point. He sure talks queer. 'Shit no,' " Willie mocked in a lispy voice, " 'I wath tired an' unfamiliar with the roadth.' Well, la dee da, an' where do you buy your pannyhose, sweetheart?" I went to Grandad's side.

"Gimme the keys," Willie demanded, sticking out his thick, stubby-fingered hand. *"Gimme the fuckin' keys!"* The skinny one pinched my chin. It hurt, but I gave no sign of the pain.

Grandad looked at me as if to say he was sorry and gave Willie the keys. We were getting in deeper and deeper. "Don't be too afraid," Grandad whispered, kneeling at my side. "They just want to have some fun." I didn't believe it.

"Yo, Marie," Buddy yelled as the trunk popped open, "smells like your old lady in here!"

"Fuck you!" a woman crowed from the backseat of their car. Willie chucked a cooler full of fish fillets onto the gravel.

"What are we gonna do, Grandad?" I whispered. I was shaking all over.

"You have to let people like this get bored. We can't act too excited. . . . Billy, I'm sorry I got us into all this." Willie, the fat one, was reaching into the plastic bag that held my blackfin.

"It's not your fault," I whispered. "They're crazy. . . .". Willie's ugly snicker drew our attention. He was maneuvering the blackfin in front of his crotch. When he had the pose he wanted, he trotted around to the side of the car and began to thrust the fish in and out of the right rear window at the woman inside.

"Hey, Marie, getta loada this hard-on!" He chortled. She laughed almost as hard as the two men. Grandad pulled me closer.

"Let's run, Grandad," I whispered.

"They'd catch me. They're half my age." Willie dropped the blackfin in Marie's lap.

"Oh, shit!" she groaned. "Thanks a pile!"

"I'm going to try offering them money," Grandad said. "Stay as far away as you can but where they can see you. If anything goes wrong, run. Find a good hiding place. They won't look for you long."

"I want to stay with you, Grandad," I said. Grandad squeezed my hand. Buddy and Willie came toward us as Marie climbed slowly out of their car.

"I have about forty dollars," Grandad said. "I'm sorry it's not more. I wish you'd take it and leave me and my grandson alone."

"You're not scared'a us, are you, pops?" Willie asked. He was rocking slightly. Buddy grabbed Grandad's belt. I could smell the beer they'd been drinking.

"Leave me alone, damn you!" Grandad shouted, pulling away. "Take the money and get out."

"We don't want your fucking forty bucks," Willie said. He unbuttoned the top of Grandad's shirt. This time, Grandad made no effort to resist. Buddy crowed like a rooster as he pulled down Grandad's zipper. My heart was a cold weight in my chest.

"You filth," Grandad said. Buddy pulled Grandad's pants down to his ankles.

"Yeah?" Willie bellowed. "And you're *shit!* Just because you drive around in that German piece of shit, you think you own the whole *fuckin' world!*" He shoved Grandad hard enough to tie up his feet in the tangle of trousers at his ankles and make him fall into the charred remains of someone's fire.

"*Stop it!*" I shouted. The sight of Grandad half-clothed and disabled terrified me. His left arm was bloodied and blackened from the fall. Willie glowered at him with an expression twisted by disgust, like Grandad was road kill or worse.

"*Muree,*" Buddy roared, "get your cunt over here and take the clothes off this kid!"

Grandad said nothing when our eyes met. Marie lurched toward me. She knelt and put her hands on my shoulders. I stepped away from her. She crawled after me. "Come 'ere," she ordered and took a clumsy swipe at me. As she loosened my belt, Grandad covered his eyes with his hands.

"Let's go, pops," Buddy said. "Take off them shorts and let us filth see how a big stud like you is put together." He and Willie chuckled as Grandad slowly pulled the clothes from around his ankles. He seemed old and beaten. It was hard to look at him. I stepped out of my slacks.

"Now the good part!" Marie cackled. Before I could resist, she was pulling down my underpants.

Willie kicked dirt at Grandad. *"The shorts, asshole!"* he shouted. *"Now!"* Grandad turned away from me as he slowly got back on his feet. While Buddy and Willie watched with sneering faces, Grandad took off his shirt, undershirt, and, finally, his shorts. Then Marie began and I turned my eyes to the sky. I became ice. I wondered why God hated us.

"Mmmmmmmmmm," she purred. After half a minute, she stopped to fill her lungs and then went back to it. It was Willie who finally noticed what she was doing.

"Fuckin' *Christ!*" he roared. The drunken woman in the hot pink pants and pink halter top had wrapped her hot pink lips around my dick and balls and was pulling at my ass with her grimy hands. Grandad was on her a half second before Willie. With one hand full of her hair and one gripping the fat pushed up by her pants, he pulled her from me. Drool spilled from her mouth as she yowled like a kicked dog and crawled away.

"Run, Billy! Run now!" Grandad yelled. He was wild-eyed. I jumped. I was off without thinking into the woods, as fast as I could; branches and briars tore into my bare skin with every step. Buddy tried to follow, but I was much faster. Instead of following a straight path, I circled back as soon as I was sure no one could see. From a hiding place near the two cars, I watched Buddy stumbling around in the underbrush. In the clearing, Willie took a wild swing at Grandad. The blow glanced off his cheek. Grandad lunged at Willie and locked both

hands around his throat. Willie buckled at the knees. Grandad went down with him, stabbing his thumbs into Willie's Adam's apple. Willie gagged and struggled desperately to get free. Grandad held on.

"I can't see shit," Buddy complained as he turned back. Then he saw what was happening to Willie. He cursed and started running. Back in the clearing, he took a wild, swinging kick at Grandad. Even forty feet away, I could hear the dull thud of Buddy's foot against Grandad's head. My stomach knotted. Grandad collapsed. Willie rolled onto his stomach, gagging and coughing.

I had to help Grandad. I left my hiding place and crept to a spot where I could get to the back of the Mercedes without them seeing me. At the edge of the clearing, I sucked air and ran so fast to the Mercedes that I crashed into the rear bumper. But no one saw. My heart was pumping like a piston. I grabbed my bag, pulled the zipper, and reached in.

The eight-inch blade of the knife flashed like an icicle in the moonlight. I moved slowly toward them. Grandad was struggling to prop himself up with one arm. My mind locked up. I couldn't think. I was too full of hate.

"Hey, look out—" I spun around. Marie, somewhere in the shadows. "Kid's gotta knife." They heard her. They saw me. I wanted to kill her for giving me away. For everything. Buddy was coming toward me. Willie staggered to his right.

"Leave me alone!" I shouted, moving closer to Grandad. My voice was high and shaky. "Leave us *alone!*"

"Dingleberry's got himself a knife, Will," Buddy laughed as he yanked a sharp surveyor's stake from the ground. He drew within six feet, and started jabbing at me. "Gimme that knife, you little shit," he ordered. I edged closer to Grandad. It wasn't the hate in Buddy's eyes that scared me as much as the hunger. He lunged closer.

"*Get away!*" I shouted. The knife blade barely missed his hand as I swung at him. I reached Grandad's side. He was trembling.

"You're dead, kid." Buddy snickered. Three missing teeth gave his mouth the look of an old man's.

"Grandaddy . . . ," I said. He shook his head. He was having trouble with his eyes.

"That old fuck was gonna kill me." Willie gagged, staggering closer.

"Grandad, tell me what to *do*. . . ."

"I can't. . . ." He shook his head again, trying to clear it. Buddy jabbed at us almost playfully with the stake.

"Stay away!" I yelled. "Leave us *alone!*" Willie grabbed a broken brick from a mound of trash.

"You two are dog meat," Willie growled. He sounded as if there were hands still wrapped around his throat. He and Buddy were circling. I couldn't keep both of them in sight. I couldn't stop shaking.

"Please go away! Please leave us alone!" I begged.

Suddenly, Grandad reached out and took the knife. His eyes had cleared. "Run when I give the word," he said. "No arguments. . . ." Willie heaved the brick. I ducked. It missed the side of my head by four inches. "*Go!*" Grandad ordered. Willie grabbed for me and missed as I shot by, into the woods. "Stay clear, Billy!" Grandad yelled. "They won't hurt me as long as you can get free!"

As soon as I was sure no one was following, I turned

back. Panting, I watched in horror from a cluster of scrub pines as Willie closed in on Grandad, holding what looked like a car battery over his head. Grandad was struggling to stand. He swung the knife protectively in front of him. Buddy was to the side, still jabbing with the stake; each time, the point got closer to Grandad's flesh. Grandad backed off as soon as he could stand. Marie was throwing up. The moonlight was fading. I strained to see the dimming images. I felt crushed.

"Grandad! Grandaddy!" I screamed, "Don't let them *hurt* you!"

"Stay back, Billy! Stay away!" I was back at the edge of the clearing when Willie heaved the battery at Grandad. Grandad moaned as he went down. They were on him like wolves in the same second.

"No! Stop it! Stop it! Leave him a-lone!" There was a flash. *The blade.* I screamed, *"Ssstoppp . . ."* Buddy looked at me. He froze for one tiny fraction of a second and he looked at me. Looked at me and raised the eight-inch blade back behind his head. Willie was looking at me, too. And Marie. And Grandad, lying naked and helpless on the ground. And then the blade flew forward through the air and plunged. Into Grandad. Into his throat. Everything was moving. Grandad sighed. His big body twitched as if an electric current had jolted it. Buddy grunted and drew back. Willie scampered away on all fours. Marie howled. My soul shattered.

"Grannndadddy!" They turned again toward the sound of my voice, all except Grandad. My face was on fire. My throat closed. Willie was moving toward me; Buddy was, too.

"My grandaddy," I sobbed. I turned and ran as fast

as I could into the woods, back to the cluster of scrub pines where I'd hidden before.

"He's gonna be okay, kid," Willie shouted from the edge of the woods. I could just make out the faint, white shape of Grandad's torso. So still. I couldn't see the knife. The blade was nicked from the time Ned had used it to pry open a casement window. "Cheap knife," he'd said when Grace noticed the nick. "Cheap knife."

"Come on, Bill," Buddy was saying. "We're gonna take the old guy to the hos'pil. Don't be 'fraid." I could barely see him in the darkness. He was going in the wrong direction. Against the half-light in the clearing, Willie was easier to see. He was lumbering straight toward my hiding place, as if he could smell me. I resisted the urge to run and crouched deeper in the undergrowth. A mosquito found my right ear. My knife. My fault. I found it for them. . . . Gave it to them. More mosquitoes joined the first. Beyond, over Delaware Bay, the moon had slid behind the trees. Willie drew within ten feet of me and stopped. I could hear his labored breathing.

"It was self-defense, kid." Buddy again, still farther away.

"Hurry up, kid," Willie bellowed. "We ain't gonna hurt ya!" I listened carefully to the sound of his footsteps as he wandered away from me.

A few minutes later, the Pontiac was in motion. I rose slowly and listened to the car's sound and watched its headlights moving away through the woods. The lights flickered quickly and passed from view, but the sound went on, fading with terrible slowness. They were gone. Or were they? I waited for what seemed like a very long time in my hiding place, and even then, I wasn't sure.

I moved, at last, with extreme caution, ready to run. I knew that one of the murderers might still be there, waiting for me. I listened. Everything was perfectly still. The moon was gone. There was a faint, gray brightening in the east. My eyes resisted the place where Grandad was lying. Turning slowly as I walked, I stepped into the clearing. No sign of them. I pressed my palms against the hood of the Mercedes as if it would make me stronger. I looked down the road, away, and as I did so, I knew inside the blackness of my heart that I had to look at Grandad. So the memory would be complete, so that in the years to come, I would know that I'd been brave enough to say good-bye.

There was no mistaking death in what I saw. No hint of life, however small, remained in the wreckage of flesh. Where blood had spilled, stains like angel wings had spread above his shoulders in the gravel. His head tilted to his right. His cheeks were drawn and sunken. His mouth was open as if giving a command. The right eye was not quite closed; the left, wide open, disbelieving, caught in that last second, searching the sky. It was a modern-art face, a face made of pieces that didn't fit. The hands I had shaken, that had held and comforted me, were bony-looking and discolored, drained of blood and life. They were frozen in a gesture of release. Beside the Adam's apple, the familiar plastic handle stuck out like some misplaced ornament. The "cheap knife," its little nick buried in dead flesh. It belonged in Grace's kitchen. . . .

While birds awakened in the tops of trees, I searched for Grandad in that wretched flesh, knowing all the time he wasn't there. I knelt in spite of what I knew and, for the last time, took the big right hand between mine. Tears poured suddenly from my eyes. My head bowed in sorrow to the ground. The sobbing seemed to come from every part of me.

sixteen

The rising sun brought color to the blood-drenched place where Grandad died. Black became red. Flies followed the scent of death to his body. I could no longer make myself look at him.

I got the handsome black-and-orange blanket from the back of the car. I held it stretched between my hands. My muscles stalled. One eye searching the sky . . . the open hands . . . the silver hair, only slightly mussed, even now . . . the neat mustache, the only one like it I'd ever seen. I wanted to cover Grandad like you do a sick person, to keep him warm. I knew I was looking at him for the last time. I took two steps forward, knelt, and drew the blanket up until it covered his face and head completely. The knife handle made an ugly bulge in the fabric. The tears stung; my chest heaved violently; the sadness exploded again. When the crying stopped, I stood without opening my eyes and turned away from the body. The keys were still in the Mercedes' trunk. I closed everything up and felt oddly surprised as the electric door-locks snapped obediently when I turned the key. The night was over.

I was hungry. My clothes lay in a flattened pile where I'd left them. The Pontiac had backed over them on the way out. I thought about Marie sucking me and pulling wildly at my ass. I shook the gravel from my things and put them on. She was like an animal. It frightened me to think she'd bite it off. She was drunk. Her lips were pink as bubble gum. Her tongue felt hot, whipping back and forth, licking so hard it almost hurt. She was crazy. She had to be.

I began to walk. The straight gravel road looked longer than I remembered. Already, the day was hot, though it was still very early. Not fifty feet from the car, a buzzing of flies drew my attention to something in the grass. The blackfin. A relic from a million years before. It looked like someone's garbage. I hated the sight of it. I kicked gravel from the road to scatter the flies. Then I heard sirens.

Again, I went over in my mind everything I could remember that might help the police put them in jail. I had written the license number of their car in a clear patch of sand near the road. I was certain I could identify them anywhere, under any circumstances. I would point the finger of death at them and never change a detail of my story.

They'd headed for Mexico or Canada, I guessed, as fast as they could. Canada, probably, it was so much closer, though Mexico seemed a more likely place for their kind.

The sirens belonged to two county police cars. They skidded to a stop a short distance in front of me. A slight breeze from the west brought a choking cloud of orange dust to the place where I stood. As it drifted slowly past, a nightmare image emerged: Buddy and Willie in the backseat of the lead police car. Laughing.

A cop opened the car door for the killers. They got out, but stayed close to the car. They wouldn't look at me. One of the cops went to look at Grandad's body. They asked me a thousand questions. An ambulance was on its way. I kept saying that Buddy and Willie had killed Grandad "in cold blood"; I didn't know exactly what it meant. The cops seemed unimpressed. Buddy and Willie had already told their story. Their being there was evidence of that. The cops kept saying they would buy me a hamburger. Buddy and Willie kept whispering to each other. Willie's throat was spotted with maroon-and-yellow bruises left by Grandad's hands. More sirens; more police cars and an ambulance arrived. Soon, there were flashing lights as far as I could see. A wiry black man in a white jacket gave me a quick medical examination and daubed my scratches with stinging orange paint. The cops and medical people discussed Grandad like a wrecked car. "What with the heat and the flies," someone on the radio said, "we'd better get this meat on ice 'fore everyone pukes." The authorization came from someone laughing.

"Hey, I'm real sorry about your grandad, Bill," Willie yelled as they were loading me into a police car. "It was self-defense. You seen it. No hard feelings, huh?"

I exploded. "You'll go to hell, you filthy scum," I shouted.

"Yeah?" Willie said. "Well, I guess there'll be one less space for us now, huh, kid?" I was spitting at the sea.

The small cop car groaned as Officer Joe Beadle squeezed his walrus body behind the wheel. "Okay, Billy," he said, "now you see that red button there? Get ready, 'cause when I tell you, I want you to push that button for me, 'kay?" He kept racing the engine to power the air-conditioning. It hurt my ears. The county ambulance was approaching from the rear. "That way, when you get back to Philly, you can tell all your buddies you were an official deputy and Officer Joe Beadle let you run his siren! How 'bout that?" The ambulance roared by. On a stretcher in the back, I could see a large man-shape, packed inside a black, zippered bag. "How 'bout it, Bill?" Officer Beadle wanted to know. "You ever run a siren before?"

seventeen

It was after one by the time Ned arrived at the police station to pick me up. Dozens of questions and signatures later, we were on our way back to Llanfair. He said it had taken Grace almost an hour to reach him at the club. He'd had a full morning of lessons. Then he realized he'd have to find someone to look after her. She was barely capable of speech when he got home.

Ned didn't know Grandad's shortcut. We went up the Garden State Parkway to the Atlantic City Expressway. You're practically on the bridge before you see a light. "The bullyboys claim your grandfather ran them off the road and when they went to have a word with him about it, he went mad, started strangling one of them, calling them filth. They say you ran into the woods and before they knew what was happening you were back with a kitchen knife in your hands. George took the knife and went after one of them with it, so they say. There was a fight, and, well, the knife ended up where it did. The police are skeptical. The two louts have quite a past between them. Nothing major. Drunk driving, fights. The problem is, all three of them positively swear it was self-defense. There's only your word, a ten-year-old." Ned was gloating. I wished he'd just go ahead and admit he was glad Grandad was dead.

"They're lying," I said. After ten years, Ned and I were still strangers. "Grandad wanted to help them. He knew the accident was his fault. He said he was sorry a million times."

"One of them was covered with strangulation marks, I gather, and the knife, you admitted yourself, it was from our kitchen. I'm not saying you're lying, Billy. The point is, under the circumstances, it will be rather difficult to prove they are."

"They made us take off our clothes. . . ."

"Yes, well they claim that was after your grandfather's attack. They wanted to teach him a lesson. They admit they were wrong to involve you in such dirty business. . . ." I couldn't bring myself to tell about Marie. I wondered if they had told the police what she did . . . if Ned knew. "I take it they were still a bit soused when they presented themselves to the police. They made no attempt to hide the fact that they'd been drinking. . . ." It worried me, but I had to admit it to myself: Willie and Buddy were smarter than they looked.

I pressed myself against the door of Ned's car, as far from him as I could get. For a second, I considered flipping the chrome lever. I would spill out onto the expressway and be run over by the Trailways bus behind us. . . . Grandad had died protecting me, a knife through his throat that I had practically handed to the killers. They would go free because there was only one of me and I was only ten years old. . . . I should have seen the stop sign and warned Grandad. I wasn't that tired. "Hey, Grandad, do you see the stop?" Everything would be different now. After a swim and lunch, Grandad and I would be riding the shortcut, our trunk full of icy fish. . . .

The Philadelphia skyline was gray on gray. The air had changed from mown grass and pine trees to refineries and fumes. Ned and I would soon be back in Llanfair, to Mom and our happy home.

eighteen

The day before Grandad's funeral, Grace's brother, my uncle Hugh, came in from Connecticut with his wife, Betse, and two of their three kids. Hugh picked up Grandad's ashes at the crematorium and, for some reason, brought them to our house. Ned said Hugh probably thought he'd have to pay more if Grandad stayed with them at the Marriott.

I can still see the box. It was much smaller than I expected, only about the size Kleenex comes in. It was neatly wrapped in heavy paper with narrow silver and white stripes. On the top, there was an envelope with Grandad's name on it. While Grace was outside talking to Hugh, I picked up the box. I was shaking. My hands were sweaty. It was heavier than you'd expect ashes to be. "George Corfield Chesterton," the envelope said. The paper was the thick, creamy-looking kind. The words were a little off center to the left. I could see where the typist had typed *a* instead of *o* in Grandad's middle name and gone back and fixed it. I remember thinking she must have been in a hurry. It made me angry.

Grace had sort of disappeared after Grandad got killed. Most of the time, she stayed in her room. She cried a lot. Sometimes I could hear her cursing. She left all of the arrangements for the service at St. Michael's Church, and the burial, to Hugh and their sister Jane. Jane had been able to do practically everything by phone from her home in White Plains, New York. I could tell Grace was jealous of Jane and Hugh. She said they'd always been a team, and that even though she was the middle child, she'd never fit in.

I hadn't been in St. Michael's since Grandma's funeral. She had belonged there her whole life. We didn't go to church. Grandma had arranged for me to be christened at St. Michael's. Ned and Grace were married there. It was considered the most prestigious church on the Main Line.

The building itself is spectacular, the kind of church where you'd expect to see a coronation. There are at least two dozen thirty-foot stained-glass windows, and seating for a good eight hundred. Nearly two hundred turned out for Grandad's memorial. I was awed to see so many important-looking people, all dressed in black. "Bunch of zombies from the bank," Ned called them, "and from those rotten, stuck-up clubs he was so fond of. They all go to each other's funerals so someone will show up when it's their turn."

"*George Cor-field Ches-ter-ton*," the minister said as the service began. Each syllable fell on me like a wrecking ball. "*Our be-lov-ed brother . . .*" The Right Reverend Richard Petrie's voice was as grand as the church. It caromed from wall to wall, column to column. His words sounded eternal, as if they were spoken in stone. They were sending Grandad to God, officially. There was no doubt. This was the end.

I sat up front, between my parents. Ned stared straight ahead. Grace sniveled and clutched my hand. Hers felt icy and damp. I thought about the fishing trip, about those last moments when Willie and Buddy were circling us. My mind drifted back to happier times . . . Christmases, sunset sails on the *Eastern Star*, hugs, smiles, and kisses. It was all over. Grandad was gone. There was only the terrible empty space he'd left behind.

The church seemed intimidating and unfriendly. The service dragged on. Each minute, it became harder for me to bear my pain. I felt close to no one and no thing. When we stood to sing a closing hymn, the words stuck in my throat.

The cemetery people had dug a neat, little hole for the box and put up a green-and-white awning over it. Grandma's name was already on the stone. There was space for Grandad's underneath. Father Petrie said more prayers. I didn't listen. A ladybug was crawling over my left shoe. I had on my green school blazer and gray flannel pants. Perspiration trickled down my back. Ned had said only, "Nonsense," when Grace asked if she could get me a summer suit. Bridget and Megan, Uncle Hugh's girls, exchanged evil looks in the shadow of their mother's reproachful frown. Suddenly, two grim men, using a sling of black ribbons, lowered the tidy box of ashes into the hole. The envelope with Grandad's name was gone. There was a shiny seal on top that looked like foil. Grace was sobbing. Ned put his arms around her, awkwardly, as if he'd never done it before. The box was no longer visible from where I was standing. It was very hot. The air smelled of fresh-cut grass. The Phillies were losing. Grandad was gone. "Good-bye, Grandad," I heard myself say. Everyone looked at me. I bit hard on my lower lip, and began to cry. I couldn't help it.

nineteen

It's Friday, my day off from Legacy Mint; that and Saturday. I work Sunday through Thursday. I didn't do the paper this morning so I got in about 3:25. If I lived at the mint, I'd have no problem getting to sleep, but the ride home usually wakes me up. I watched a rerun of "T. J. Hooker" and ate a can of tuna, which I washed down with bourbon. I have eleven cans of tuna left and when they're gone, I won't buy any more. I saw a thing on TV about how they kill millions of porpoises every year netting tuna. The sea and its creatures are like God to me.

I woke up around noon and cleaned the apartment. There's laundry equipment in the basement. After I've done the cleaning, I go down there and run the wash. It's usually a couple of loads. Some of the tenants just load the machines and leave. I'm not about to take a chance on somebody waltzing off with one of my uniforms, not at $118 apiece.

On the second and fourth Fridays of each month, I

drive down to Atlantic City. I can't afford to gamble, but I like the action. I like to escape. I'm happy enough most of the time just working with my computer or watching television in my apartment, but a couple times a month, I like to get away.

Atlantic City is where I met Cinnamon. I've known her two years. We have rapport. She calls herself either a dancer or an entertainer, but the fact is, she's a stripper. There hasn't been any sex yet, although I've been aroused when I was with her, and I'm quite sure she knew it. Unfortunately, the place where she works has very strict rules about employees dating the customers. Still, I expect us to be intimate eventually. As long as I've waited to have sex with a woman, I want everything to be right the first time: the right woman, the right mood, the right environment, plenty of time. I've read about people doing it on elevators, between floors. The idea disgusts me.

By three, I'm showered, shaved, and ready to go. Since it's June, I've switched over to the tan sport coat and dark brown slacks. Today, I go the whole route and put on a tie. It's dark brown with blue paisley things in it. It goes well with the light blue shirt.

If the traffic's not too bad, you can get to Atlantic City from my place in 90 minutes, but on a Friday afternoon in June, forget it. I make it in 106 minutes—not bad, considering. My car is a black Dodge Daytona. I got a good deal since it was rental. I bought the extended warranty. True, the Daytona might be more suitable for a teenager, but at that time in my life, cars weren't on the bill of fare, and whatever thirty-three-year-old security guards are supposed to drive I doubt would interest me.

I park in a lot near the Sure Thing, the lounge where Cinnamon works. In winter, you can park on the street. I've brought her candy. I usually do, or flowers. She seems to prefer the candy. Actually, I bought a case of it on sale. I didn't tell her that. I'm sure she would think it was presumptuous.

It's very dark inside the Sure Thing. They have a bouncer at the door to collect a five-dollar cover charge. I fumble with my money for a few seconds while my eyes adjust to the light. I know the bouncer recognizes me, but he just mumbles the standard greeting, even though I speak to him by name. It irritates me. I've been a good customer, to say the least.

The rock music is throbbing, "Total Eclipse of the Heart"; the atmosphere is one part air to nine parts cigarette smoke. I don't smoke, but I got so used to the smell of it in prison that clean air smelled strange to me when I got out. Even so, my eyes sting. Melanie, one of the hostesses, offers me a table near the stage, but I head for the bar. I like to check things out before I commit myself.

Brandy, one of my favorite bartenders, is on duty. She greets me with a big smile. "Hey, honey, where you been keeping yourself?" She was off the last two times I was in. She's wearing a red satin blouse that shows off her great cleavage, and black fishnet panty hose that rise over the sweet spot between her thighs and cheeks. A black bodysuit thing covers the legal minimum. Twenty seconds after I sit down, I'm in love with her ass.

I say, "I've been on vacation in the south of France." She gives me a cocktail napkin and a look that reads out somewhere between "Bullshit!" and "What the hell are you talking about?" "What can I do for you?" she says.

Suck my cock. "Rum and coke. Have one yourself."
She makes my drink and pours herself a shot of root
beer schnapps. We touch glasses. "Cinnamon around?"
I put a twenty on the counter. She takes it.

"In the back changing. She came in five minutes before
you." Brandy puts a fan of two fives and two ones in
front of me and swishes off to another customer, a black
guy in an expensive suit. I sip some drink and swing
my barstool toward the stage. The girl dancing must belong to the day shift. She's got boobs like fried eggs and
an abdominal scar. The deejay makes some wisecracks
that don't go over and plays something by Springsteen.
It's not a bad crowd. Maybe fifty guys. Construction
types off work for the day. Husbands. College twerps.
A couple of women: one young and dead-eyed sitting
by herself at the bar, probably after a job or a quick
twenty. The other one's about fifty, antsy, chain-
smoking, sitting at a table with two much younger guys
who act bored. I don't get it.

A pretty blonde with a face like a twelve-year-old
starts dancing on the second stage. There are three stages
altogether. One's still dark. The girl with the fried-egg
boobs is replaced by one I call Silicon Sue. She's older
than I am, but well preserved. It doesn't matter; no one
cares about her face. I'm getting into it. I wave at Brandy
for another drink.

It's twenty of seven by the time Cinnamon finally
makes an appearance. I have no idea what she was doing back there. I know some of the girls go backstage
and get high between dances. They're required to dance
three songs; then they can hustle the customers for

drinks or go grocery shopping. It doesn't matter as long as they're ready to dance when it's their turn. Cinnamon told me she made over thirty thousand last year. All tips, all cash.

She starts for the deejay booth; then she notices me. I avoid eye contact and turn a little as if I haven't seen her. I guess I'm peeved. I have no right to be. She didn't know I was here. "Hi, pumpkin!" she says. "How you doin'?" I can't help smiling. She plants a little kiss beside my ear. As she swings onto the stool next to me, her knee brushes my thigh. She's got on this sort of bathing-suit thing that's covered with gold bangles. Her boobs bulge out of it like fat scoops of ice cream begging to be licked.

"I'm great," I say, "now that you're here." I wave at Brandy to bring us drinks. "Here's a little something." I hand her the candy. Her eyes light up.

"Oh, thanks, Steve. You're really sweet, you know that?" She kisses me again in the same place, just as I hoped she would. Her stockings are like shiny gold film over the smooth flesh of her legs. It's hard not to touch. "You going to be able to stay awhile?"

"If that's what you want."

She laughs. Brandy sets the glasses in front of us and takes ten dollars. "Thanks for the drink," Cinn says. She takes a quick sip through the straw. It's soda of some kind in a cocktail glass. We've never talked about it, but I found out that there's no booze in the dancers' drinks, even at six bucks a pop. I must have bought her ten of them one night and matched her drink for drink. I'm on my ass and she's dead sober. Finally, while she was in the john, I checked her drink. Ginger ale. I felt like I'd been royally screwed. I got all set to unload on her, but then when she came back, she pressed against me and smiled this incredible smile, and I just couldn't stay mad at her. After all, she doesn't make the rules in this world, any more than I do.

"Is the candy okay? Now that it's summer, maybe you'd rather have flowers."

"It's fine, really. You don't mind if I share it with the other girls, do you? I mean, no sense in me getting fat all by myself." We both laugh as she pulls a cigarette out of the little red leather case she keeps them in. There's a loop on the outside that holds her lighter. "I'm up next."

"Me, too!"

She slaps my arm playfully. "You talk that way around your mother?"

"Who do you think that is?" I point to Silicon Sue. Cinn laughs again. Her voice is a little raspy from all the smoking. I guess she's about twenty-six. She knows my age. Her hair is cut short. It's blond, probably from a bottle, but very becoming. She's about five-eight in heels. I love her makeup. Silver eye shadow. Glossy red lips. She has on these long, shiny gold earrings that sparkle like chandeliers. Her eyes are lavender-gray, big as Diana Ross's. I try not to stare at her. Sometimes, when we're talking, I realize I'm not looking at her at all.

"Have you been okay?" I ask. "Everything going all right?"

"Oh yeah, you know, same old shit. My landlord wants to raise the rent so me and my girlfriend are looking for another place."

"Any prospects?"

"Nah. Everything's getting so expensive. Hey, if you hear of anything . . . Oh shit, you live in Philly, I forgot. . . . Christ, I'm on." She drops her cigarettes behind the bar and hops off the stool. "Good to see you, Steve. Hang around if you've got nothing better to do; I'm on till two. Smile!" I pull my face into a smile and blow her a kiss as she trots off to the main stage. She's left the candy on the bar. I don't know whether to put it with her cigarettes or just leave it there.

She's dancing a Rod Stewart song. Easy tempo. She struts it back and forth; the costume stays on. This is the tease. By the end of the third number, she'll be naked except for pasties and a G-string.

I was disappointed in our conversation. Cinn seemed distant. I order another drink and put out a fresh twenty. Brandy takes the empties but doesn't wipe the bar. It's wet. The condensation from our glasses soaked though the cheap napkins they use. I take a wad of them from a stack nearby and dry the area in front of me. I feel myself getting depressed. I'm not even watching Cinn dance.

Two goons in motorcycle outfits move into the space where Cinn had been sitting. I can't see around them. *"We are young, heartache to heartache. . . ."* I put the candy behind the bar next to her cigarettes and take my drink to a small table beside the stage where she's dancing. I can't catch her eye. She squats in front of some greasy kid with a folded-up five in his mouth and pulls out her G-string. He stuffs the bill in there and starts laughing. Cinn is on her back now writhing on the floor for the college boys. She licks the tip of a finger and runs it along her crotch. Every guy around the stage is whoop-

ing and whistling, except me. They throw money. . . .
"Love is a battlefield. . . ."

Cinn spots me and winks while she is picking up bills
from the dance floor at the end of her set. I told her my
name is Steve because I don't want to take any chance
of her recognizing my real name. I've found I like being
someone else. A grinning black girl takes the stage.
Cinn's ten minutes' work appears to have been worth
about twenty-five dollars, tax free. Not bad considering
the educational requirements for the job.

I find an empty table away from the lights, where
Cinn can join me. Melanie takes my order and promises
to tell Cinn where I'm sitting. By the time the drinks
come, all three stages are working.

When Cinn finally comes out of the dressing room,
my drink is gone. She's got on a spectacular new costume: a royal blue body stocking with sequin designs in
all the right places. I straighten myself and pull her chair
closer to mine. I'm ready to wave when she starts looking for me, but she never does. Instead, she goes straight
to a table with a couple of guys in business suits and
sits down. They act like best friends. A waitress stops at
their table. I see Cinn ordering. I look at the six-dollar
glass of ginger ale I've bought for her. *"Blue jean beauty
queen . . ."* Every bubble glows blue-pink in the rays of
the black light that hangs above me. Wasted. I order a
new drink for myself and try to get off on the tall redhead prancing on stage two. Cinn has her arm around
one of the hotshots. They're laughing it up. Another girl
has joined the party. I feel like an ant. I know Cinn sits
with other men when I'm not here, but I don't let that
bother me. It's her job, and she hasn't picked them in-

stead of me. I kill my drink and walk out.

The night air is damp and soured by fumes from cars, bars, and restaurants. The Atlantic Ocean is only a thousand feet away but you can't smell it, or hear it either. All the sounds are people sounds. I'm sorry I came. I had important things to tell Cinn. But the mood is spoiled.

My car glistens in a coat of dew. I get in and realize I have no heart to make the long drive home. I close my eyes and see the swaying roundness of her hips and buttocks. The nipples. The breasts. The moist lips. I can still hear her music and feel its beat. I loosen my belt and zipper and take some air. My hand goes where I know it shouldn't. I feel the heat.

Soon, Cinnamon is with me, and though we know the time and place are wrong, neither of us is stronger than our desire.

twenty

Charles and Deidre Howe reside in Boulder, Colorado, in the fashionable Mapleton section. Their children, Andrew ("Drew"), age five, and Elizabeth ("Lizzie"), seven, are in private schools. Mrs. Howe drives the Volvo station wagon; he has a BMW convertible. I don't know the color of either car.

I have no record of prior marriages for Howe. Mrs. Howe's marriage to Leonard Poul, a flutist, was annulled in 1978. I assume he was impotent. In this past year, the Howes have had medical expenses related to her reproductive organs and young Lizzie's asthma. They carry a million in life insurance—on Deidre.

She is the daughter of Thomas and Penelope Cummings of Winnetka, Illinois. Mr. Cummings was heir to a huge chunk of Illinois Central stock and served in various executive capacities with the company until his death. Mrs. Cummings, née Balfort, is a descendant of meat-packing money old enough to have lost any scent of the stockyards.

Mr. Howe, in his sinecure as a "trustee" of the Eli Gentry Foundation, shares in the fun of bestowing the millions of dollars in grants that the foundation hands out each year, usually in the humanities. Eli Gentry, an old-fashioned cattle baron, was Mrs. Howe's great-grandfather. Mr. Howe's "job," as far as I have been able to learn, consists of flying around the country and allowing his ass to be kissed by grant recipients and would-be recipients. As they say, it's hard work, but somebody has to do it.

Mr. Howe's personal history is sketchy. No hometown newspapers to comb. No hometown. In fact, during the five years prior to his marriage to Deidre, Mr. Howe held three different jobs and lived in four states. Part of the time, he was unemployed. Among the companies he worked for were a big hotel chain and a penny-stock brokerage. In 1984, he was arrested on a DUI in California. The charge was dismissed. . . .

In the early days, as Howe's life unfolded before me, I could scarcely believe how accurately I'd typed him. Everything was true to form. Nothing I've learned about him since has changed that. Oh, he runs the Boulder Marathon and coaches Lizzie's soccer team. He even played a part in *The Pirates of Penzance* last year. You might think he was a real straight arrow, but all it took was one look at the man's face and I knew. I just knew.

twenty-one

It's 11:35 Friday night. I'm sitting in briefs and a tank top on the green love seat I bought from the Salvation Army. I have the thermostat for the a.c. set at seventy-five, but it feels hotter than that. It went over ninety today. In my hand is a glass of Old Yellowstone. Neat. I have a pleasant buzz going. The room is dark except for a faint glow from the night-light in the john. On the radio, some asshole is ranting about skinheads. The place is clean. All the laundry is done for another week. I have nothing to do. I took all the cleansers, brushes, sponges, and other junk out from under the kitchen sink today and gave that space a good scrubbing. I do it every month. Also today, I tossed the kalanchoe plant that had been dying on the windowsill above my kitchen sink. No loss, I got it free at True Value. Next Friday, I'll be back at the Sure Thing. I'm looking forward to it, but this is my off week. I pick up the phone.

It's two hours earlier where Howe lives. I've called before. I pretend I'm selling something or collecting money for charity. It's nice to stay in touch.

Lizzie answers on the fifth ring. She should be in bed. I hear a TV in the background. "Hello, honey," I say, "may I speak to your daddy? I have something important to tell him." She drops the handset on a hard surface. I'm using a light Spanish accent. I vary the voice each time. She yells for her father. They turn down the TV. She's telling him it's someone important. You better believe it, sweetheart.

"Hel-lo." His voice, all charm. Perhaps he's buzzing a bit, too.

"Hello, Mr. Howe?"

"Yes."

"How are you tonight, sir?"

"Fine, who is—"

"That's great, sir. This is Steve DeJesus of Vector Securities. I'm sorry to bother you on a Friday night, sir, but a friend gave me your name and said he thought you might be interested in a special offering we have coming up next week. Might that be right, Mr. Howe? Could you spare me a few minutes to tell you about the kind of investment opportunity that comes along once in a lifetime?"

"I'm really not—"

"Do you follow the market, Mr. Howe?"

"What friend gave you my name?"

"I really don't know, sir. We have you down as a referral."

"I have a broker, Mr. . . . ?"

"DeJesus, sir. Are you strictly a conservative investor, Mr. Howe? Or do you think you might consider taking a businessman's risk to earn several times your initial investment?"

"Mr. DeJesus, I'm just not interested. I'm going to hang up now." It's at moments like this that I'm especially glad I bought a phone with redial. Three rings.

"Hello." A tad curt this time.

"Hello there, Mr. Howe. Steve DeJesus. I'm afraid we were cut off. Must be having trouble with our phone system again. Sorry, sir."

"Look," he barks, "you are irritating me. I'm not one bit—"

"One question, sir, and I'll hang up. A yes or no answer is all I ask, Mr. Howe. Fifteen seconds more. I'm just trying to earn a living, sir."

"Get on with it."

"Do you still butt-fuck that little girl of yours every chance you get?"

This time, it's my turn to hang up. I do it quickly so he doesn't hear my laughter. I go into the kitchen and turn on the overhead light so I can see the calendar. Over the months and years, I've logged all our calls. Not once has he ever given me the feeling that he or his dear wife recognized my voice. I note in my own private shorthand the time and nature of the conversation. I'm not usually so offensive, but this phase of our relationship will end soon. So really, I have nothing to lose.

twenty-two

It was strange how lonely I felt right after Grandad died. We hadn't even lived in the same house, and we didn't really see that much of each other. I guess the difference was I knew he was there. He called me at least twice a week, and we usually did something together about once a month. It would have been more often, but Ned resented Grandad's interest in me. I never knew why. It wasn't as if Grandad was cutting in on time Ned wanted to spend with me.

In addition to the phone calls and the outings, Grandad and I had always written to each other. His secretary typed the letters he sent me. The bank stationery was quite elegant. Grandad's name was printed in raised letters near the top. Underneath, it said, "Chairman." Sometimes he'd send me a key chain or a penlight or some other trinket the bank was giving away. When I was small, I sent him drawings I'd made. One day a few weeks after he was killed, I realized I could still write to him. I got excited. It was like getting a little piece of him back.

July 28

Dear Grandad,

It feels really dumb to be writing to a dead person but I miss you a lot and my parents arent any good to talk to. The thing I miss most about you is talking to you and the way you used to make me feel all happy inside. I hope maybe you will know I'm writing to you in heaven or your ghost will find out. Anyway it makes me feel better even if you don't answer. Thank you for all the money you left me for when I'm 25. Ned was really mad because he thought you would leave mom a lot of money. He wants to sue for more of your money but mom doesn't want to. They had a really bad fite about it. I was lissining on the 2nd floor. Mom was crying a lot. Ned says uncle Hugh and aunt Jane don't give a dam about us. Last night I had to push mom up the stairs from behind and she started to fall over backwards on top of me and it really scared me. I still love her but I don't like to take care of her like a baby. I wish you were here to help. Sometimes I get kind of made at you for dying. I didn't see the stop sign either so maybe it was my fault. I still dream about what happent almost every night. I get sad when I think my life will never be as good as before you died. Someday I know I will be in heaven with you. I hope you don't think this letter is to stupid. I'm going to hide

it where nobody will ever find it but you or me. I
love you.

Love,
Billy

Before the lawyer read Grandad's will, Ned obsessed for
hours calculating how much we would get. He treated
Grace like a movie star. But alas, Grandad had made
some bad investments and blown his income on "personal pleasures." The bottom line was, Grandad's whole
estate was less than half a million. He'd left the bulk of
that in trust for his six grandchildren. After the lawyers
and taxes and everybody else took their cut, Grace's
share wasn't enough for the mortgage payment on 929
Ammons. So much for Ned's plan to open the "Main
Line Academy of Tennis." He was so pissed, it was actually funny.

To get even with Grandad, Ned wanted to yank me
out of Westfield Academy. He wrote the school a long
letter instructing them to send him the $500 deposit
Grandad had paid for the fall term. Grace would have
none of that. It was one of the few times she refused to
play doormat. I remember her saying, "It's the only
thing about our lives that isn't shabby." She said she'd
sell some of Grandma's jewelry to help pay for it. At
first, I thought she was worried about my education, but
the more she talked about it, I realized that she just
wanted to go on being a "Westfield Mother." It didn't
matter that she never helped out at the thrift shop or the
Christmas bazaar. That green-and-gold Westfield sticker
in the back window of her old Audi separated Grace
from the masses.

twenty-three

One afternoon that fall, there was an incident at the train station. Except for two old black women, who were in overcoats despite the warm weather, everyone waiting for the train was a Westfielder. Roger Ormsby and some other kids from my class were passing around a can of beer. There was a bench at the far west end of the platform that I considered my own. I plopped my books down there and took off my school blazer and tie. Near the bench was a tall clump of grass that had pushed its way through the asphalt near the tracks. Chunks of pavement the size of brownies stood practically on end at its rim. As I bent to yank a blade from the clump, Roger Ormsby's shadow darkened my hands.

"Hey, McIlvain," he said, "my dad says you're going to school on charity this fall. How's it feel?" I felt my face turn red. Uncle Hugh, a Westfield alumnus like Grandad, had negotiated a deal for my tuition with the school's board of managers. Ormsby's father was on the board.

I said, "Why don't you go drink some more beer or something, Ormsby? Leave me alone." In addition to being fat, Ormsby had big brown eyes with long lashes and greasy brown hair. Even at ten, you could tell he was going to be bald when he grew up. His face, with its turned-up nose and big buckteeth, always reminded me of a beaver.

"If you're gettin' a free ride," he said, "*I'd* like to know about it. My dad's payin' full tuition for me and my brother, plus givin' money to the school besides." Two others, Ronnie Strauser and Clyde Stitch, stood smirking next to a rusty lamppost ten feet away. Stitch had wrapped his school tie around the beer can. I got up.

"Look, Ro-ger," I said, "I'm not getting charity. My parents pay for me the same as yours." I had grown over the summer, but so had Ormsby. He was still two inches taller.

"Liar! They had to ask my dad's permission to give you charity. I heard him tell my mom all about it. You probably couldn't go to *public* school on what your old man makes." Strauser and Stitch thought the crack was pretty funny.

"What's it going to take to get rid of you, Ormsby?" I asked. I could feel the fight coming. Ormsby considered himself a big jock.

"Just admit you're gettin' charity . . . and say thanks to everyone whose parents give money to the school. You can start with me and these guys."

"Fuck off," I said. Ormsby's rubbery lips formed a smirk as he took half a step back and looked at the others. I doubted that Stitch and Strauser would gang up on me. Ormsby was the kind of kid everyone wanted to see in a fight.

"You guys hear this kid?" he laughed. "Pretty big mouth. Well, maybe he's not on charity"—he was looking right at me—"but I could name probably a hundred people who would swear his mother's an alk." We lunged simultaneously. Stitch and Strauser closed in. Ormsby pounded my back as we tussled. I got a leg behind his calf and pushed. We both went down. I landed on top. My weight drove the wind from him. Gasping, he grappled for my face and throat. I whipped a fist across his left cheek. He howled. I was doing much better than I expected. "Waste him, Billy," Strauser urged. A crowd was forming. I felt good. I hit him again, and again, driving my fist into his mouth, nose, and cheek. The more I hit him, the harder I hit him. It was exhilarating. He panicked. "Let me up!" he screamed. "Let me up! Help me, you guys!" He tried arching his back and rolling to escape. I kept punching. The crowd was cheering me. There was blood on Ormsby's face and on the pavement behind his head. Suddenly, he was sobbing like a baby. He stopped trying to attack and covered his face with his hands. I sat back on his chest. The crowd hovered, gawking at the fallen hotshot. Paul Schuyler was smiling at me.

"Let me up," Ormsby begged. I felt ten feet tall.

"I don't want you to come near me again the rest of your life, Ormsby," I said. I grabbed his throat and squeezed. When he tried to push my hand away, I squeezed tighter. "Did you hear me?" He gagged some response. I let go of his throat, rose up on my knees, and sat down hard on his stomach. "Huh, Ormsby?"

"Okay, okay," he wheezed.

"You promise?"

"Yeah. Promise. Please get offa me," he whined. I yearned for an excuse to hit him again. Pounding him gave me a rush.

Tears spilled from Ormsby's eyes as he stood up. There was blood in his nostrils and at the corner of his mouth. The whole side of his face was swollen. I backed away. Strauser waved to me as the crowd of onlookers moved down the platform. I savored their admiring looks.

"You're gonna get thrown out of school for this, McIlvain," Ormsby warned from a safe distance. "My dad's gonna sue for sure." I didn't answer. He was just trying to save face. The crowd was regrouping near the station building. I was alone again. The idea of getting thrown out of Westfield didn't bother me very much, but it scared me to think that Ormsby's father might sue. Ned would be furious.

During the ride home, I visualized the terror in Ormsby's eyes as I pounded him. I'd even scared myself a little. Since Grandad died, something I couldn't name had changed inside.

twenty-four

Oct 4

Dear Grandad,

You won't beleive this. Those two guys who killed you named Buddy and Willie are suing for $2,000,000.00. The one you strangled claims he can't work because he has black outs and the other one says what he had to do to you caused him cycological damage and he has to see a doctor the rest of his life. Ned got so mad he went away by himself for 2 days and mom practally never stopped crying the whole time. Uncle Hugh says you had $1,000,000 insurance but if they win there wont be anything left for us kids. I wish I could kill Buddy and Willie. One good thing was I liked it when Ned was gone. Evrything was a lot more peacefull. Mom is still pretty bad. She keeps saying why does evrything have to be so ugly all the time. She told me to enjoy my childhood becaus these are the best years of my life. To her evrything is

Ugly Ugly Ugly Ugly. Our house might be the ug-lyist of all. She doesn't even try to clean anymore. There are piles of dirty dishes and rotten food in the kitchen. She has Morris Grocery deliver food and haff the time she doesn't even put it away. Upstairs there are all these trash bags. Yesterday she opened her door to talk to me and the smell from in there was so bad I almost got sick. A couple of times I tried to clean up but it made me really sad or something and I had to stop. I stay away as much as I can. I guess I'm kind of scared. Some-thing bad is going to happen. I can tell. I just wish I could hide until it's over. I still think about you evry day and wish you could be here. Sometimes when the phone rings I think its you for a second calling me the way you used to. The world is a pretty dumb place without you. I would give any-thing if you could come back.

Love,
Billy

twenty-five

A few weeks after I beat up Roger Ormsby, Paul Schuyler, the richest kid in my school, asked me to spend the weekend at his house. Ormsby had told everyone that Paul had cystic fibrosis. It was true, but Paul didn't want anyone to know. When Paul invited me, I figured it was just because he was grateful that I'd trashed Ormsby.

I'm not sure why my parents got so wired about that weekend. It was as if they thought some of the Schuylers' money and prestige would rub off on them and make everything all right. They had me waiting at the curb fifteen minutes before the Schuylers' car was supposed to come for me. Grace was in a panic that one of the Schuylers might see the inside of our house, or her. "I'm not looking my best right now, sweetie," she told me as Ned was trying to hustle me out the door. "Tell them I had tickets to a concert."

"At nine in the morning?" Ned asked.

"Oh, I don't know," she said. "Tell them something,

and be sure they know you're a Chesterton, darling. One of the Chestnut Hill Chestertons. And whatever you do, don't let them in this slum when you come back."

The Schuylers sent a gray, chauffeur-driven Jaguar that smelled of leather. Paul was in the backseat. Woodlawn, the Schuyler family mansion, was only fifteen minutes from our house, but it was in another world, protected by electric gates. I got spooked as we drove in. Paul seemed different. He was the king's son and I was the scruffy serf. I thought about asking them to take me home; I felt unworthy of such a place, but it was too late. We were pulling into a fancy little stable that had been converted to a six-car garage.

The house looked like a castle. It was made of gray stone and seemed to have chimneys everywhere. It sat at the top of a hill. Acres of gently sloping lawn and neat plantings wrapped around it like a green skirt, trimmed at the hem with a ruffle of woods that blocked any immediate sign of the outside world. Far below, through the light haze of an early October morning, I could see the graceful curves of the Schuylkill River. I had only dreamed of myself in such grand surroundings.

Paul's mother was young and beautiful. She treated me like visiting royalty; my nervousness vanished. That evening, she taught me how to play backgammon. We sat across from each other at a little table in their den. There was a bright fire crackling nearby. Paul and his father were playing Parcheesi.

"One of the things I like about this game," she told me as she set up the board, "is that it's half luck and half skill. When you win, of course, you take credit for being a skillful player, but when you lose, it's pure bad luck. . . ." She laughed girlishly and went on with the instructions. I'm sure I was staring at her every minute, but she never let on if it bothered her. She had some magical quality I couldn't resist. She seemed to sparkle. Her thick light-brown hair flowed in shining curves around the delicate features of her face. Her pale blue eyes were innocent one minute and danced with mischief the next. Her nose and cheeks were sprinkled with tiny freckles. She was wearing a light sweater the color of raspberries that showed off her large, welcoming breasts. I wanted to touch her. Her name was Claire, and I think I'm still a little bit in love with her. Halfway through the evening, I asked her if she'd ever been in the movies.

"Why, Billy," she laughed, "what makes you ask that?"

"I don't think I've ever seen a lady as beautiful as you." My voice was as low as I could make it. I could tell I had embarrassed her. I felt terrible. "I'm sorry. . . ."

"No, Billy . . ." She put her hand over mine. "I'm afraid I've never been very good at accepting compliments. That was a lovely thing of you to say." I was glad that Paul and his dad were still concentrating on the Parcheesi board. "I was in a few shows in college, just in the chorus. I always felt very awkward. Is it your roll?" My palms were dripping.

"I guess it is," I said. I laughed dumbly as I tossed the dice.

"I'm afraid I don't know your parents," she said, as she sat back in her chair. "Is your father a lawyer?"

"He . . . he's in business, sports equipment. He owns a big factory."

"Oh, that must be interesting. I'll bet you enjoy going there with him." I was sure she knew it was a lie.

"Yes. It's kind of far away." I wanted desperately to change the subject but my mind was blank.

"I enjoyed chatting with your mother on the phone the other day. I'm surprised our paths have never crossed at school. There are times when it seems I'm there *con*-stantly."

She couldn't possibly believe Ned owned a factory. She knew where we lived. "She stays at home pretty much," I said.

"Oh?"

"It's her heart. She has to stay in bed a lot."

"I'm sorry, Billy. I didn't know."

"That's okay."

"I'm afraid this game isn't going your way."

"I guess not."

"Well, remember, just blame it on bad luck." Paul and his dad were approaching the table, just in time to see me lose.

More than his many comforts and his wealth, I envied Paul his parents, his mother most of all. It seemed terrible to waste her on a boy who would die young. I would have given anything for the love and countless advantages Paul took for granted. The rest of that night, I tried to imagine a way that he and I could trade places. It seemed that everybody would be better off in the long run, when Paul was gone. It was a tantalizing possibility. My mind was still churning long after the last goodnight.

When I gave up on sleep, I got out of bed and went to the window of the large, comfortable room they'd given me next to Paul's. The view was to the north. A million lights twinkled at me from the far hills near Conshohocken. The huge house was dead silent. The world seemed solid and serene. I couldn't understand what was happening. For no apparent reason, I began to cry.

After Paul's father made a big breakfast for everyone, we all went to church. Paul's great-aunt Agnes came home with us for Sunday dinner. For a little while that day, I felt like part of their family. It probably helped that Aunt Agnes kept confusing me with Paul. That afternoon, Paul and I spent hours exploring the woods and fields around his house. We had fun, but it was hard for me to keep my mind on our imaginary adventures. I kept thinking that I didn't want the weekend to end, and the more I thought about it, the faster the time seemed to go by. Finally, the sunset ended our play. The time had come for Paul to do his homework and for me to go home. Thanks to my charm and good luck, I suppose, Claire Schuyler decided to drive me herself.

As I settled into the Jaguar beside Mrs. Schuyler, I realized what a big investment I had in her opinion of me, and suddenly, I was more afraid than Grace that a Schuyler might set foot in our house. What was in that house, human and otherwise, did not go with the image I had tried to project of myself.

As the electric gates parted to let us pass into the real world, my mind searched for words to convince Mrs. Schuyler not to take me home, but there were no words, and if there had been, my throat was too dry to speak them. After a dozen minutes of winding, leaf-covered lanes, the Jaguar took Hampton Avenue on a yellow and we were in Llanfair. I cleared my throat and waited for the lady beside me to ask directions. I prayed that "the slum," as Grace called it, had burned to the ground.

"Isn't *this* nice," Mrs. Schuyler said as we pulled up. "What a cozy home!" Her lie made me angry.

"Ah . . . We're redecorating," I said nervously as we approached the door. She seemed incredibly out of place in my front yard. "The house might be a bit of a mess."

"Oh, don't even think about that, Billy," she said cheerfully. She was so smooth. "It will be nice to meet your parents. I'm anxious to tell them how much we enjoyed having you."

There was no response to three rings of the doorbell. I was incredibly relieved and about to suggest that Mrs. Schuyler leave me with a neighbor when she walked along the front porch to a window. I followed. At the sight of Grace, I felt my face flush and a cold lump swell in my throat. She was passed out on the floor between the couch and the coffee table. Mrs. Schuyler went back to the door without speaking. It was unlocked. I wanted to run. We went in. Grace was in her raggy bathrobe. Her hair was matted; her feet were bare. My face burned with shame. The coffee table was cluttered with crumpled Kleenexes, dirty ashtrays, glasses, and an empty vodka bottle. The room air reeked of cigarette smoke and the sour smell of Grace's body. I stepped away from Mrs. Schuyler. I felt diseased.

Grace must have sensed our presence because she stirred as we approached. When she found us with her bleary eyes, she struggled briefly to sit up, but it was no good. She sank back, clinging to me with pleading eyes and a feeble smile. I knew she wanted me to make it right, but I had no idea what to do.

twenty-six

I sit with my legs spread wide. Cinnamon stands ready in the space between them. The bawdy smile on her lips is all for me. The music begins. *"Take me to where love is...."* The costume is new. Black simulated leather, lots of straps and metal stud-work. She starts to move, swaying easily. Men at the tables near us are looking at her. I want to tell them to turn their fucking eyes toward one of the stages. What's happening between Cinn and me is strictly private. She squats a little and swings her knees between my thighs. She rises and shows me the proud lift of her haunches. Even in the smoky air, I savor the sweet scent of her perfume.

"I love your perfume," I tell her. She doesn't hear me. I repeat it a little louder. She turns toward me again. As she does so, she peels off the bra part and hangs it around my neck.

"Thank you," she says. She puts her hands on my shoulders and leans across me so the tender curve of her long neck is under my nose. "Even better up close, huh?" She laughs.

"The closer the better!"

Her dainty earrings are rhinestones clustered like grapes. As she straightens, she brings her nipples within an inch or two of my face. I want desperately to touch, to suck. "I'll get you some," I say. "What's it called?"

"Roman Flower, but really, you shouldn't."

"I want to. I'm going away, Cinn. Don't miss me too much!"

"Vacation?"

"Important business. Something I've been working on for years."

"Good luck." She blows me a kiss with her fingertip and turns, working closer to me with each revolution. Her ass nearly touches my face. I feel her heat. I'm hard. I hope she's noticed.

"I'll miss you," I say.

"Me, too." Suddenly, she bends at the waist, puts her hands on my thighs, and lowers her head into the space above my crotch. Now she has certainly noticed. Her head bobs over my dick. Her hair whips my face. Harder and faster. I don't want her to stop. I want to show myself to her. I want her to taste me. Marie. I bite the inside of my cheek to help control the urge to hold and kiss. The music stops. The fantasy is over. Before I can protest, she's pulled the bra from my shoulders and is fastening it.

"That was beautiful, Cinn."

"You make it easy, Steve." She frowns a little.

"Sorry," I say. "Something took my mind off business." I'm embarrassed. I hand her a twenty and two fives.

"It's twenty," she says.

"Ten's a tip," I say. "Don't forget me while I'm away."

"You're too good to me, Steve." She kisses me lightly below the ear. "Stay away from loose women on that vacation, huh?"

"You bet!" I laugh.

They're calling her name to take the stage. I get sad as she walks away. I'd give an arm for any sign that she cared.

It's almost closing time. I sit like a pile of crap on my barstool. Cinn missed her last set. She's hiding from me, or off with another man. I am so sad. Within days, I will transcend the past and no one knows or gives a particular shit. If Cinnamon knew, she would care and understand. I ache to tell her. I know we are meant to be joined.

I save the little red straws they put in the drinks. It's a way to track expense and consumption. Eleven drinks so far tonight. Eleven. Too many, but normal for me. I don't feel drunk, but I wouldn't bet the ranch on passing a Breathalyzer.

There is only one stage working now. Felicity's up. She's small but cute. Black hair with loose curls. Amazing eyelashes. A baby smile. Her tits are bold: sex apples ripe for plucking. I think she's an addict. There are ten other customers. Some of them are boyfriends. Some want to be. A Vietnamese woman comes in a couple of times a night with long-stem roses in clear plastic sleeves. Horny, lovesick fools like me buy them and give them to the dancers in place of the words we cannot say.

Brandy checks the clock behind the bar. It's set thirteen minutes fast. "Bar time." In another minute or two she'll offer last call. Then, bang, as soon as they have all the money, the lights go up and they start grabbing glasses. Party's over. End of fantasy. Go to hell, go anywhere, *leave*.

Suddenly, Cinn is here. I didn't see her coming. I'm resurrected. She's mounting the third stool to my right. She's in street clothes, a stretchy black halter top and tight jeans. She's tense, maybe a little drunk. She lights a cigarette. I don't think she knows it's me sitting here. My throat is dry, but I speak.

"Buy you a drink?" She frowns at the sight of me. "I don't mean to intrude. I know you're on your own time."

She sighs. "Just tell me this," she says, "are all men total assholes, or what?" Her eyes dare me to disagree.

"Most are," I laugh. "Some are trying not to be." The deejay announces last call. "How 'bout the drink, Cinn? You look like you could use it."

She studies me as she expels a plume of cigarette smoke. "Hey, Brandy," she says, "Double Seven and Seven. Steve's buyin'."

"I'll have the usual, Brandy," I say. "Double, too."

Brandy gives Cinn a look. Cinn does a thing with her eyes and Brandy pours. Real booze for Cinn. A first. I am pumped with excitement and a little scared. I give Brandy a fat tip to impress Cinn. Real drinks are cheaper than the fake ones. Cinn is looking at me in a way she never has before. I can't read it. Silicon Sue joins Felicity for the last dance of the night. Sue's plastic tits are the only parts are of her that look awake.

"Cheers, Cinn," I say. It seems apt.

Cinn knocks down a third of her drink. "Thanks," she says. "I don't need this, but I need it, if you know what I mean."

"I was waiting for your last set."

"Sorry. I got tied up backstage."

"Man trouble?"

"Yeah. . . . No, asshole trouble. Never mind. I'm not gonna cry anymore."

"It's okay, if you want to, I understand."

"Thanks. You're sweet, Steve."

"I just want to be your friend, to help, if I can." She takes another big knock and gives me a smile.

"So why are you sitting way over there?"

I move to the stool next to her and practically knock it over climbing on. I wonder if she can tell how nervous I am.

She hooks her arm through mine. Her eyes are all red. "Steve . . ." She presses her thigh against mine. If I wasn't hard before, I am now. There's a steamy smell about her, under the booze and smoke and perfume. ". . . you heading back to Philly right away?"

"Well, soon. I mean . . . there's no rush."

"I could use a ride. I can call a cab if it's not convenient, but it's not far out of your way."

"I'd love to."

"It's just that I was expecting a ride, and the king of the assholes flames out on me, you know."

"Sure."

"You won't get weird on me or anything, will you?"

"Hey," I say, "we're old friends."

Cinn and I finish what's left of our drinks and stand to go. A couple. I'm grinning like Christmas morning; I can't help it. The dregs watch with envy as we leave.

Cinn loves the Daytona. I ask her if she was expecting a garbage truck. She laughs. Her reaction pays back every cent I spent for the car. I hold the door for her. She has new respect for me: I'm a human being, someone with an identity beyond the smoky shadows of the Sure Thing. Cinn is the first woman who's sat in my car. Actually, she's my first passenger, period.

As we drive, she talks on about her boyfriend. *Ex*-boyfriend. I'm supportive. I tell her to talk out her anger. I know how to talk to women from watching TV. She lights a cigarette. It gives me an chance to show off the electric sunroof. I envy the stretchy halter top caressing Cinn's breasts.

There's almost no traffic. The ads say AC never sleeps. Tonight, it's not asleep. It's dead.

I have no rubbers. I feel embarrassed about stopping to buy some. I've never bought them. On the inside, they just handed them out. I decide to wait. Maybe she has some. I assume she was intimate with her boyfriend. I can't stop looking at her.

We head for the expressway. She says she lives at the Gull Inn, a housekeeping motel across the bay in Pleasantville. I'm so hard it feels like I'm cutting myself on my zipper. I wonder if I'll know what to do. I wonder if she'll know it's my first time.

The Gull Inn is a dump. I had always imagined Cinn

in a tidy condo. Her unit is second from the end. There's a light on inside. We splash across the lot and pull in next to her car, an old Duster. Yellow, I think.

"Hey thanks, Steve," she says. The sound of the phony name startles me. Everything else is so real. "You're a doll, you know? I mean, I really appreciate the ride, and you listening to me bitch about Gene all the way over here. There's a lot of guys wouldn't put up with that."

"I've been wanting to do something nice for you for a long time." She looks at me with grateful eyes and smiles kindly. She cups her hand against the side of my face and leans over and kisses my lips. She's never done that before. No woman has, except Grace. I can't believe the sensation . . . so sweet and tender. Sexy, but kind, too. Electrifying. Before I can respond, she leans back again. "I can't figure you," she says. "You're a nice-looking guy, smart. You drive a real nice car. Don't you have a girl?"

"No . . ." I'm flustered. I can't believe she has no idea how I feel about her. "I work alone a lot. I just don't meet people." •

"I think you're cute," she laughs.

"I think you're the sexiest woman alive."

"Liar, but thanks."

"And the best kisser!" She leans over and kisses me again. This time, she moves her mouth all over mine. I put my arms around her. I feel her tongue on my lips. I touch it with mine. I'm afraid I'll come in my pants.

"I have a bottle inside, Steve," she snickers, "if you're thirsty . . ."   •

I can't let her go. The sensation of her bare skin against my hand, the warmth and weight of her body against mine . . . it's a thousand dreams come true. Wet dreams. "Practically dehydrated," I say.

"Pardon me?"

"Hell, yes, I'm thirsty." I release her as she leans back. My crotch is wet, but I haven't come.

"Good, we'll celebrate the death of Gene." She gropes for her door handle.

"Wait, I'll get your door. Hold on."

"You're weird, you know, but I like it."

I get out and lock my car door. There's a smell . . . like a dead cat. But I need air. I take my time rounding the car to get Cinn's door. The parking lot is full of puddles. There's a narrow strip of bulkheaded fill across the road. A hundred yards off is the bay. In the mud flats near the bulkhead are four crooked rows of rotting pilings. I open her door.

"Oh, shit," she says. "That mud's gonna wreck my shoes. Hold on, I'll take 'em off."

"No, I'll carry you."

"Are you for real?"

"Sure. I work out." Used to.

"Okay, how 'bout a piggyback? I ain't had one of them since my old man."

"You've got it!" We laugh as she twists herself up onto the doorsill. I stand close so she can use me for support. We're both a little drunk so it's clumsy, but fun. Finally, she climbs onto my back, wrapping her legs around me, hanging them over my forearms. She hitches herself tight against me. I feel the heat of her crotch against my back. I walk toward her front door.

"Hey," she says, "this is great! How 'bout a little gallop?" She bounces as I jog toward her door. "Come on, stud, don't quit!" Soon, I'm trotting back and forth on the concrete apron in front of the motel. I'm whinnying like a horse and she's cheering me on. We're both laughing. She weighs nothing. It's three o'clock in the morning; God has answered my prayers.

Finally, lights go on in one of the units and we hear someone cursing. It's time to head for the bottle Cinn mentioned. At her door, she kisses me again. This time, our genitals are pressed together. I let my hand slip down over her ass. My universe is reduced to that moment and its precious sensations. I don't care if I ever go home or back to work. She bites my cheek and leads me by the hand into her place.

The young black woman stretched out on the drab sofa is an unwelcome surprise. "Steve, hon, this is Shadow, my roommate. Shadow, this is my friend, Steve."

"Hi, Steve." She's good-looking, about twenty-five. Close-cropped Afro; lavender sweatsuit, bare feet. There's a TV going. Cinn closes the door.

"How come you're up, Shad?"

"Gene called."

"Shit."

"I couldn't get back to sleep." Shad stubs out her cigarette and drinks from a can of grape soda. "He wants you to call him. He sounded pissed."

"Yeah, he's pissed all right. Steve, I better call, you know; otherwise, he'll just keep callin' all night. He's like that, you know, real stubborn. Won't take a minute." She pats my face and goes to the bedroom in the back of the unit. She closes the door behind her. Shadow and I stare dumbly at each other. Then she smiles.

"It's *Rocky II*," she says. "Pull up a chair."

Through the closed door and above the sound of the TV, I hear Cinn cursing at the ex-boyfriend, the alcoholic itinerant roofer. White trash. Silently, I cheer her on. I accept Shadow's offer of a drink: bad whiskey in a plastic cup with a single half-frozen ice cube. Shad pours herself one. I recognize her now from the Thing, day shift. She wears wigs. She's checking out Cinn's new boyfriend: me.

"Hey," she says, "don't worry about me. If you and Cinn want privacy, I know how to stay out of the way."

"Thanks," I say. I give her the wink. She understands.

Cinn's place looks better from the outside. Inside, it's a sty. The black vinyl sofa under Shad looks like a Goodwill reject. Underneath everything is a matted green shag carpet. The holes are the best thing about it. I'm planted in a grimy upholstered chair with burn marks on the arms and a bad wobble. Next to the tiny kitchen area in the back is a round Formica table with three mismatched metal chairs. On the wall above the TV, there's a water-stained picture of the AC boardwalk. The place reeks of cigarettes and mildew. I'm disappointed in the way Cinn lives, but no less horny. I see her in a new way—not merely as a beautiful woman but as someone leading a hard life. I'm sympathetic and determined to help. I wonder how long she'll stay on the phone.

It's the fourth commercial break in *Rocky II* since I sat down and Cinn went to phone her ex. My erection is gone. My head hurts. Shadow has crashed. I pour myself another drink. I have an uneasy feeling about the situation. I can't allow myself to get mad. I cannot allow it.

I take my drink quietly to the door of Cinn's bedroom and listen. I cannot make out her words, but it sounds friendly. The hope drains out of me. I sigh and start back to my seat. Maybe they're trying to end it as friends. I check myself in a wall mirror near her front door. I sit down. Her place is filthy.

Nearly an hour after we arrived, she comes out of the bedroom. The makeup is gone. The hair around her forehead is wet. She's a mess. The black halter has been replaced by a baggy, pink Mickey Mouse T-shirt with a hole at the left shoulder. I barely recognize her. She squints at me oddly through the smoke of the cigarette dangling from her lips and pours herself a drink. I stand.

"Sorry," she says. Either she forgot I was there, or figured I'd taken the hint and left. She leans against the counter near her piss-pot kitchen sink and looks at me sideways. The sexy friendliness is gone. She flicks some ash into the sink. "Look, you need to go, Steve." She sounds nervous. "Gene and me, we came to an understanding, you know. I feel bad about keeping you waiting, I really do."

I move in and gut-punch her. The glass drops from her hand and shatters. Behind the look of amazement on her face, there is awe. I rip off the T-shirt and mount her. I'm in. Molten steel. She moans and shudders under me. My hands take her breasts. I pump her full of jit. She smiles and tastes it with her cunt; her eyes glaze over. She says she loves me. Melts. Too late. I grab the grimy throat and choke her. Her eyes bulge. She sobs. She says she loves me. No mercy, bitch. I come again, and again.

"Steve?"

"Sorry."

"I lose you there for a second?"

"I'll go," I say.

"I feel real bad, you know."

"There was something I wanted to tell you."

She yawns for the second time. "Hey, I'll see you at the Thing, won't I? Next week? First drink's on me."

"Next week is too late."

At dawn, the sun cracks the clouds behind me as I hit the high point on the Walt Whitman Bridge. I'm exhausted, hung over. It's only five-something and already the bridge is clogged with commuters, an open sewer of our brain-dead work force. Vainly, I work my dick with spit and the memory of Cinn's passion. The pink innocence of the new day bathes the Philadelphia skyline in false hope. The world is vile and meaningless. I am an abomination in it.

I will soar from the ashes. The Light of Redemption blazes before me.

twenty-seven

Ned was fucking the lady next door the night Grace tried to kill herself. That's hindsight. At ten, I probably couldn't or wouldn't have put a name on what he was doing. The notion of my parents having sex, independently or together, would not have occurred to me.

It was about six months after the couple next door to us split up that the neighbor lady started calling with things for Ned to fix. Before long, it seemed like he was always going over there and staying for hours. Her name was Debbie. She had bright orange hair and always wore a lot of blue eye shadow. She reminded me of Ronald McDonald.

When things started happening, it was probably around one in the morning. I was watching *The Creeping Unknown* on the kitchen TV. It's funny how little details like that stick in your mind when something terrible happens. I loved watching old horror movies, but I always got scared. Some nights I checked three or four times to make sure all the doors were locked.

The monster was dragging his deformed body down a cobblestoned London street. Big Ben was striking the hour. A beautiful blind girl, a flower seller, had fallen asleep in a doorway. Her clothes were rags but she had the face of an angel. You knew she was going to get it. The monster got closer. His arms and legs were four times normal size. His face was a mass of grotesque bulges. The flower girl moved. The monster saw her. His eyes went wild. He went for her, to get her blood. He couldn't help himself. Clouds of fog swirled around him in the moonlight. A trail of glowing pus marked his path. The violins on the soundtrack went crazy. My heart was pounding like mad. Then suddenly, there was some fat guy on the screen selling hairpieces. I turned to run to my room for candy and there in front of me was this pale, robed woman, standing perfectly still in the doorway, like a ghost. My blood froze. It was Grace. I have no idea how long she'd been standing there.

"Mom! Gosh, you scared me," I said. As I drew close, I could see tears shining on her cheeks in the blue light from the TV. There were little puddles at the bottom of each eye. She was whimpering. My heart sank. "What's wrong, Mom? Why are you crying?" She put her arms around me and began sobbing. She had such a sour smell. Some of her tears splashed on my face.

"I love you, Billy," she sobbed. "Do you know that, sweetie?"

Tony the Plumber was on again telling about his famous discounts for senior citizens.

"Sure, Mom. I love you, too." I wondered if I could get her to leave before the movie came on.

"Do you, darling? Do you really? I know how hard

it's been for you, with Mother not feeling well these last few months. You've been so brave. I just feel like such a failure. . . ." She cried violently. Some black guy on TV was telling who his guests would be on "Community Focus." The movie would be on any second.

"It's okay, Mom. You'll feel better soon. You've just been upset about Grandad. . . ."

"Can you ever forgive me for humiliating you in front of Mrs. Schuyler? God, how you must hate me for that! You probably wish you didn't have a mother. . . ."

"I love you, Mom. I really do. Why don't you try to get some sleep? I'll bet you're really tired." I nudged her toward the stairs.

And now back to our feature. . . .

"I'm not going to disgrace you ever again, Billy. Or worry you. You'll never have to be ashamed of me again. . . ."

"That's great, Mom." The girl in the movie was shrieking. The monster snarled. I tried to get a peek but we were too far into the hall. "You wanna watch with me, Mom? It's a really neat movie." She stopped moving.

"Billy, I want you to know I always loved you. Just remember that, darling." She took my face in her hands. She was smiling that pathetic, little-girl smile of hers behind the tears. I couldn't understand why she had to act so weird. She pulled me close. "Mommy always loved you. I loved you more than anything else in the world." She held me tight against her. Her body shuddered against me as she cried. I got scared. Then, suddenly, she stopped. "I'll leave you alone, now," she said. She let go of me. "You want to get back to your show."

"Uh, that's okay, Mom. . . ."

"No, no, I know how awful it is, having to put up with me. Enjoy your movie." She started up the stairs. "I'm so glad you have things that make you happy. Good night, Billy."

"Uh, g'night, Mom. . . ."

Police were at the scene of the murder. An angry crowd had gathered.

"Love you," she said. She blew me a kiss.

The scene had switched to the offices of Scotland Yard, where scientists, military, and the police, had gathered to make a plan to destroy the creature.

Grace had broken the spell. I couldn't get back into it. My thoughts went back to her time and again. I watched indifferently as soldiers with flamethrowers herded the howling monster toward the spires and buttresses of an ancient cathedral that was undergoing a face-lift. I felt drained. I felt sad and angry. The monster sought refuge on the great scaffold that had been erected in front of the cathedral. Below him, workmen attached giant cables that would direct all of South London's electrical current into the metal structure.

The monster climbed hopelessly on the scaffold, higher and higher. Upstairs, at about the same time, Grace was digging into her wrists with a razor blade. On the direct order of the monster's former commanding officer, two hundred megavolts of electricity surged into the scaffold. Almost instantly, it began to melt, collapsing in flames to the ground. Screaming with anguish, mental and physical, the monster fell like a fiery comet. As blood from both wrists splattered on her robe and the white porcelain sink in front of her, Grace swallowed a full bottle of Nembutal capsules. In the last few smoky.

seconds of his existence, the features of a British space hero were once again recognizable in the shriveling monster's flesh. He seemed at peace. Then he was gone, a wisp of vapor carried off by a breeze. I always rooted for the monsters.

It was time to go upstairs, to sleep, but I resisted. I didn't want to be alone with my thoughts. I watched a long string of stupid commercials, including a mini-epic for senior citizens' auto insurance that featured some has-been movie star and a phone number. I wondered how many old people would call in for their free, no-obligation booklet and ice scraper at quarter of two in the morning. I yawned and tried to rub the sleep from my eyes. A rerun of "M Squad" came on. I changed channels. Six bored people on a discussion show . . . A hundred giddy people in feathers and sequins prancing around in the finale of an old musical . . . I turned it off.

The kitchen was suddenly silent and very dark. My eyes adjusted slowly. An afterimage of the TV screen seemed to glide across my view. The motor of the refrigerator kicked on. There were lights next door. I realized that Ned was still over there. "A brief appearance," he'd said. "They're having a party." It made me angry, but I didn't spy. I didn't want to know more. My eyes adjusted to the darkness.

I sighed and made my way to the kitchen door. An odd light from upstairs filled the front hall. I realized it was coming from the little bathroom I shared with Ned. I climbed the stairs slowly. Three-quarters of the way up, I could see over the top step and into the bathroom. She was leaning over the sink, still in her robe. Her forehead was pressed against the mirror on the medicine cabinet. She had both hands in the sink. She wasn't moving.

"Hey, Mom, whatcha doing?" I ran to her. Her face was as white as the tile. Her eyes were closed. The bowl of the sink was bathed in blood. Her hands were palm down beside the drain. A bloody razor blade lay beside the soap dish. "God, Mom what did you *do?*" I was shouting. She opened her eyes drowsily and smiled at me. "What should I do, Mom? Please tell me! What should I *do?*"

"You should be in bed, Billy," she said dreamily. "Don't pay any 'tention to me, darling, jus' go to bed. I'll be fine." The bright bulb overhead bathed her in light, making little reflections in her yellow hair. The front of her was splotched with blood. It was everywhere, even on the floor. She seemed so peaceful. She closed her eyes again and went back to wherever she had been. I was terrified. My mother. *My mother.* Bleeding to death.

"Mom, you've got to sit down." I put my hands at her waist and guided her toward the toilet seat. My insides swirled. "No, Billy! Go 'way!" She was angry, but so weak. Her knees buckled suddenly. She was able to right herself. I pushed harder.

"Sit on the toilet!" I yelled. *"Sit!"*

"No!" she shrieked pathetically. Her knees buckled again. One of her slashed wrists nearly touched my face as she grabbed for my shoulder with a bloody hand. The cut was little more than an inch, straight across the veins beneath her skin. It dripped steadily onto my shirt, penetrating the fabric. Red dots. It scared me. I recoiled; I shoved her away.

She found the front edge of the toilet seat but slipped to the floor with a jarring thud. I burst into tears. I could feel the warmth of her blood on my shoulder as it soaked through. She let out an awful moan. "Oh dear God," she cried, "why can't I *die?*" She looked like a broken doll, bent forward, her chin almost touching her knees.

"Mommy," I sobbed. "I love you. Let me help."

"I'll be okay, Billy," she said. She didn't look at me. "It's just like in the movies. You'll see. I'll be fine." She turned her head and smiled her little-girl smile at me. The bloody wrists were turned up in her lap. The flesh was pink where she'd cut herself. "Just like in the movies," she had said. I looked into her weak and miserable face and hated and loved her. Then, as fast as I could, I ran to the downstairs phone.

My heart was racing. I turned on every light as I tore into the kitchen. It took the ambulance service four rings to answer. The woman who took the information sounded like a robot. My mother was upstairs dying, and the ambulance lady was bored. Couldn't she care? Couldn't she *act* like it meant something to her?

I had to tell Ned. I knew I should go back upstairs and check her, but I couldn't look at her again. I would go next door. There was nothing I could do for her. I wasn't a doctor. I didn't even know first aid. Next door.

I had just stumbled outside when the phone rang. The robot checking to see if it was a prank. Too many children lately sending them on false alarms. How many seconds wasted? How many seconds does it take to die?

A surface root caught the tip of my right sneaker as I tore into the Centrellas' yard. I went sprawling across their walk. Barely aware that the heels of my hands were badly shredded, I stumbled quickly up the steps and rammed a thumb against the doorbell. After it chimed, there were no sounds, only my rapid breathing. Some party. The lights were still on, at least, very low.

It was Sunday, the seventh, 2:21 AM. I wondered if this would be the last day of my mother's life. I hit the bell again, three times. It was strange to be standing on the Centrellas' porch, looking at my house. I had never seen that view of it before. In all the years we'd lived next door, I had never stood on that porch. Until now.

"Yes, what is it? Who are you?" The sound of her voice startled me. She was peeking out over the chain lock on her door. "Are you Billy?" Pot smoke drifted into the space between us. I stepped back, full of anger and disgust.

"Yes, I need to see my father right away."

"What is it? Is something wrong?" She had on a floor-length robe with a fluffy collar. She acted groggy. Several candles burned brightly in the small slice of room visible behind her.

"I need to see him now. It's an emergency." She was keeping me outside. There was some kind of low music. Something weird, like springs in a cartoon. *Boinngg*, only low. Swami music. I wanted to kill her.

"My God, what is it?" She was flustered. She craned her short neck toward our house. "Fire? Is it a fire? We were just having a party. . . . I'm not sure your father's still here." She looked over her shoulder, into the part of the room I couldn't see.

"It's all right, luv. Everything's perfectly smashing." Ned was drunk.

"Just a minute," she said and shut the door in my face.

I paced. It was a minute or two before Ned appeared. With every second that passed, I hated him more. I thought of Grandad. If only he were alive. Finally, I heard Ned fumbling with the door latch and saying something I couldn't hear. He opened the door wide to show himself. She was out of sight to one side.

"Right, Billy, what's up?" He stood unnaturally erect, doing his best to look sharp.

"It's Mom. . . ." I was choking on the words I had to say.

"Go on." His shirt wasn't tucked in at the back.

"She's cut her wrists." I heard Mrs. Centrellà gasp. Ned grimaced. It took a while to see things in the darkness.

"You call? Did you call an ambulance?" Ned asked.

In the moment before I answered, I noticed that his fly was wide open. "Yes," I said, "I think she's passed out." I started to cry again. I hated Ned even more for seeing it. I made my tears stop. I took deep breaths. "What are you going to do about it?"

"I'll be right there, of course. . . ." Something was making Ned hesitate. I wasn't sure what. "At least you've called. Did they say how soon . . . ?" At that instant, headlights rounded the corner at the end of the block, catching me briefly in their beams. A police car, no flashers or siren. It pulled up abruptly at the Centrella house. An ambulance siren warbled in the distance. I stared at Ned. "Christ, they think it's here!" he groaned, turning sheepishly to Mrs. Centrella. "Be a love, will you, Debbie? Find my shoes. I'm 'fraid I have no idea where they are."

Mrs. Centrella found Ned's shoes while a pair of policemen trotted up her front steps. She tossed them down in front of him and stepped back quickly into the shadows.

Ned did his best to act sober, explaining that he'd just come over to see if the neighbor lady would look after me. I said nothing. More seconds went by. He tried to work his feet into the shoes without the cops noticing. They noticed, and I was sure they smelled the pot smoke, too. Finally, Ned stepped onto the porch. He patted my head and said not to worry; Mrs. Centrella would see that I had everything I needed.

The ambulance arrived as Ned and the cops were cutting through the hedge into our yard. I watched from a corner of the Centrellas' porch as the paramedics hurriedly unloaded a stretcher and equipment cases. I wondered if Grace was still alive. The thought of her death terrified me; I had no desire to get closer or see more. Behind me, Mrs. Centrella opened her screen door.

"Why don't you come in, Billy?" she said. She looked at me expectantly; her chest rose and fell rapidly with each nervous breath. She wanted to rise to the occasion, but she was so stoned it took all her concentration just to stand there with her tits hanging out. I just stared at her. "How about some cocoa and eggs, honey?" she said.

"Go fuck yourself," I said. It was the first time I spoke that way to an adult.

There was a wonderful old horse chestnut tree growing at the edge of the parking lot by the Methodist church. In summer, its vast canopy of leaves provided shelter from the heat and passing storms. I hid at the base of it while the emergency people tended to Grace. It looked like all the lights were on inside our house. It didn't take them long to bring her out. She was on a stretcher. I couldn't tell whether her face was covered or not. They were moving quickly; I guessed that meant she was still alive. Kids in an old heap pulled up to watch. Ned got into the patrol car with the cops. The spectacle was awesome and terrifying. The ambulance didn't leave. I wondered desperately what was wrong. Then they drove off, the cops leading the ambulance. No sirens now; there was no need at that hour. The teenagers dumped some beer cans on the street and peeled out.

It took me a while to build up the courage to go inside. It was strange in there. Between us, Ned and I had turned on every light. The lights and litter reminded me of a stadium after a game. The resident sadness was there, only deeper than usual. There was a sense of peace.

Out of habit, I went into the kitchen and opened the refrigerator. There was a saucepan half full of soup Grace had heated for herself and abandoned. On top of the refrigerator was a fresh carton of her cigarettes, next to the cookbook she never used. It struck me wrong that a person's things are unchanged when they cut their wrists, or die. Her shoes were waiting for her upstairs whether she lived to wear any of them again or not. The soup was waiting to be eaten. It had been so strange to see Uncle Hugh driving Grandad's car after he died. People care so much about their things. People die, their things go on. They become other people's things; they become trash. I poured the soup down the drain and rinsed out the pan with hot water.

My legs felt dead as I began climbing the steps. The bright bathroom light spilled into the upstairs hall. I closed my eyes. The horror of finding her there ran through me again like a poison. I could see her at the sink, spilling her blood as calmly as she used to paint her nails. The razor blade. The fall. "Why can't I die?" The cuts. "Just like in the movies." And the blood. "Mommy always loved you."

I was past the bathroom and nearing the attic steps when I opened my eyes. Suddenly, I felt angry. She hadn't done this only to herself. She had also done it to me. Instead of going up to my room, I went back.

There was far more blood than I remembered. It made me gag. There were places on the white tile where she had smeared it like finger paint. The little trash bucket overflowed with paper wrappers and protective strips from bandages and surgical dressings. The razor blade was gone. I covered my mouth, shut off the light, and slammed the door. I leaned over the stair rail for several seconds, fighting off the urge to throw up.

I wondered why all the lights were on in her room, why her drawers were open. What were they looking for? What did they find? Clothes to wear in the hospital? What? I went in. It had a stale and musty odor, yet there were hints of her in better times, scents of powder and perfume. I hadn't been past the door in months. The room was diseased. From the bed that had once been the sleeping place of both my parents, a tangled mass of sheets and blankets, mottled with the stains of a hundred drunken accidents, spilled onto the floor. Overflowing ashtrays on each of the night tables were surrounded by drinking glasses clouded with greasy fingerprints.

The family's photo albums were in a heap in front of Grace's closet door. Some were open, some closed. From the general look of things, I guessed that Grace had thrown the books at the door in a rage. My insides knotted when I noticed my parents' wedding album. The beautiful white leather cover had said "Ned and Grace" in flowing gold script; right below that was the date of their wedding in smaller letters, also gold. She had stabbed and ripped and gouged the cover with something like scissors or a knife. There was virtually nothing left of it but shredded cardboard.

Her top bureau drawer was open. Nestled among her slips and brassieres was a bowl of moldy brown food so badly decomposed I couldn't even recognize what it was. As I was trying to imagine what could have led Grace to put a bowl of food, complete with a spoon, in a drawer of her underthings, I noticed something shiny beneath a bra. It was a vodka bottle, half gallon, empty. One led to another, and another, all around the room. From the stacks of shoe boxes in her closet to the sweater storage cases beneath the bed, there were empties, partial empties, and full bottles hidden everywhere. Everywhere. The quantity blew me away. I had never imagined how much Grace drank. Even seeing the evidence of it, I couldn't comprehend just what it meant.

I'd piled eighteen bottles on her bed when I was through, assorted brands and sizes. Two were unopened. Five were anywhere from half to a third full. The rest were empty.

I looked around me. Grace's room had given up its secrets—sick, sad, sorry place that it was. As I turned to go, one of the bottles slipped to the floor with a thud. I picked it up by its neck and hefted it like a club. The vodka sloshed merrily inside; so clear, like water. I'd once heard Grace announcing to someone on the telephone that you can't smell vodka on a person's breath. Maybe *she* couldn't. I raised the bottle over my head and stood poised to throw it at the image of myself in her mirror. I just stood there like that . . . until the bottle became very heavy and my arms began to hurt and I began to feel very sad. Finally, I put it back on her bed where it wouldn't roll off again and then I went upstairs. It was much too late. I was far too tired. I didn't know if I still had a mother. I did know that for the second time in four months something bad had happened that would change my life forever. I couldn't do anything about it right away. I could only make up my mind not to let anything like that ever happen to me again. And go to sleep.

twenty-eight

December 8

Dear Grandad,

I gave Mom an ashtry I made out of alumum at school because she hasn't had any alcol for a month. Isn't that great? I'm really proud of her because I know she's scared about Ned being gone. I'm scared too. I don't know what's going to happen to us. I try not to think about it or I get upset. Ned's been gone almost 3 weeks. He went to San Diego in Calfornia and took all the money. We threw his clothes out. I hope he never comes back. Our house is pretty clean now. Aunt Jane who I don't like had 2 funny ladies here to clean while Mom was sick and now she has a lot of energy so she cleans all the time. It even makes me nervouse she cleans so much.

Mom talks to uncle Hugh on the telephone a lot in Conn. She says we won't be able to pay the bill when it comes. She and uncle Hugh are trying to

figure out what we should do. I guess we are going
there for Xmas wich I'm not happy about because
I hate his kids. Mom and I went to Howard John-
son's for Thanksgiving wich was neat.

I sure love Mom for not drinking. I asked God
to make things better for us now. I still love you.

Love,
Billy

That first month Grace was struggling to stay off
booze, I felt myself loving her in a way I never had before. I could tell she was going through hell, but with
each day, I got a little more confident she was going to
make it.

Christmas was the opportunity to show my feelings. I
sold an old watch of Ned's to one of the janitors at Westfield and searched every shop on Main Street for something special. It was hard to find anything very
impressive in my price range but I finally settled on a
huge box of chocolates I found at Variety Discount. It
was as broad as a dinner tray and at least three inches
deep. The cellophane had red ribbons and holly printed
on it. It seemed like a good deal, but while I was admiring it later at home, I discovered some fine print that
said there were only ten ounces of candy inside: my special gift was mostly cardboard and air. Eventually I decided that the huge box was a gift in its own right. I hid
it under my bed and went out and bought a bag of Hershey's Kisses to go with it.

twenty-nine

Uncle Hugh and Aunt Betse lived on the shore of Long Island Sound in the elegant private community of Faire Haven, a quick walk from the Greenwich train station. Their minimum-wage Jamaican housekeeper, Joyce, raised their three kids while they searched selflessly for life's meaning in high-powered Manhattan careers.

The area reminded me of the Main Line. The slate-roofed colonial was the favored architectural style, always huge, with two or three chimneys, and a pair of stone lions guarding the front door. Some of the older properties were surrounded by tall wrought-iron fences with spear pickets.

Uncle Hugh's house was one of a small minority constructed entirely of wood. It was a white, three-story Victorian with dark green shutters—quite stately, but somewhat austere. Their driveway was horseshoe shaped. A neat boxwood hedge bordered the entire property, which was quite flat.

Our third-floor rooms were intended to be servants'

quarters. Our bath had an old-fashioned tub and no shower. My room was half the size of Grace's. The mattress sagged like a hammock and had a fetid odor. Grace, I think, felt about as comfortable there as I did. Uncle Hugh's daughter Bridget called me "Wee Wee."

Early Christmas morning, seven-year-old Cousin Randall woke Grace and me by pounding furiously on our doors and demanding that we come down immediately so he could start opening his presents. I thought about saying I was sick. Two days with my rich cousins had virtually killed my interest in the holiday.

The night before, we'd gone to a candlelight service at the church Hugh's family attended. During the recessional, while they were all singing "Joy to the World," I found myself spellbound by the fine, caramel-colored hair of the young woman standing in front of me. It cascaded in gentle curls nearly to her waist, where it swayed and shimmered just inches from the bright little flame that danced at the tip of my candle. As the knot of ministers shuffled solemnly past our pew, something odd happened. I was seized by an urge to thrust the candle into the young woman's hair and set it on fire. It appalled and frightened me to think that my mind was capable of such an impulse, yet the more I thought about it, the more tempted I was to act. As if to test myself, I moved the candle slowly closer to the woman's hair; another inch and the delicate ends closest to the flame would have blackened and shriveled from the heat. If she leaned back, the mass of curls would have burst into flames: she would be scarred for life. My body tensed with excitement—they were all so full of themselves. . . . Before anything happened, the song ended and Bridget

gave me a shove. I'm sure I wouldn't have done anything. But just thinking about it had made me feel better.

As I pulled on my flannel robe that Christmas morning, I could hear Grace stirring next door. Halfway down
the first flight of steps, I remembered her present and
turned back. While she was taking a bath the day before,
I'd sneaked it from its hiding place in our car to a new
one underneath the bed in my room. The mere sight of
it had raised my spirits. It was truly the grandest box of
candy I'd ever seen. As I carried it proudly down the
stairs, I could smell the bayberry and evergreens below.
Carols were playing on a radio. A warm, excited feeling
came over me.

When I walked into the living room, Megan, Bridget,
and Randall, who'd each been allowed to open one present, were jealously eyeing one another's loot. Hugh was
on the hall phone apologizing to Aunt Jane for waking
her up. Aunt Betse, Hugh's wife, was ensconced at one
end of the living-room sofa with her bare feet tucked
under her and a crisp copy of the *New York Times* between her hands. I found a good spot and carefully
placed Grace's present under the huge tree.

"Merry Christmas, William," Aunt Betse purred. Her
husky voice made everything sound sarcastic.

"Merry Christmas, Aunt Betse."

"Is your mother about yet?" she asked, peering over
the little half-glasses she used to read.

"Yes. I heard her before I came down."

"Good," Betse announced, "we're all waiting."

Betse and Grace were opposites. Betse was dark and
sturdy-looking, completely sure of herself, competent,
domineering. Her glossy black hair was pulled into a

shiny bun at the back of her head. Her small eyes were hazel. She always appeared perfectly made up. Grace had once said that Betse made her feel like a rag. I had fantasized that Betse wasn't human.

After ten minutes of stares and cracks from my cousins, I went upstairs to get Grace. I knocked lightly on her door.

"Billy, is that you, darling?" she asked brightly.

"Yes, Mom. They want you to come down." It took her a minute to unlock the door. Once she had, she swung it wide open and knelt to give me a big hug.

"Merry Christmas, my darling Billy," she said grandly. "I just can't seem to get my makeup straight this morning." She went to her mirror and gave her cheeks one last, playful pat with her powder puff. "I guess you just can't make a silk purse out of a sow's ear," she laughed.

"Should I tell them you're coming?" I asked. She seemed so nervous.

"Don't bother. I'll only be another min! We'll go down together!—You know, darling, there was one thing I always wanted for Christmas when I was a young girl ... oh, until the time I was nearly twenty, I guess. You'll never guess what! A greenhouse! I wanted a place where it would always be pretty, where there would be flowers all year. It's always summer in a greenhouse, you know. Do you think it's a silly dream? I'll bet you do!" She looked at me whimsically and retied the belt on her robe.

"It sounds nice," I said. A sick feeling spread through me. She knelt again in front of me. The gaiety was gone. There were tears in her eyes.

"Do you think I'll ever have my greenhouse, Billy? Is

it just a silly dream I should leave behind?"

I stared into her face and realized I had begun to sweat. There was a strange, strangling tightness above the pounding in my chest. I hadn't seen Grace like this for months. Not since the last time she was drunk.

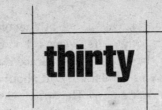

thirty

"**H**ello, Mrs. Howe?"

"Yes, who is this?"

"I'm sorry; my name is Martin Ross. You don't know me, but . . . Mrs. Howe, I'm afraid I have some bad news."

"Go on."

"I believe your husband is having an affair with my wife."

"No . . ."

"I know how you feel, Mrs. Howe. I wouldn't call you if there were any doubt."

"Mr. Ross, my husband and I are happily married. This is absurd."

"I would have said the same thing. I have three children, Mrs. Howe. The oldest is just eight. I'm desperate to save my marriage. Please listen to me. I understand you and Mr. Howe have children also. Is that right?"

She sighed. "Yes, two."

"I became suspicious one day a few weeks ago. My

oldest, Mary Francis, called me at the office from a neighbor's. Grace, my wife, wasn't home. The kids couldn't get into the house. Later, Grace claimed she'd had a flat. There was something odd about her manner so I checked. The car's new. The spare was still in the trunk, never used. The car was dirty. If one of the tires had been off the car, the hubcap would have had finger marks where the dirt had been disturbed. None of them did. The following week, Grace joined a fitness club, or said she had. She started going to work out in the evenings. All this time she was acting . . . well, anxious to please. She'd always been considerate, but now she was always doing little things for me, always excited. She'd come in all flushed and almost giddy after her workouts. I remembered, in college, the boys always thought they could tell when a girl had had relations, when she acted like that. . . ."

"For the love of God, Mr. Ross, make your point. None of this has anything to do with my husband."

"I'm afraid it does, Mrs. Howe. I hired a detective when I became suspicious. My wife's 'fitness club' is a motel on Twenty-eighth Street. That's where she's been meeting your Charles. I have pictures of them there."

"I don't believe it."

"I know how you feel. I'm still in denial myself. I thought that if we both confronted them tonight, perhaps the shock would end it. I can't believe Grace would just throw over our marriage for an . . . affair."

"I'll have to see the pictures first."

"I understand. I have your address. Prepare yourself. There are some of them together in your BMW, kissing quite passionately. I felt ill when I first saw them."

"Oh Jesus . . ." Finally, tears.

"I know; it helps to cry. Let's hope we can convince them to come to their senses."

"I suppose I should thank you. I just don't know what to say."

"There's one other thing. When was the last time you and Charles had relations?"

"Excuse me?"

"I know, it's none of my business; I just don't think either of us should take chances. God knows who else they've had sex with."

thirty-one

April 22

Dear Grandad,

I'm thinking of running away. We have been living on the thrid floor of Uncle Hugh's house since
Xmas. I hate it. It was only supposed to be a visit,
but Mom got loaded and Uncle Hugh decided we
should move in so Mom could get help. I hate my
cousins and they hate me. I'm the only kid in Faire
Haven that goes to public school. I feel really sad
all the time. Sometimes when I try to study for
school I have to read the assignment four or five
times just to know what it says. I hope I'm not
going crazy. The school isn't too bad. At least you
don't have to wear a coat and tie. The other kids
don't bother me which is good. I thought they
might try to give me a hard time because I'm new
but they leave me alone pretty much. Sometimes I
pretend I'm a spy or something and thats why I
have to stay away from the other kids.

The only trouble with running away is I don't know were I would go. We still have our house in Llanfair but their trying to rent it. Uncle Hugh said we should sell it but Ned won't sign the papers.

Mom is changed so much you practally wouldn't rekanize her. She goes to Dr. Woodworth 3 times a week. He's a psychiatriost. Then she goes jogging and rides Aunt Betse's bike and goes to the spa. All she does is talk about herself which is pretty boring. Uncle Hugh says she's spending too much money but she says she will pay him back every penny when she sells the house someday. Mom has not been drunk since Xmas. I wish she would pay attention to me sometimes. I don't know if I will run away or not.

Love,
Billy

At times that spring, Grace was someone I didn't know. Actually, she was a whole group of people I didn't know. The jock thing amazed everyone. She pedaled, twisted, dieted, lifted, and swam herself into incredible shape. One day, a woman at the fitness place told her she looked like Grace Kelly. That was all my Grace needed to hear. She started wearing her hair the way the princess did and coloring it to match. She looked fantastic. It was like the real Grace had come out from behind the clouds to shine for a while.

Earlier in the year, Grace and I had been strangely close: fear, loneliness, and the shared misery of being at Hugh's. That, and her trying to kick booze. The most intimate period began one night in January. She came to my room. I heard her crying and pretended to be asleep. She sat on the bed and combed my hair with her hand. After a few minutes, she slipped under the covers with me and held me against her. We spent the night like that. There were other nights, after that first one. I feel embarrassed revealing it, but at those moments our love was dearest to me. We lay close enough that our bodies touched. We helped each other. We hugged and kissed and took turns saying everything was going to be okay. It was as if we were married or brother and sister. In the morning, we'd have long, whispered conversations, and when we were sure all of Uncle Hugh's tribe were out of the house, she would kiss me, and then we'd get dressed.

Things were different between us by the time of my birthday, May 6. I was turning eleven and as far as I could tell, no one in the house knew or cared. It was a Saturday. When I got up, Grace was already at her health club.

She finally showed up around noon and whispered that she was going to take me out for lunch. It had to be a big secret because she didn't think Uncle Hugh and his family even knew it was my birthday and she didn't want them to think they had to do anything for me. We went to a ritzy place near Greenwich called the Candletree Inn. I'd never heard of it, but I could tell Grace had been there before. She seemed excited. Later I found out why.

The lunch was passable. Grace talked nonstop about her favorite subject: herself. She was thinking of becoming a psychologist, she said. Her shrink, Dr. Woodworth, had convinced her she could do almost anything with her life. He had helped her so much, she thought she might get a PhD and try to help other people the same way. She also wanted to write. She was sure that millions of women were suffering in the same kind of destructive relationship she'd had with Ned, and she wanted to help them by putting all of her experiences in a book. After she'd sworn me to secrecy, she announced that she'd already written the first chapter. I thought she'd be flattered when I asked to read it. Instead, she got huffy and said it was much too grown-up.

She gave me my presents at the restaurant: a woven elastic belt, a set of monogrammed handkerchiefs, and a copy of *Ann Landers Talks to Teens about Sex*. "It's out of print," she said as I unwrapped it. "I had to call all over to find a copy. It's for your protection, Billy. Times have changed since I was your age. I'm not sure for the better, but we have no choice except to go along, do we? Do you like it?" I still remember the creepy feeling I got when I saw what it was. For a second, I wondered if it was a mistake, if the bookstore had gift-wrapped the wrong book. "Do you like it, Billy?"

"Mom, I'm only eleven," I reminded her.

"You don't like it," she snapped.

"Oh, I do," I said. I flipped the pages under my thumb as if to prove it. "I really do."

"You're getting to be so handsome," she said. "The girls are going to be *all over* you in a few years!" She seemed to like the idea. I guess I was blushing. "Don't be embarrassed! You should be proud! Your father was certainly handsome. I'd have to give him that, but I'd say you owe your good looks to your grandfather. Sometimes you look so much like him I get goose bumps! Tell me something, darling," she said. She leaned toward me and lowered her voice. "Do you have a special girl, you know, someone you're really fond of?" The question hurt me. I remember the way she sat there across the table, grinning, so eager for me to say yes. I wondered what reason she had to think I had any friends at all, boy or girl.

"Uh, not right now."

"Well, don't you worry, darling," she laughed. "When you're seventeen, I'll probably have to protect you from the other mothers!"

I'd only been in a coed school a few months at that point, and I didn't feel any different about girls than I ever had. Even so, I sensed the day was coming. Peggy Meissinger and Janet Bickford, two of the girls in my class, were getting breasts. A lot of the boys talked about them. The talk made me uncomfortable. I felt threatened by it, the same way I felt threatened by those little boobs. But I looked. Everybody looked, even the girls. We wondered who would be next.

Grace wanted to go for a walk after lunch. Behind the inn, there was a path that wound through gardens to a duck pond. On the far side of the pond was a stone bench sheltered by the swaying branches of a weeping willow tree. Grace led me there without speaking and sat down. There was plenty of room for me beside her on the bench, but her manner put me off. I stood back until she motioned to me to sit down.

"Billy," she said in a soft voice, "you cannot imagine the pain of being alone. That's what my life has been for the past twelve years . . . with your father. Just three days ago, I shared this bench with a special new friend.

At your age, you can't begin to understand what that means." I made tracks in the dust below the bench by swinging my feet.

"Who?" I said.

"I mustn't say, not yet. It really isn't important that you know. . . ." There were hundreds of cigarette butts hiding in the tufts of tall grass around the bench. I wondered how many of them were hers. "I feel hopeful for the first time in my life. Nothing worthwhile is ever easy, but I've made a start. . . ." My left foot unearthed a metal pull-tab. "I feel that what's good for me is good for you. As my life improves, yours should, too. Do you understand?"

"Sure, Mom."

"Perhaps next year or the year after, I'll give you a new father for your birthday! Tell me what you think about that!"

"Great."

"Be happy for me, Billy," she said brightly as she stood up. "For the first time, I'm glad to be alive."

Grace's thoughts were far away as we drove home. She was smiling and driving rather fast. In six months of life without Ned, it had never occurred to me that she might want another man. I felt threatened by this mystery boyfriend, even though I had no idea who he was. I knew it couldn't be her psychiatrist. From what she and Uncle Hugh had said, he was rich, married, and had her totally outclassed. I decided it was some muscle-bound creep from the Y or the health club where she spent so much time. I sat there beside her in the car, and the more I thought about it, the angrier I got. She looked so smug. I knew she wasn't thinking about me. I was her son; I had been through it all with her. I was the man in her life. She had no right to replace me. She had no right to shut me out.

When we got back to Faire Haven, I shut myself in my room. After I stuffed the handkerchiefs and belt in a drawer, I flopped down on my bed with the book. I still thought it was the dumbest gift I'd ever received, but I was curious. I looked, but there were no pictures of girls without any clothes on. There was nothing about how you do sex or what it's like. There was nothing about what Marie had done to me when Grandad got killed.

It had taken me a long time to admit to myself that her mouth felt good sucking on my penis and balls, even as scared as I was. It made the guilt a lot worse. The shrinks in juvenile detention made me spend a long time dealing with it. It was hard for me to accept the fact that my enjoying what Marie did, or not enjoying it, did not change the fact that she did it. Grandad was dead and that was that. Marie didn't kill him. I didn't kill him. And nothing I could do would bring him back.

From the window of my room, I could see Grace sunning herself in the middle of Uncle Hugh's backyard. She was lying on her back on one of those lawn chairs that fold down like a cot. She had on huge sunglasses and a skimpy bikini made out of shiny, dark pink material. Her body glistened like ripe fruit in the sun. I wished she would cover herself. It made me angry to think of someone looking at her, like Cousin Randall or "Uncle" Stanley, the lush next door who Bridget said kept trying for a feel. While I was watching, she rolled over to bake her back. After she'd wriggled herself into a comfortable position, she undid the top of her bikini and poked the bottom down enough to show the top inch or two of cleft in her butt. I turned away, wondering who, besides Grace herself, would have the pleasure of examining her tan. Then, scarcely aware that I was even doing it, I went to her room.

I had made regular inspections of Grace's things ever since the night she tried to kill herself. Usually, I was motivated by anger. It didn't matter whether I had any reason to think she'd been drinking. I did it to protect myself. There would be no second collection of vodka bottles for me to discover.

The inspections usually followed the same pattern. In the first rush of anger, I would check the area around her bed, the nightstand, under the pillows, between the mattress and box spring . . . then I would go to her bureau, and, finally, the closet. As the search progressed, my anger would burn off. At the end, I usually felt guilty, and a little foolish.

This time, there was something new on her closet shelf under a stack of shoe boxes. It was a yellow tablet, the large, legal-size format I associated with serious, grown-up work. I folded back the cover. Grace had crossed out two titles, "Patient Relations" and "Bedside Manner," before finally settling on "The Affair." I decided that this must be what Grace had been talking about, "her story," the one she wanted women everywhere to read. I went to her window and was relieved to see that she was still proudly displaying her new body on Uncle Hugh's lawn chair. As fast as I could, I replaced everything just as I had found it, except her tablet. That went with me to my room.

I locked my door and pulled the painted chair they had given me to the window. I could see that Grace hadn't put very much of her story on paper, but that was okay. I was eager to see how she'd begun.

The Affair

We both knew it was wrong from the start. He, married, a doctor. I, also married (unhappily), his patient. Neither of us had been unfaithful before. My husband, my handsome English adulterer, had never been anything *but!* We told ourselves we were lonely and that there was no harm in lessening each other's pain. That was so true! But there was something more, a powerful physical yearning that wouldn't die!

My husband hadn't touched me for almost two years. I was desperate for the comfort of a human hand. His wife, he confided, was frigid and lay there like a stone when they made love. Only the coldest of women could be unresponsive to a man so truly sensitive and caring.

My "H.W.," Harold Wadsworth, M.D. (not his real name!), reminded me at first sight (Was it Love at??) of handsome movie stars I've admired on the silver screen: He has the cool blue eyes of a Richard Burton, and the rugged, handsome features of a Robert Preston. *My* superstar is ever so much younger than they, of course! We were attracted to each other right away but kept our true feelings secret for a month. Then, one Friday, after an especially exciting and meaningful hour, he asked me to join him for *a drink!* A drink? Me, the Alcoholic? Have a drink with my psychiatrist? We both laughed at what he'd said. We went to Café Pierre, near his office. I felt self-conscious. Would everybody stare? He walked in proud as a peacock, and ordered "the usual" (a dry martini with a cocktail onion) and for me, Perrier and bitters, a new treat.

We had talked about my sexual frustration in his office. Now it was to be *his* turn! He was so honest, I tried hard to understand how much he hurt. It wasn't long before we knew what had to be. He seemed so shy about bringing it up. (If only he had known how I yearned to have him inside me!) He mentioned a spot called the "Candlestick Inn." I heard myself saying "yes, yes" even as my love was saying we should *truly* share. . . . I wanted him more than I could *bear!*

We drove excitedly, like children, through the night. I snuggled close to him on the seat of his beautiful car, feeling like Cinderella in modern clothes. H.W. was certainly a prince!

The inn was even more lovely than he'd said, my prince's castle, lit up like a diamond in the night. I grew nervous as he checked the parking lot for familiar cars. I was like a shy, silly girl trying to look inconspicuous as he got us a room and ordered champagne. Once again he'd forgotten that I don't drink! Could it be that my prince was nervous, too?

The room was darling. I felt like a bride. He poured the champagne and gave me a tiny sip! Naughty girl! It was delicious, but not nearly so much so as he! Our first kiss sent shivers down my spine. I felt like jelly and clung to him like a little girl. As he held me, I sensed his powerful presence against my thigh.

We turned off all the lights, except for a single candle on the mantle of the tiny fireplace. He stood still, like a statue, while I unveiled his strong body to my adoring eyes. . . . Yes, I confess, he was so big, I couldn't help staring and wanting to touch. . . . Then, before I knew what was happening, I'd dropped to my knees and was kissing him with the hunger of long-denied lust! Whoever would have thought I could be so bold?

The first time I read "The Affair," I felt disgusted and betrayed. Over twenty years later, that hasn't changed. Of course, I've read worse, but it wasn't my own mother writing. In the finale, she gushes about her "delicious throbbing," and her "unlimited ecstasy"; then it's "the fiery eruptions of my pelvic volcano." It ends, "To be continued, I hope!"

thirty-two

It's hard to breathe and I'm trembling. Not because of what I am about to do but because of where I am: Jitters and sweaty palms after a millennium, hardly surprising.

The old key doesn't work. I pick the lock and step inside. It's foreign to me only for a moment. Cosmetic changes cannot mask what it is. It bristles with memories. Like roaches and silverfish, they seethe beneath its surface, eating their own feces.

I am drawn upward. To origins. My childhood bedroom. A cute office now with a PC and a fax machine. My throat is parched. I hear my parents screaming.

The owners are out, a Vietnamese couple in their thirties: Mr. and Mrs. Thoa. They don't know. I have tried to warn them, but they hang up. They have a restaurant in Ardmore. The kids are there with them now. Very hardworking. Never back before eleven-thirty. It's just nine now, and dark; I have plenty of time.

The smell of the place is different. Furniture polish

and new carpet. Not cigarettes and decay. If I think about it long enough, I gag.

My parents' bedroom. Pleasant on the surface, but wallpaper and carpet cannot hide history's vile stain. I hear Ned's dirty laugh through the closed door of his "study." I enter the bathroom where Grace slashed her wrists. Is the small, dark spot my mother's blood, or do I imagine it?

Tentacles of Handi-Wrap stretch from each room to a five-gallon plastic jug in the kitchen. The jug is tightly capped. It is full of gasoline.

I want to explore further, but I am suffocating. I cannot go on until this part of me is gone. Grace is with me in the kitchen, crying. I will ask the Thoas' forgiveness. They won't understand.

I assemble a small stack of books, half the height of the gasoline jug. I place the stack next to the jug and stand a highway flare on top of it, leaning against the jug. When the flare burns down and melts the jug, the gasoline will ignite. I will be miles away. The trailers of plastic wrap will carry the flames to the other rooms, each drenched with gasoline. In an hour, 929 Ammons will be hazardous waste. Billy's funeral pyre. I pull the shades and curtains in the front of the house and open windows in the back so the flames can breathe.

Tears stream down my face as I light the flare. For so long, for so many years, I had hope. The circle is closing.

thirty-three

Dear Grandad,

I am going to a new school, Sand Creek Elementary School. It's near Medford, N.J. I don't like it too much. All the kids seem really babyish. I'd rather be around grown-ups. It's the third school I've been to in nine months.

Grace and I have been living at a place called the Gaillard Centre. Uncle Hugh made her come here for her Alcoholism after she ran away with a salesman named McCrary and they got drunk in Penna. McCrary gave her a set of steak knives with plastic handles for a gift and she started to cry. It was pretty bad. She told everybody she was going to spend the weekend with a friend from college but she didn't come back when she was supposed to and I got really scared. I thought maybe she had run away or something and left me with uncle Hugh and his rotten kids. Uncle Hugh called the police, and they put her car on the Teletype Machine for all the states around Conn.

Grace was supposed to meet Dr. Woodworth for the weekend but he didn't show up which is how she met McCrary. It think it's pretty gross. I never saw uncle Hugh so mad as when he found out Grace was screwing around with her psychiatriost. He said he wouldn't pay any of Woodworth's bills. He should of hired some guys to kill the crummy creep.

That same weekend, while Uncle Hugh and his lousy family were at their club, I tried to get drunk drinking kalua and cream de mint but all I did was throw up. Cleaning it up was real fun. YUK.

The first two weeks Grace was at Gaillard, I had to stay by myself at uncle Hugh's. His kids kept teasing me about Grace being a drunk and I almost ran away. . . .

During this reign of abuse by my cousins, there was a landmark event in my life. Although what I did was justified, I could not bring myself to tell Grandad. I cherished, and still do, not only Grandad's approval but his sheltering regard for my innocence.

It happened one afternoon when I was alone in my uncle's house. Almost alone. My relatives' dog, Laddie, an ill-bred collie who barked constantly, was there, too. I'd been living at Hugh's nearly six months and the dog still gave no sign of recognizing me. Laddie was the best-loved member of the entire family. Laddie, in fact, was the only member of the family to whom any of them were ever affectionate.

I was in the kitchen, making chocolate milk. Laddie was asleep in his basket bed. When I tossed a spoon into the sink, he woke and started to bark at me. He wouldn't stop. As I stared into his stupid, barking face, something exploded. I got so angry I started to shake. I hated him for not knowing me. I hated him for being loved.

There had been an outbreak of pet poisonings in north Greenwich. The local paper had thoughtfully printed the details. I don't believe in coincidence. I copied the pattern. The magic ingredient was antifreeze. Sweeter than corn syrup, the paper had said, and quite lethal. In the bowl Hugh used for his cereal, I made a stew of hot dogs and Prestone for Laddie. He loved it.

What happened next surprised and scared me: Nothing. Laddie went on about his business. Everything was the same, except he was nicer to me. It gave me the creeps. I decided the paper had purposely left out some important fact about the poisonings. But they hadn't. Laddie started vomiting the next day. Three days after that, he was dead. Hugh's whole family got hysterical. I was sure they could read the guilt in my face; but no, they weren't in the habit of looking at me. I gloated secretly as they moped about. Not because Laddie was dead; that was incidental. It was the sheer joy of knowing I had hurt them.

... The third week someone is at Gaillard, their family is supposed to come and tell the Alcoholic what they think is wrong with them and everything like that. I was the only one from our family who came. In one of the cyco-dramas, I pretended to be you which was really fun. I also got a chance to tell Grace I don't like her to drink and I wish she would spend some time with me. She seemed different to me when it was all over, like she was really smaller or something. Now I know everything about her.

After Family Week, Grace wanted me to go back to Uncle Hugh's. I said no. I wouldn't go back there for anything. I got really mad. I think I scared her. I'm getting to be almost as tall as she is now by a couple inches. Anyway, she let me stay.

When Grace's time was over, she said Uncle Hugh didn't want us at his house and she didn't want to go back anyway. She got a job as a maid at Gaillard which really surprised me and we moved into an old Navy barricks that they divided into rooms. Gaillard used to be a Navy place in World War 2. Grace likes living here because it's kind of like a big family. Most of the other people on the staff are Alcoholics too. I worked for Fletcher in the yard this summer and made $87.00 which I gave to Grace because we don't have any money. I like living here pretty much too. There are no kids around. We are getting along better than before. We talk and stuff and tell jokes which is nice. I started calling her Grace.

In September, one of the new Alcoholics tried to kill himself and Grace found him and saved his life. His father was really greatful to Grace. He's a rich real estate developer from Trenton, N.J. Grace says he's a Multi Millionare. His name is Gomo Bellarosa and he offered Grace a job at a new devellopmet at Princeton, N.J. near where you went to college. We get to live in a really neat house (she says) and have open houses every weekend. Grace likes him but she says he talks bad and she thinks he looks like an eggplant. She's been trying to re-decorate the house like The Main Line in her spare time. I think she's scared of so much responsibility but she says we have to go because it might be our last chance. I'm a little scared too, but it will be nice to live in a fancy house for a change. I sure hope she doesn't start to drink.

Maybe things are really going to be better now. I love you.

Love,
Billy

thirty-four

Within months after we moved to Ravenswood, the new development, demand for houses soared throughout the Northeast. Grace couldn't have picked a better time to get into real estate. People were paying more for some properties than the asking price. It was crazy, but that didn't stop her from taking the money.

·At first, I was sure she was going to blow it. She couldn't accept her own success. The first time she got a contract, she had a panic attack. She was positive the deal would fall through and there would never be another one. She was wrong, and I think that surprised both of us.

We lived in a model called "the George Washington." It was over six thousand square feet. The day Grace took me to see it, I could hardly believe I was going to live in a place like that. It had bathrooms bigger than the living room of our house in Llanfair. Grace was so anxious about getting fired when we moved in that I had to tiptoe around and act like I was living in a museum.

She said her job with Con-Land was the first thing in her life that was truly all hers and she was determined not to fail.

Unfortunately, during those first, anxious weeks, Buddy and Willie's lawsuit came to trial, and Grace had to ask her boss for time off so she could drive me down there to testify. She was furious about having to miss work.

January 5

Dear Grandad,

Buddy and Willie are going to get $750,000.00 each for killing you. Uncle Hugh says the lawyers and crummy doctors who testafied will take a big part, plus the I.R.S. but I still think it sucks. There is something wrong in this country. The insurance has to pay most of it, but even so, there won't be any trust funds for me and the other grandchildren. I wish I could kill Buddy and Willie and the crooks who testafied for them. I thought lawyers and doctors were supposed to be honest.

Also Grace sold our house in Llanfair. I didn't know anything about it. Now we have no place that's our own. She said my father changed his mind about selling because he wanted to go to Australia. I asked her if he got a job as a kangaroo.

That's about it. I really miss you. I still wish you could be alive. Wish us luck!

Write soon! (joke)

Love,
Billy

P.S. Don't worry about Buddy and Willie. I'm going to get both of them.

I blamed myself for Buddy and Willie's windfall. I actually believed if I had told the jury that Marie gave me a blow job, it might have changed their verdict. The problem was, I couldn't talk about Marie in those days. I couldn't stop thinking about her, either.

The trial was in Philadelphia because that's where Grandad's estate was. The insurance company lawyer told me to look hurt and innocent when I testified. We rehearsed different expressions in his office until we found the right one.

When I heard the verdict, I ran out of the courtroom and locked myself in a stall in the men's room. I cried and begged God to kill me.

I'd been in the stall about fifteen minutes when I heard people come in. Buddy and Willie. Somehow, I knew it even before they said anything or moved to the urinals, where I could see them through the gaps in my stall. At first, they just stood next to each other taking a piss. Then one of them started to grunt like a pig. He did it a couple of times, then he started doing it faster. Then the other one started doing the same thing and soon they were both grunting and barking and howling like dogs and dancing with each other all over the men's room. They were lucky I didn't have a gun. I wanted to shoot off their balls and make them eat it.

As it turned out, the prospect of losing a million dollars caught the attention of the insurance company. They filed an appeal right away, and this time, they sent in the A Team.

thirty-five

When we moved to Ravenswood, I had a half year of elementary school to finish. That was my fourth school in two years, so I'd gotten used to changing. It was no big deal; I simply stayed away from the other kids. They already had their little groups and friendships, so they didn't bother me. By the end of junior high, I was getting to know a few kids, but mostly I kept people at a distance.

It was the same for Grace. After Ned, Dr. Woodworth, and the salesman in Pennsylvania, the last thing she wanted was some man to mess her up. We kept to ourselves. Sometimes she would talk to me about her work and I would try to help her figure things out. Occasionally, I escorted her to company parties.

Sometimes it seemed as if we were just floating, not connected to anything. Grace had put her "dear brother and sister," as she called them, out of her life. There was no one in the world we could trust, or even talk to, except each other. Still, each year we lived there, I saw less of her.

I never heard anything from my father, not even a postcard. It hurt that he could forget me so easily. I hadn't forgotten him. Sometimes, Grace and I would sit around and make jokes about him, but, in a funny way, I wanted him back. I thought it might be different since Grace had quit booze and was making money.

The only real sore spot between Grace and me was my grades. The curriculum my first year at Bowker Junior High was comparable to the fifth grade at Westfield. Still, all during those years at Ravenswood, the teachers kept saying I could do better. I was an "underachiever." I guess I achieved as much as I really wanted to, which admittedly wasn't very much. Except for English, which I liked and was pretty good at, I worked just hard enough to avoid failing grades. I told Grace it was the best I could do, but I don't think I fooled her. Earning big bucks had made her ambitious. She wanted me to transfer to the Hun School or Lawrenceville, but my grades were too low. I could tell I was falling out of favor.

I didn't lose touch with Buddy and Willie, although I was somewhat distracted by the frequent changes in my life and body. During the trial, I had learned where each of them lived and what sort of lives they led. I anticipated the resolution, but I hadn't settled on a specific plan. Patience, I knew, was my best hope. I had absolute faith that the time would come, when I was larger and stronger and able to deal with them on their own terms. I called each of them regularly, no less than once or twice every month. Usually at inconvenient times: the middle of the night, early on a Saturday morning. Each time, I used a different voice and some new mode of harassment. I rejoiced in their anger. The sound of their voices kept my hate alive.

thirty-six

My trip to Boulder to visit the Howes will coincide with the annual meeting of the Gentry Foundation. Not that the event is of any interest to me, but it's a way to make sure he won't be out of town while I'm there.

I've told my supervisor at Legacy that I'm going to spend my week's vacation camping in the Pocono Mountains. I thought I should make it clear that they won't be able to reach me, and that my "plans" should involve something so dull that no one will ask any potentially embarrassing questions when I get back.

I found a postcard of the Beverly Wilshire Hotel that I've written and addressed to Cinnamon, and sent in an envelope to the Beverly Hills postmaster for remailing. Often, the stamps on postcards aren't canceled, but I didn't want to take a chance.

The night before departure, I don't sleep. In the morning, I do all my usual chores around the apartment and eat a light lunch of leftovers from the China Dragon. There are now no perishables in my refrigerator. I am unexpectedly calm. At 2:05 PM, I catch a bus to the Broomall Arby's, where I connect with a van to Philadelphia International Airport.

Ninety minutes later, I'm in seat 19A, searching the landscape below for the ashes of 929 Ammons. It's a dinner flight, but because of the time difference, it will only be midevening when I get in. The view to the west from my window seat is arresting: majestic thunderheads in the scarlet glory of a setting sun. Suddenly, I'm in it. Soaring. I'm oblivious when they bring the food. In my heart, I know Grandad is with me.

Denver is surprisingly flat. There are mountains to the west, but at quite a distance. The shuttle from the car-rental place takes me to some teenaged twit who delivers an irritating sales pitch intended to make me rent a more expensive model and spend as much on redundant insurance as the basic daily rate for the car. I listen patiently and turn it down flat. Zit Face turns off the charm.

It's nearly nine, but still light. I have decided to stay in the Denver area as a precaution. I find the Motel 6 listed in my directory. A few blocks north is a twenty-four-hour adult bookstore that advertises "live girls." Handy for those late-night, literary cravings. I register as Steve Hancock. The accommodations are basic, but clean and well ordered. I begin to unpack my things. Suddenly, the excitement is too much. I decide to drive to Boulder and check things out.

It takes a little over half an hour. A clerk in a convenience store gives me directions to the street where Howe lives. I hadn't realized Boulder is a college town. Though I'm sure classes are over for the summer, there are many young people around. Howe's neighborhood is on the west side. It's dark, but I can see that the houses are big, old, homey things, somewhat Victorian. The streets are wide and lined with overhanging maples. Howe's place is a large two-story brick with white shutters. Corner lot. I park across the street.

There are lights burning on both floors. I see her Volvo in the drive. No doubt his BMW is tucked snugly away in the detached garage I see at the back of the property.

The sweet night air bears the scent of an evening shower. I drink it in. A calico cat that had been curled up on the landing at Howe's front door stirs itself and slinks off into the shrubbery.

At last, I'm here.

thirty-seven

Brad Hines, Eric Muloski, and I shared a bus stop all through junior high and into high school. As it happened, Grace had sold both families their homes. A "Paul Revere" for the Hines family and a "Marquis de Lafayette" for the Muloskis.

Brad Hines was a charming, athletic kid from a prominent, cohesive family. Not terribly bright, but pleasant enough. Unfortunately, Brad was so handsome and generally blessed in all aspects of his life that you were left with no choice but to despise him.

Eric Muloski, aka "the Wimp," was a shy, frail kid whose parents' frequent battles kept the neighborhood gossip mill spinning. Eric was also brilliant. For all these good reasons, of course, it was considered practically toxic to be seen with him, and though the three of us often chatted, the school bus never caught Brad or me within ten feet of Eric when it pulled up. Still, I was fond of him. Like me, Eric was an only child and, from all appearances, equally lonely. I was glad, when the time came, that I was there for him.

Grace was at a party somewhere the night it happened. I was restless, and there was nothing on TV but crap like "Andy Williams' Christmas in Vail." The house was even gloomier than usual. That afternoon, the cleaning people had set up our fake Christmas tree. I decided to go for a walk. The walking wasn't as good in Ravenswood as in Llanfair. The houses, like the people, had no soul.

A smoky three-quarter moon shone through a layer of wispy clouds. A few houses had Christmas lights. There was a crust of old snow on the ground. It was strangely quiet. It's always quieter when there's snow. If I stood very still, I could hear the traffic on Route 1 three miles away.

I started walking on the street, but it was icy so I cut across people's yards. The snow made a nice crunching sound. After I turned the first corner, I heard something. I wasn't sure what. I stopped to listen. I was in the middle of Eric's front yard. His house was dark except for the welcome light and a dim glow from somewhere in the back of the first floor. After a few seconds, I heard the sound again. It was coming from the house Con-Land was building next door. It was a combination of sounds really, like coughing and a thumping noise.

They were still framing the new house so it was just a skeleton. As I got closer, I could see the silhouette of someone standing on a box on the second floor. The person was pushing at the box with his feet and twisting from side to side. It gave me a spooky feeling but I was curious. Soon, I could see the noose of wire running between his neck and the joist over his head. A boy's voice told me to run up there and stop the suicide, but I ignored it. It was an old voice.

When I got to the top of the temporary steps to the second floor, I could see that it was Eric. All the hair stood up behind my head. My mouth opened as if I were going to cry out, but there was no sound.

He had tied himself into the wire noose and apparently intended to kick the wooden box from under his feet, but the box was too big for him to kick out of the way so he was stuck there swinging and kicking and gagging. I didn't let him see me at first. I just watched. I felt sorry for him but I knew how unhappy he was. Death was what he wanted. After a couple of minutes, I went to a place where he could see me. His eyes got big and he shook his head at me. I smiled and pulled the box from under his feet. I hoped he could see my smile.

Right away, his gagging got worse and there was a terrible look of anguish on his face. He knew he wasn't going to go quickly. He didn't weigh enough. I stepped forward and hugged him and pulled down on him and told him it was going to be okay. I knew I was doing the right thing. After a few minutes, he was still. I took a few steps back and said a prayer for him.

Somewhere nearby, they were singing carols.

thirty-eight

Her name was Karen Clarke. I was standing behind her in the cafeteria line at Palmer High. I should have known something was going to happen because all I could usually smell when I was shuffling along in that line was boiled cabbage and pizza, but this time, all I could smell was her, and she smelled great, like baby powder, but sexy. We were passing the salad display when a couple of the old women who worked there started yelling at each other and the line stalled. Karen turned to me and said, "Can you believe them?" I'm not sure what I said, I was so flustered, but she agreed with it, and we just kept talking away like that until the line started moving and she turned her attention back to the petroleum waste they called food at that school.

"Karen," I blurted out, "would you like to go to DQ after school?" I didn't know where the words came from. I felt like a ventriloquist's dummy. She turned and smiled again, a soft, sweet smile. There was probably enough metal in Karen's mouth for the grill of a BMW, but I didn't see it. I was caught up in the magic of her blue eyes.

It was funny, as we walked along the sidewalk after school, I stopped thinking about her and started thinking about the mere fact that she was there, with me. I couldn't get over what I'd done. Her breasts really got to me. They weren't large, but even under the fuzzy, powder blue sweater she was wearing, they were assertive. I mean, they stuck out in a way that said, "Hey, look at us. We're some really fantastic tits."

I talked a lot. I guess because I was nervous; I wanted to show how smart and charming I was. I assumed that's what I was supposed to do. She acted impressed. I impressed myself. The words just seemed to flow. While we were waiting for a green, she caught me checking her out and shifted her books in front of her to cover up. After that, I made myself look at the trees and cars, even the dirt in the street, anything but her, but I could still see her. Her hair was blond, layered in soft, bouncy curls along her head. She was springtime; and she was mine.

I bought sundaes, hot fudge for me, hot caramel for her, and a large fries. Then I led her to the most private booth I could find. She was beautiful. I had never seen a girl as beautiful in my life. I still couldn't believe I was there with her. I tore the pouches of ketchup for the fries and she squeezed. We both liked our fries swimming in so much ketchup that you couldn't pick one up without getting it on your fingers. She was complaining about school and dumb assignments. . . . I had trouble following the conversation. She had breasts, *real breasts*.

"...Really," Karen moaned as she nibbled a fry, "I

couldn't be-lieve it when they made us write 'What I Did
on My Summer Vacation' for the four-thousandth time.
I never dreamed they made you do that kind of kid junk
in high school. God, we're practically grown up."

"We had to write it, too," I said. "I wrote 'None of
Your Business' in big red letters and handed it in. . . ."

"Oh, wow! Neat!" Karen giggled. "Did you really do
it?"

"Absolutely," I assured her. She was laughing too
hard for me to admit that it wasn't true. "Last week,
when we were supposed to write a biographical sketch
of a famous American, I wrote about Eric instead."

"Who's Eric? You don't mean Eric Bloomfeld, the senior, do you? He's a nerd."

"No. Eric Muloski, the kid who killed himself at
Christmas. He lived in my neighborhood, around the
corner, actually."

"You *knew* him?"

"Yes. We were kind of friends, you know, from the
bus stop. My mom sold them their house. His parents
were splitting up. He was really shy, but they said he
was a genius."

She shook her head. "Bummer."

"Some guys who were working on the house they're
building next to his found him. He was hanging from
the joists on the second floor. He hung himself with electrical wire. . . ." She pulled a spoonful of caramel sundae
from her mouth and held it while her tongue made a
quick cleanup trip around her lips. Lips. Marie. "The
police said he must have snuck out of his house in the
middle of the night"—Karen's lips were ripe and
glossy—"and gone over there and done it. He'd been

dead for hours when they found him." I could almost feel her sucking me.

"Gross. . . . God, that's horrible. You didn't *see* him or anything, did you?"

Her eyes got huge when I nodded. "He looked really peaceful. It was the first time I ever saw him when he didn't look sad, or worse. I was happy for him. I wanted to go to his funeral, but my mom said it was private." She was leaning forward in a way that made her nipples rub against the edge of the table. "Some people are hung up about death," I said. "Not me, I've seen it before." Her eyes locked with mine. I had an erection. I needed her strawberry lips to taste my cock. I couldn't think of anything else. That's probably how Grace got in without my seeing her.

I couldn't believe my rotten luck when I saw her standing at the back of a line of three people waiting to order. Suddenly, I felt this terrible guilt and shame, as if I were being disloyal to Grace merely by sitting there with Karen. Forget about what I'd been thinking. The man at the front of the line got his order and went to a table. All of a sudden, my heart was pounding and I started to sweat.

"Billy?"

"Huh?"

"What's the matter? You look like you've seen a ghost or something." Karen looked in the direction I'd been staring.

"No, I . . . Sorry. It's okay." Grace was at the head of the line, her back still toward me; I had this panic feeling like I had to run for the door.

"I was wondering, would you like to come over to my

house and do homework? My parents don't get home for hours and my brothers are both away at school. . . ."

"I'll be right back . . . ," I said. All I knew was that I had to get out of there so I could breathe. There were two doors. Either way, I had to go by Grace. I turned my head away from her and walked as fast as I could. Along the way, I nearly knocked over a table where three black guys were drinking coffee. The entrance was jammed with some fat woman and about ten obnoxious brats. As I pushed past them, one of the brats started to cry.

I was probably running by the time I reached the back of the building. There was a fenced place where the dumpsters were. I went in there and tried to catch my breath. It took a long time. I felt like a total asshole. I tried to think of excuses to tell Karen. I stuck my head outside the trash thing and looked for any sign of Grace or her car. I checked one side of the building, then the other. I cut around the back of the auto parts place next door and got a good view of the parking area in front of the DQ. No sign of Grace's car. I couldn't risk going back in. I was drenched with sweat. I decided Karen would figure I was a head case no matter what I said to her. I went home feeling awful.

That night, I waited up for Grace; I had to find out if she'd seen me. She was later than usual. She claimed she'd spent the whole day near Philadelphia looking at property. I didn't know whether to believe her or not.

I managed to avoid Karen for about a week, but one day I was working in the computer lab and she spotted me. I assumed she would dump on me, but instead she was quite kind about what had happened. She said she hoped she hadn't done anything that bothered me, and told me she always had a big birthday party in March and that I'd be invited. Her kindness touched me, although if she'd been hostile, I wouldn't have felt as bad about disgracing myself.

Every day, I checked our mail for the invitation to her party. Unfortunately, before it came, we had moved again.

Grace came into my bedroom one morning a little after six. Usually we hardly saw each other before night. I had to catch the school bus at 7:40, and she always watched some business show on cable and did her workout. This particular morning, she came in and sat on the bed next to me. We were totally out of sync. She was dressed in one of her drop-dead business outfits, and had a cigarette and a cup of coffee going. I was half-asleep and half-naked. She kissed me and said good morning. I sat up. Her cigarette smoke was disgusting. Grace had never smoked inside before we bought the house.

"I hate to disturb you, honey," she said, "but I have some exciting news: I have a new job. It's a wonderful opportunity for me."

"Great." I yawned.

"It's going to mean some adjustments and inconvenience, but it's a real step up. Con-Land has been optioning acreage out near West Chester for some time. They want to do another project like Ravenswood in some of the old horse country, but we've had to be very discreet. Well, two weeks ago, the last piece of the puzzle fell into place and the board has decided to do a phase one—a hundred and sixty homes. And guess who they want to be the sales director!"

"Who?"

"Me!" If she'd been smiling any harder, I think the skin on her face would have split. "Isn't that exciting? Not bad for four years with the company, huh? From pouring coffee at open houses to selling a fifty-million-dollar project? Aren't you happy for me?"

"Sure."

"But what?"

"Are you saying we have to move back to Pennsylvania?"

"I don't think it's a matter of *have to*, Billy. I see it as *want to*. I've found a stunning townhouse for us in Haverford, near the Cricket Club. If you apply yourself the rest of the year at Harriton High, I'm sure we can get you back into Westfield in the fall. We're back, Billy. Don't you see it? On our terms, not living like the hired help in Llanfair. I should think you'd be delighted."

I was feeling too many emotions for so early in the day. I knew in my gut she felt defensive about the move or she wouldn't have waited till morning to tell me. I was glad for her—not as glad as she was for herself—but glad. I just wasn't glad for me. "Why did you keep it such a big secret?" I asked.

"Secret? There was no secret. Nothing was certain until a day or two ago. I didn't want us to get our hopes up. Can't you be happy for me? I've worked hard for this, Billy."

"When do we move?"

"Two weeks. I had to sign a lease for the first of the month. Look, I was going to surprise you for your birth-

day, Billy," she said, "but maybe this is just as good a
time. I've decided to give you your own car as soon as
you're sixteen." (There was a girl at Palmer who said
her mother bribed her with new bedroom furniture
every time they were going to move.) "Now, does that
make you feel better?" Grace said.

I should have told her how I felt about changing
schools and houses again, and how much it hurt me that
she was just dumping this whole thing in my lap. Instead, I said, "New or used?" I was only fifteen.

"The car? Well, actually, I'd planned to let you have
my car." It was a four-year-old white Chevy Nova, with
a tiny four-cylinder engine; a permanent stench of cigarette smoke; and a nasty shimmy over fifty from the
time Grace plowed into a telephone pole after an ice
storm. I wanted a car. I had wet dreams about cars, but
Grace's was to what I wanted like badminton is to pro
football.

I rolled away from her and said, "What will you
drive?"

"Really, Billy," she said, "I'm starting to get irritated.
I've come in here to tell you some wonderful news and
now I've given you a car, and you act like I've commit-
ted a crime, for God's sake."

"Sorry," I said. I'd disappointed her. I felt a weird
sense of responsibility for Grace's emotions. It went back
to when she was first trying to quit booze. I was always
afraid that she might start again if I did anything to upset her. "I didn't mean anything. I just wanted to know
what kind of car you're going to get, that's all. I'm happy
for you about the job; really, I am. I just don't feel very
well. . . ."

"I've got to go down there today with my team to look for offices. It may run into dinner; I'm not sure. Don't wait up for me. I think when you see the new house and realize how nice it will be to get back to your roots, you'll see this move differently. I'm sorry, I just can't live my life to please the whole world."

thirty-nine

Saturday morning. I drive to Boulder and find the main post office. It's a few minutes after nine. General Delivery for Steve Hancock? The clerk is gone too long. My heart sinks. I imagine the worst. Cold sweat. I keep checking the exits. Finally, he returns with it. My package, apparently intact. I go to the Trailways depot, rent a locker, and leave the parcel. No need to open it, I know what's inside.

To the Howe residence. I park on the opposite corner this time so I can see more of the house. The day is brilliant, not a cloud. The air is surprisingly cool. Through a thin hedge that runs along the sidewalk on the west side of the property, I can see into the backyard. There's a swing set, a plastic wading pool, and what appears to be a sandbox. The whole package is so homey. You can almost hear the cartoon shows on the big family TV and smell the bacon and eggs (or would it be pancakes?) cooking up in the kitchen. As far I can tell, they're still in there. The Volvo doesn't appear to have budged since last night.

Just after nine-thirty, I get a jolt. A male jogger, to whom I pay no particular attention as he approaches, swings up the Howes' front walk and lets himself into the house. It's Howe. I get goose bumps. I wish I'd paid more attention when I first saw him. Still, everything fits: He's slender, a little less than six feet. The features are fine. The hair coverage is good for someone his age. He's still handsome, as he was in the honeymoon photo. Not surprisingly, the jogging ensemble is *trés* chic: a loose-fitting red jacket embellished with jaunty white stripes, and on the bottom, those black stretch tights that look like they'd be all the rage in San Francisco. I scold myself for not locking in on him sooner. Adrenaline surges through me.

At ten-fifteen, as the entire Howe family emerges through the front door, I start my car. Everyone's dressed for the pool. Mom, a bony blonde in dark glasses, has a bundle of towels under her left arm; Dad's carrying a cooler. Do I perceive tension between them? Surely nothing's awry in the ideal marriage. The kids are predictably cute. Little Andrew's got Mom's yellow hair, and Elizabeth, in a huge sun hat, has Dad's light brown locks. Both kids have blow-up pool toys, nearly as big as they are.

When the Volvo is halfway down the block, I shift the Subaru into drive and start following. As we roll along the shady streets, I see bicyclists everywhere, all in racing attire and pedaling what appear to my ignorant eye to be serious machines. I wonder if they arrest males here for not owning a jockstrap.

The lot at the Boulder Country Club is nearly full. I hear cheers coming from beyond the low-slung buildings. It's all very swank. Golf course, tennis courts, swimming pool, and a fabulous view of the mountains. I slip the Subaru into the first open slot. The Howes park three rows closer to the clubhouse.

Once the Howes have gone in, I repark the Subaru in a space from which it's easier to observe the buildings and the Howes' car. For comfort, I pull out Charlie Crystal's porno playing cards. Strange, I still think of them as Charlie's though I've had them nearly twenty years. . . .

At eleven o'clock, I wonder if I should be making better use of my time. I'd like to inspect the Howe car at close range, but I don't want to risk being spotted on the off chance Mommy or Daddy comes back for something. . . .

Hi, *Niggeria*. The Queen of Spades. My special pet. A gorgeous black girl with huge tits. Except for her crown, she's naked, but she's holding this scepter thing with a rubber prick on the end. Crystal and I hung out together the summer we were fourteen. He gave the Queen to me and said she'd help me "spray the ceiling." He was right. As soon as I could, I went back to his house and swiped the whole deck.

At eleven-thirty, a set of sprinkler heads pops out of the ground to my right and starts watering my car, as well as a section of lawn. I take it as a sign I should be elsewhere. The Howes have been at the pool nearly an hour, but, given the cooler, it's a safe bet they're planning to hang out with the other beautiful people at least through lunchtime. I decide to pay a visit to their house.

On the way, I stop at a pay phone and call their number. I know it as well as my own. It's the same recording I've heard many times before: dear Charles expressing the family's regret that no one can answer the phone "quickly," to imply, I suppose, that everyone's home, heavily armed, and poised to confront all intruders. I repeat the call several times in case someone is there who might be irritated into answering. There's no response.

I park on the street next to the Howes' backyard. There's a Nissan pickup a few feet ahead of me and a green Karmann Ghia convertible near the corner. I don't feel conspicuous, but I take a few minutes to reconnoiter. It looks and feels okay. I pull on a pair of latex gloves and get out of the car. The sidewalk is clear. I cut through the hedge and trot up the wooden steps to the Howes' back entrance as if I'd done it a thousand times. I knock and wait and knock and wait. No sign of life in either of the adjoining properties. Unlocked breaker box and phone interface just this side of the east corner. Convenient. Suddenly, a fat, old dog emerges from the cool darkness under the steps. Part Irish setter from the look of him. I prepare to flee if he barks. But no, he lumbers up the steps and waits to be petted. I oblige. I must commend the Howes on their choice of watchdogs. The lock is an old Kwikset dead bolt. A challenge on the order of whacking off for a well-equipped graduate of the Pennsylvania State Pen. I'm in; 12:07 PM. I give myself five minutes.

House is probably fifty years old. Kitchen looks about three. Probably a fifty-thousand-dollar remodel, not that I'm a judge of such things. Dirty breakfast dishes here and there. Cold cereal yet. Tsk tsk. Everything's elegant. Very Waspy, right down to the paintings of English hunting scenes on the dining-room wall and the sterling-silver tea service on the sideboard. Nice stereo in the den. A personal computer. Huge TV. A showplace of home electronics. Ten of me could probably get by on what the Howes spend on toys and entertainment. In the front hall, my spine turns suddenly to ice as I notice the control panel for a security system. I look more closely. It's off. Too much trouble to punch the numbers. Maybe they use it only at night. Too bad they didn't arm it when they left this morning. Too bad for them.

I go to the master bedroom. An antique four-poster dominates. More electronics. Another control panel by what I assume is his side of the bed. Family pictures on the walls. Her nightstand is well stocked for sexual fun. A variety of unguents and a rubber device that looks like a tiny Frisbee. For birth control, I suppose. Yum yum. Something touches me, I jump. A cat snaking between my legs. Deep breaths drop my heartbeat below triple digits. I go to the dressers, his and hers. His is full of the usual things. Quantity and quality are consistent with his lofty station. I love her undies, silky, lacy, naughty, all sorts of luscious colors from mauve to tacky red. I want to stuff my pockets with them for later fun. But no; I settle for a kiss.

There's pee in the toilet in the children's bathroom. I flush it without thinking. Andrew's room. The good life. The best of F. A. O. Schwarz. The toys are transitional. From baby to boy. I'm jealous. I wonder if the Howes would adopt a thirty-three-year-old. Probably not this one.

Time to go. Vanity, a whim . . . I want to leave some small sign of my visit. Mash a flower? Microwave the goldfish? Too cliché. I slip the ten of clubs into the box of Froot Loops cereal on the kitchen table. It shows a bitchy blonde I baptized Vixen doing a be-kind-to-animals number with a German shepherd—something to help young Andy rise and shine.

Never fear, Vixie dear, I'll be back.

forty

The place Grace rented for us was a sublet in a complex called Wyncliff Place. I saw immediately what appealed to her about it. It was quite elegant with its French Provincial architecture and fountains and hedges and statues. It even had a security guard at the front gate. I hated it. I was the only person living there under thirty-five.

The school was a school. It was bigger than Palmer and older. There were some appealing girls, but I had made up my mind not to become involved until Grace bought a place and we were permanently situated. She was interested in finding an old farmhouse out along Brandywine Creek near her new subdivision.

In early May, just before my birthday, Grandad's insurance company finally ran out of gimmicks to delay paying off Buddy and Willie. The company's lawyers had worked the appeals process for four years, all the way to the state Supreme Court. Finally, a hearing was scheduled to decide whether the $750,000 awards to

Buddy and Willie were excessive. But then, half an hour before the hearing was supposed to start, the insurance company lawyers settled with the killers' lawyers for the original amount. This time, Buddy and Willie were the losers. Their lawyers took a lot more than they would have without all the appeals. On top of that, Willie had had to live on disability and the income from a menial job for four extra years to keep up the pretense that he suffered from blackouts; and Buddy had been paying a psychiatrist the whole time to prove he had permanent emotional damage from stabbing Grandad. I guess Buddy and Willie were pretty pissed, but the settlement still cleaned out everything Grandad had left for me, so however angry those bastards may have been, it was nothing compared to the way I felt.

The night I found out, I was making dinner and watching an old western on TV. I thought I was alone, but Grace blew into the kitchen and startled the hell out of me. She had on a slinky black dress, gloves, and lots of jewelry. She usually looked pretty good, but this time she looked like a movie star. I guess she'd been back in her room getting dolled up and I didn't know it. Anyway, after the usual conversation about what kind of day I'd had and how I shouldn't wait up for her, she casually told me that Buddy and Willie were about to get paid off. I guess I just sat there acting as if I'd been socked in the face with a bag of rocks because we didn't talk about it. She was in her usual hurry.

When she was gone, I closed my eyes and I was back in that clearing trying to keep the flies off Grandad's body. I was ten and that terrible, lonely feeling came over me. I started to cry; I cried like I would never stop.

I hated myself for crying. I hit myself for crying, again and again, in the side of the head. It hurt and I got angry, but I kept pounding on my head anyway. Then the crying stopped and I could see clearly: The injustice was finally complete, just as I was about to get a car and a driver's license. The timing was perfect. Suddenly, for the first time in weeks, I wasn't depressed. I was excited.

forty-one

My birthday was on a Friday. Right after school, my Sears driving instructor took me over to the state police barracks where you take the driving test. I didn't think I'd be nervous, but I was. Very. Actually, the only thing I did wrong was to try to start the car when it was already started. Fortunately, they don't dock you for that.

As soon as I got home, I started searching for the keys to the Nova. (Grace was driving a brand-new Thunderbird by then, courtesy of Con-Land.) I searched everywhere and eventually decided that Grace had purposely hidden the keys so that she could make a ceremony of the presentation. That morning, she had coyly instructed me to dress for a special evening.

While we lived in Ravenswood, I'd started to work out. I was never jock material, but I liked the way it made my body look. Anyway, I worked with the weights for a while before I got ready to step out with Grace. I always did it with music and usually in Grace's bedroom. One wall was completely mirrored.

After I had a shower, I put on a shirt with French cuffs, a tie Grace had given me for Christmas that had little foxes sewn into it, and my dark gray suit. I looked pretty sharp. As a special treat for Grace, I splashed on some after-shave she'd bought me.

By a quarter past seven, I was starting to wonder if this was going to be one of those nights when Grace had promised me she'd be early, only to blow in around eleven o'clock. Also, I was halfway through my third news show of the evening and getting not only quite bored but very hungry. About twenty-five past seven, I heard Grace's key in the front door and I shut off the tube. As the door swung open, I stood to greet her.

"Billy," she gushed, "I want you to meet my very, very dear friend, Marty Shoemaker!" She swept across the room toward me towing some clown in a business suit. Both of them had these huge, shit-eating grins. I felt as if I had two noses or something.

"How're ya doin' there, big guy?" the clown asked. "Hey, sorry if we're a couple of minutes late!" He grabbed my hand before I could back away and started pumping it. Grace was moving packages from the doorway to the kitchen counter. "Hey, that's a pretty good grip," he laughed, pretending to be in pain. He reeked of booze. I wanted to walk out the front door.

"Billy," Grace squeaked, "isn't this wonderful, having a new friend to help us celebrate your birthday? I told you tonight would be extra special!" She didn't seem to be drunk.

"Hey, it's my pleasure," Shoemaker said. "I hope it's okay with you, Bill. I told your mother, no more of that

Billy stuff, now that you're sixteen. You know, Grace, he's even handsomer than you said; bigger, too." He winked at her. "Hey, I hope you like steaks," he said. "Mom and I practically bought out the 'Le Booserie' out in Wayne. Actually, don't worry about it. Mel Goldberg, the owner, we're old golf buddies. Hey, I'm a T-bone man, myself, how about you, Bill? Sirloin? Delmonico?"

"Mr. Shoemaker is president of Docu-X Systems, Billy . . . Bill. I'll never get used to that. They're in the suite next to ours." She seemed so nervous, so anxious to please.

"Stop by anytime, Bill. I'll give you the grand tour. It's a new franchise, but in five years, we'll be the biggest mobile shredder on the East Coast. Piece of cake. The Watergate thing was a gift from God."

"Great," I said.

"Say, Grace," Shoemaker laughed, "what's a man gotta do around here to get a drink?" I watched from a distance as they located a big bag from the state store and Grace pointed him toward the glasses and ice. He tossed three cubes into a tumbler and filled it with vodka. After he carefully sipped the top off his drink so it wouldn't spill, he ambled over, all smiles, to join me at the kitchen table. Grace, meanwhile, fussed nervously with the bags and boxes she'd brought in.

Shoemaker wasn't ugly at least. He was probably six feet, an inch taller than I, and had dark wavy hair. He was thin and looked like he was in reasonably good shape for someone forty or forty-five.

"Whew! Long day," he groaned. He lowered himself into one of the dinky chrome chairs at the kitchen table. The table itself was black glass and chrome. I'd never liked it because it seemed unfriendly to me, if that's possible for a table. "Hey, love the place, Grace," he called out over his shoulder. He pulled a silver cigarette case from a pocket of his gray trousers and popped it open. "Looks like the Phils are gonna have a lock on the cellar again this year, huh, Bill?"

"I don't know," I said. "I never paid that much attention."

"Right on! Doesn't leave enough time for chasing girls!" Shoemaker laughed again and pulled hard on his cigarette. "How's the chef doing out there? I'd be happy to give you a hand with those steaks! Over forty bucks for three steaks, Bill. Can you believe that?"

"Everything's under control, I think," Grace said in her cheeriest voice. "Can I freshen your drink?"

"Not quite," he said. "I'm powerless to defend myself if I get drunk!" They both chuckled. I noticed Shoemaker's cologne for the first time, an unusual musty-sweet scent, like garbage.

"I sure hope you and I are going to be friends, Bill," he confided. "I think the world of your mom, I really do. She's tops. I don't know how much she's told you about me. I've got two daughters. One's in college: Rusty, down in Florida. The other one is a senior in high school out in Dayton. That's where I'm from. Jamie, she's still living with her mom. Jan and I separated the year before last. I'd been with IBM since Korea. They transferred me to Hartford a few years back and, well, the new job just wasn't right for me. I tried consulting for a while. . . ." He seemed to lose his train of thought. I couldn't imagine why this total stranger was suddenly telling me his life story, but it sounded as if he'd done it hundreds of times before. "Hey, somebody stole my drink!" he exclaimed suddenly, springing from his chair.

In the kitchen, he made himself another huge vodka-on-the-rocks, sipped the top off, and went to nibble on Grace's ear. They were talking in voices only a fool and a drunk would think I couldn't hear. Shoemaker was telling her what terrific friends he and I were getting to be. She couldn't have been more pleased. When he'd had enough ear, he said, "Hey, Bill, how about opening a few presents?"

"I thought we might wait until after dinner," Grace said meekly.

"Hey, Bill doesn't want to wait. This is *his* birthday. Let the guy do what he wants!"

While the potatoes au gratin boiled over in the oven and three beautiful steaks grilled on the Jenn-Air, I was presented with two ties, three shirts, a biography of Nixon, a Beatles album, and an "advanced chronome-ter" that told the time in three parts of the world and could wake you by sound, vibration, or both. Shoemaker told me he'd picked it out. I took one look at the stupid thing and made up my mind that it would never touch my wrist. The car keys? Grace told me I could dig them out of her purse.

While Shoemaker poured himself another drink, Grace set the dining-room table. It was the first time we'd used it. It was almost nine when we sat down to eat. The potatoes were dried out; the steaks were prac-tically cremated; and the Stouffer's spinach soufflé was still ice-cold. But there was lots of wine: two bottles of Marty's favorite cabernet sauvignon. Grace permitted herself only a sip, but with Marty cheering me on, I matched him almost glass for glass. I could tell Grace was either angry about my drinking, or just jealous, but she didn't say anything. She just kept giving me The Look.

By the end of the meal, Grace was getting all sloppy about my growing up and I, with a nice buzz going, had started to wonder if I'd misjudged the boyfriend after all.

"You know," Grace sighed, "I can't tell you how happy it makes me that we can all be together for this very, very special occasion. I can't believe my darling Billy is actually sixteen. The next thing you know, he'll be going off to college and thinking about a family of his own. My Billy, Mr. Shoemaker—"

" 'Marty,' please."

". . . Marty and I have been seeing each other nearly two months now."

"She come into my office wanting to use the phone. I said, 'Great, just leave a dime on the desk. . . .' "

"I want you to know, he's a very, very special man, and very dear to me."

He leaned across the table and kissed her awkwardly on the lips. "That goes double for me," Marty assured me with a wink.

"I haven't told you about . . . us, because, well, frankly, I felt uncomfortable after everything that had gone on before. But, Marty decided that—*we* decided that—it was wrong to shut you out. So, our friendship will be three ways from now on."

"Sound okay to you, Bill? Someday soon, we'll run in to the Vet and show those Phillies fans what cheering's all about." All I could manage was a queasy smile. The room had started slowly spinning.

"There's one more thing I want to say, Billy, Bill. I know you're anxious to have your cake—"

"And eat it, too!" Shoemaker laughed. Grace gave Marty a heavy look and took his hand.

"Marty will be staying here, with me, some nights. I know you're old enough now to understand. We love each other very much and people who love, who love each other the way we do, want to be together all the time." She looked anxiously at Marty for approval. He was rechecking the second wine bottle by candlelight to be positively certain it was empty. She released his hand and reached for her cigarettes. "God," she muttered, "what I'd give for one lousy glass of champagne." Warm wine had begun rising like mercury in my throat.

"So, Bill," Marty said, coming suddenly to life, "you won't mind sharing the orange juice with an old guy like me, will you?"

"No," I said, barely opening my mouth. "No" was not just the only response to anything I could imagine, it seemed to be the only word I could say.

"Super!" Shoemaker cheered. "Guess I'll get my toothbrush from the car!" He and Grace shared a little laugh.

"Well," Grace gushed, "is everybody ready for ice cream and cake?"

A dark expression twisted Shoemaker's weary face. "Christ!" he moaned. "I had a feeling something was wrong when we walked in here! I *forgot* the goddamn cake! I put it down in the butcher place so we could buy meat, remember? I never picked the goddamn thing up again. Christ! We walked right out of there without it! Twenty-three fifty! Can you believe that?"

"When I didn't see it, I thought you'd just left it in the car for a surprise," Grace said pleasantly. "Oh well, maybe we have some cookies. We've got plenty of am- aretto raisin ice cream. I'm sure of that! Wait'll you try it, Billy! It's Marty's favorite!"

"Forget it," I said through clenched teeth. "I'm . . ." The mouth clamped suddenly shut. Cold sweat ran like Niagara. Deep breathing didn't help. They kept staring at me, waiting for me to speak. ". . . throw up," I said at last.

As I heaved dinner into the toilet, I could hear the two of them in the dining room, still laughing.

forty-two

In the dream, everything was white: the room, the sheets, the snow outside, even the sky. It was like the inside of an empty refrigerator or a scene from some crazy foreign movie.

Bad as it was, however, the whiteness was the least of it. I felt as if a clay pipe had been jammed down my throat and my chest had been strapped with steel. I couldn't breathe or swallow. To complete the job, they'd stolen my brain and filled the empty space with lead. I couldn't think or move. Time stood still.

When I closed my eyes, there was a picture show: vivid colors, familiar faces, yet different, stretched or crushed. Sounds were strange, hard to hang on to, or identify. I was warm, sweating. My feet were blanketed with snow. Grace was young and beautiful. Pink. She held me in her long arms. Ned stood beside us, golden, handsome. It was a summer day. He kissed her. He screamed and kicked her. He kicked us bloody. And left us sobbing on the ground.

It was night. I was wet and cold. Everything for her greenhouse was stacked neatly beside the garage. I found the place they'd made for it beside the living room. . . . Under snow. She was drunk. She had a gun and shot me. She screamed and shot me. The world went red. There was thunder in my heart and I went down.

Then it was morning. My pain was gone. Grace was lying in the bed beside me. I had just been born.

forty-three

I dragged into the kitchen about seven-thirty. The place smelled like an ashtray. His jacket, tie, and shoes were in the living room. Just looking at them, I got hurt and angry all over again. I didn't want to see him coming out of her bedroom. I felt out of place in my own home. I wrote her a note. Something like, "Thanks for a great birthday. We have a history paper due Monday so I thought I'd do some research. If it gets late, I'll grab a hamburger on the way home. Love, Billy." I figured that would buy me the whole day. I should have put a PS: "I hope Marty has syphilis," but naturally, I didn't have the guts.

I felt horribly conspicuous behind the wheel of a car with no adult present, but of course, nobody was paying any attention. It was a beautiful day. That's one thing about my birthday. Around then, so many trees and bushes are blooming. I had all the windows open in the car and the radio blasting away.

An eerie feeling came over me in South Jersey, traveling those old roads, remembering the last time—in Grandad's Mercedes. In some ways I felt grown up and different, but inside I was still ten-year-old Billy, missing his Grandad. But you can't go back; you can never go back. For every door that opens in front of you, another one closes to where you've been.

In Buena, I stopped to buy gas. Wonderful smells were drifting across the street from an Italian bakery. As I got into the car to go, a tiny cloud cut in front of the sun and made a monstrous black shadow that sailed down the road where I was headed. For a second, everything got cool and quiet. The hair on the back of my neck stood up. I thought about turning back. Then the shadow was gone. I needed to talk to somebody.

I had forgotten that the marina parking lot was covered with broken clamshells. Otherwise, everything looked the same as I remembered. I parked and started walking toward the dock. The sun shining on all that white made it really bright. The air smelled fishy. The sky was like a postcard. A girl went by on a bicycle and smiled at me. I started to feel better.

I looked all over for the *Ebony Witch*, but she wasn't there. In her berth was a speedboat called *Easy Money*. After I'd been up and down all the docks twice, I asked an old guy who was replacing some of the rotten boards in one of the walkways about her. He knew right away.

"Oh, yeah," he said, "Stan Buch's boat. Yeah, he lost her about three years ago."

"In a storm?" I asked.

"No," the man laughed. "The bank took her. We had a couple bad years. You musta heard about it. Shit washin' up on the beaches. Raw sewerage. You know, mothers was takin' their babies out for a dip and there's turds floatin' by. Business dried up like that. Buch had a lot of debts, hospital bills mostly. They took his boat. He worked mate on the *Sea Gal* for a summer, but that was no good. Last I heard, he and the missus was back in Tampa and Buch was doin' odd jobs weldin' for people."

"What about the *Witch?*"

"Shit if I know. She probably went for a song. You know, the way things was around here then and with her being as old as she was. What do you care? You kin to Stan?"

"No, I just went out on her once with my grandad. We had a really good time."

"Wish I could help you, fella." He lit a cigarette. "You might call Conroy Auction back in Vineland. They handle a lot of stuff like that. Come to think of it, there was a rumor Stan snatched her back off the bank one night and took her out and sank her. I never believed he done that. Stan would of sooner shot his wife than sink that boat. I think it broke his heart when they took her away."

I sat on the edge of the dock for a while and watched the weekend boaters go by. The sun was warm but there was a cool breeze from the ocean. As always, the gulls were swooping and squawking as they searched for food. It was a beautiful afternoon, peaceful, too. In a few weeks, the summer season would be under way and the place would be swarming. I imagined that on the night of July Fourth, some kid would go out bluefishing from the marina with his grandad, and they'd have themselves the time of their lives. Of course, the kid wouldn't be me, and the grandad wouldn't be mine, and the boat wouldn't be the *Ebony Witch*. That would never happen again.

It took me close to an hour to find the place where Buddy and Willie killed Grandad, but I just kept trying different roads until I had the right one. They'd put a traffic light and a MiniMart at the intersection where the accident happened. That fooled me the first time through, but once I identified that place, it was simple.

I got a lump in my throat as I took that last turn. I remembered how scared I was that night and how I prayed that they wouldn't follow us in there. Even six years later, I checked the rearview mirror a couple of times driving in.

The spot where the actual killing took place was totally different: no more gravel road, no more surveyor's stakes, and no more trash dump. Now it was "Ocean Acres—a year-round, waterfront community by the Sylva Corporation." There were canals on both sides of the road and houses that backed up onto them. Some of the houses had boats. Where the road ended before, you could go right or left. Either way, there were more houses and more canals. Instead of turning, I pulled onto the shoulder. Straight ahead was a little white house with one of those cutesy anchor-and-chain fences around the front yard. There was a kid about twelve out front shooting baskets. Shooting baskets where I'd hid naked in the underbrush and watched my grandfather get killed. Nothing was the same as that night. There was no place where I could get close to those memories. It didn't seem right, the way everything changes.

Gagne's Bait-Tackle-Boats was a few miles north, all

alone at the end of a sandy road near a little village called Reed's Beach. I stopped at a safe distance and left the motor running. It was really shabby, much worse than I anticipated. The main building was a shack that didn't look like it had been painted in a hundred years. Instead of regular windows, it had big, overhanging shutters. The shutters were propped wide open with two-by-fours, but there didn't seem to be anyone around. Even so, my stomach was in knots. On one end of the building, you could still read where somebody had painted BREKFEST-LUNCH. It looked like the house specialty would be flies. Nailed to the wall beside the front door was a big white-and-blue sign that said "Business For Sale" and gave a phone number. For a sign, it really improved the looks of the place.

The property backed up on Delaware Bay. The parking area around the shack was bordered on the south and east by tall marsh grasses. Just north of the shack, the land was bulkheaded, and a little spit of channel about fifty feet long cut in from the bay. They had about two dozen rental boats as far as I could tell. Most were still stacked up on the beach, but three of them bobbed like nursing piglets against the east end of a floating dock in the channel. On the north side of the dock was a skiff with a big outboard. I had been sitting there maybe three or four minutes, checking the place out, when his voice came out of nowhere and startled me.

"What's on your mind, kid?" He moved between me and the sun. I tried not to show how badly he'd spooked me.

"Nothing. I'm just . . . somebody told me you have boats for rent." He was looking in the back of the car.

Maybe he thought I was there to steal from him.

"You don't exactly look like you come down for a day's fishin'."

"No, I'm ... it was just an idea I had. ..." He was hard to see with the sun behind him. I couldn't tell whether he recognized me behind the baseball cap and shades I'd worn to hide my features. He was older, shorter, and fatter than the picture in my mind. I was trying not to panic, being so close to him, talking to him. Buddy. I decided he didn't recognize me. I'd changed more than halfway from kid to man in the years since he'd last had his beady eyes on me.

"I ain't really open yet. Just gettin' the place straighten' out." He wasn't wearing a shirt, which, with his body, was a big mistake. He had saggy little boobs with wispy tufts of white-blond hair at the nipples. An ugly scar went downhill to the left from his navel. The stringy blond mustache looked a little thicker, but he had lost even more of the skimpy fringe of hair around his head. He had on paint-splotched khaki pants and grimy running shoes. Five cans of a six-pack dangled from his left hand and the sixth, open, was in his right. "My 'frigerator's busted," he said. "The neighbor's lettin' me keep my beer and shit over her place till I get it fixed." He smelled like he looked. Buddy. The Killer.

"I don't rent the powerboats to no one under eighteen without a deposit, but it don't matter because I ain't got the motors serviced yet. Maybe by next weekend. Tow boats run twelve for the tow out and back includin' the first hour and three bucks an hour after that. Once you're at the channel, you can use the oars but don't go no further than you can see my marker buoy. Time starts when we leave the dock." He took a couple of gulps and waited for my answer. When I drove in there, the last thing on my mind was renting a boat, but somehow, it seemed like such a weird idea, I thought it might be fun to play along.

"I didn't bring my fishing stuff," I said.

"Three bucks a rod, includes one rig and your dipsy. Ten-dollar deposit. Extra rigs an' weights is two-fifty. I'd take at least a couple extra. Best fishin's at the wreck an' it eats lines. Good for me; bad for you." He waited for me to laugh at his funny. I did and right away got mad at myself for it. "Tell you what," he said, "we only got two hours decent light left tops. You give me fifteen, you can fish till seven, and I'll throw in the road rental. Bait and extra rigs is on you. How's that?"

"Okay." If you didn't know what a scum Buddy was, you might think he was a reasonably nice guy.

"You can park it over the office. We'll get you fixed up inside and you can pay me."

"How come you're selling? I saw the sign."

The stupid smile disappeared. For a second, I wondered if the question might lead him to recognize me. "I won the lottery," he said.

"That's great," I said.

"It could of been greater. I'll tell you this, I learned the people you really got to watch out for in this life are the ones that's supposed to be on your side."

My question didn't have a great effect on Buddy's mood. In the office, he dropped the small talk and concentrated on assembling the stuff I needed. I thought about asking him some more questions about winning the lottery, but decided not to press my luck. His office was a shit heap. There were beer cans and candy wrappers all over the place. Near the door, there was a little display case with fishing stuff in it: reels, knives, and scalers, things like that, but mostly knives. He seemed to have a thing for the big, ugly ones, more like you'd use on a gorilla than a fish. While he was putting his beers into a metal cooler, I grabbed one of the knives. It had a laminated wood handle and a seven-inch blade. I shoved it under my sweatshirt. My heart started thumping. Just taking the thing gave me a rush.

The skiff Buddy used for towing was an eighteen-footer with a fiberglass hull and a sixty-horse Evinrude on the stern. On the covered part back of the bow, there was an aluminum flange that looked like it was meant to hold a windshield, but there was no windshield. I stood on the floating dock while he got on board to start his motor. As I watched him, a strange sensation came over me. I felt my free will slipping away, yielding to some great power beyond myself. I was being sucked empty and refilled at the same time. When he turned his back, I must have pulled the knife from under my sweatshirt and unsheathed it, because the next thing I knew, I had it in my hand. My chest got tight. I held the knife point-up in my right fist, behind my back. The veins in the side of my head were throbbing. It was like a dream. Sounds got dull and fuzzy. My peripheral vision blurred. I could see only Buddy Gagne. Only his torso. Only his gut as he turned. Turned. He was talking. I couldn't understand the language. He put his foot on the dock to get off the boat. He smiled at me and, as if that were my cue, I whipped the knife from behind me and thrust it into his gut. He groaned. He fell over backward into his skiff. He just lay there in the bottom of the rocking boat looking at me with this incredibly stupid expression. I felt like I'd been looking at a movie. "You lousy shit," I said. "You killed my grandad."

I hadn't consciously intended to do it, not any of it. I'd only wanted to look, to plan. But it had happened because it had to. *Had to.* As if, for six years, that very moment and series of actions had been destined to occur. He was trying to crawl out of the boat. My head was going to explode. He was trying to yell. I freaked. I looked frantically for something to hit him with. There was a paddle on the dock. I remember it was bright red. I raised it as high as I could over my head and swung it down, edge first, against the top of his skull. It skipped off the bone and left an eight-inch gash in his scalp, but it made no sound.

I was in the boat with him, heading into the bay. It took about fifteen minutes, heading southwest, to reach the channel. I threw the anchor. It was lonely out there. In the summer, there would have been boats all over. I couldn't see the west shore of the bay at all. A few miles to the northwest, there were two big tankers and a freighter anchored. They sat heavy in the water, probably waiting for dock space in Philadelphia. The Jersey shore was five or six miles to my east. There were houses and a beach, but you couldn't see any of the details. The current and the wind were going in almost the same direction, strong enough to make a wake behind the boat, though it wasn't moving.

For a long time, I just sat there. I couldn't make myself look at him. At random intervals, frisky waves slapped the bow and sent spray flying into the boat. My sweatshirt and jeans got soaked. I felt miserable, lonely and sad. I was so scared.

Where I was anchored, if you looked south, you could see straight to the Atlantic Ocean. There were some big, puffy white clouds piled up out there that afternoon. I started staring at them. I really got into them, I guess, because I stopped feeling cold and lonely. For some little piece of time, I felt as secure as I used to sitting on Grandad's lap. I could hear his voice, but there were no words. I could feel him near me, but he wasn't there. I had this feeling of being in touch with my whole life, as it had been, and as it was. Ned was there, and wasn't; Grace was there, drunk and sober; Grandad was there, and not; I saw the places I had lived; my teachers; even Grace's new boyfriend, Marty Shoemaker. All of it seemed empty and far away. I don't know what it is about the ocean; it always makes me think like that. I like it, but it makes me sad.

When I came back from outer space, one of those big, fancy racing yachts was rounding the cape just south of me. Her sails were puffed out like pillows as she tacked into the bay. After a few minutes, she cut right between me and the setting sun. All the water around her was shining gold. It was one of the most beautiful things I've ever seen.

I rose slowly from my seat and turned to look at Buddy. The blood from the gash in his head had run over his face and turned black. The knife was buried in his gut up to the hilt. There was blood everywhere. I turned away from him again and threw up over the side. I was shivering. My knees were shaking. On land, it would have been warmer, but the wind was blowing off the water, which was no more than forty-five degrees. I wondered if Grace had started to worry about me. I wondered if she was fucking Marty Shoemaker.

Across the water, people were turning on their house lights. I figured I'd covered myself with Grace until seven or eight, max. The earliest I could get back, pushing it, was ten. I'd call her from the first pay phone and tell her I'd run into some friends. Losing my driving privileges on the first day would be a disaster.

I sucked in as much air as I could and climbed over the seat back to get closer. His skin had started to discolor. I looked away for a second and took more air. Then, with both hands on his belt, I lifted with all my strength and rolled him over the side.

Though the light was fading, you could see blood swirling like black ink into the water around him. I might have expected to feel good about his death, but I didn't. His mouth was wide open. I heard him choking. He was already dead.

I hauled in the anchor and turned on the ignition. The old Evinrude wouldn't kick in. I held my finger hard against the starter button and prayed. It looked like the shore was moving, but it was me, drifting toward the sea. I was about to panic when the motor sputtered and coughed. Then, finally, it caught.

I eased her back to where Buddy was and put the shifter in neutral. He was just floating there. By morning, he could be on the beach. The boat started to drift over him. His mouth was full of water. His eyes were wide open. I reached into the water and pulled the knife from him and used it to cut the anchor line from its cleat. I knelt and got the line around his neck. Suddenly, his left arm rose out of the water like it had a mind of its own. His cold, white fingers brushed my face. I jumped back, sucking air and realized it hadn't happened. It was impossible. He was dead. My skin got tight and prickly. I couldn't breathe. I heard him drift under the boat. I could see a star in the sky above me. The wind had slacked off. I caught him on the other side of the boat and tied a good knot around his neck. I stood over him with the anchor in my right hand.

With the shore lights blinking on and the star above me, I felt a kind of peacefulness. Something good was with me all of a sudden. I threw the anchor and watched as it pulled him down. The white shape of his face was all I could see, and pretty soon, there was nothing. Buddy was gone.

I threw his knife in after him, then headed for land. The salt air smells different at night, rich and full of life. I knew I was looking for a piece of shoreline with no lights, but that was all. The first place I picked was wrong. For a while, I thought I might have to beach the boat and hitch a ride, but my eyes got used to the poor light and finally I found it, a lot farther north than I had estimated.

Once I tied up, I worked nervously in near-darkness washing blood and fingerprints from the boat. In the shack, using an old flashlight from my car, I wiped everything I thought I might have touched. I could actually feel the blood surging through me like electricity. A sudden gust lifted one of the big window shutters behind me and the prop fell out. The sharp slam sounded like a cannon. I ducked. I was sure someone had shot at me.

When the Nova's tires finally rolled onto Route 47, it was night. Still, I could feel everyone staring. The world had changed again. There was a brick in my throat.

I don't really know what I thought about Buddy being dead right then. My mind was obsessed with getting home. It must have been after nine. I knew Grace would kill me, but I thought that if I could just get there and get in bed, everything would be okay. I started rehearsing stories out loud to explain why I was late and hadn't called. I thought about what it was going to be like to face her with Buddy's death fresh in my mind. I wondered if she would be able to tell that something big had happened and I was holding out on her. I wondered what it would be like to live with it . . . not being able to tell, wanting to tell. I wondered if she had called the cops. . . . I had good news. Good for both of us. I imagined myself in the distant future, telling her in detail what I'd done. Her expression went from shock to admiration. She wouldn't tell. She couldn't tell. She kissed me and told me I was brave.

I was so excited when I got home that I could hardly stand it. There were lights on. Of course, she was waiting up. Even her T-Bird looked anxious. She would be so glad to see me, then really angry. "I hope you've got a good explanation for this, young man. If not, you're grounded for a year. I've been worried sick. . . ." I could see the little puddles of tears at the bottoms of her eyes. "I'm really sorry, Grace," I would say. "I didn't mean to upset you. . . ."

Inside, there was no Grace, only the stale, empty smell the place got when no one had been there for hours. The lights had come on by timers as they did every night if no one switched them on first. The note I'd left for her was still on the hall table where I'd put it. There was one for me on the door of the refrigerator.

Dear Billy,
    So glad you were able to sleep in. Marty surprised me with matinee tickets to *A Chorus Line* so we're rushing to New York! (I'm so glad you two hit it off!) I'll call if there's time. Please—*no* driving, and *no* parties. See you Sunday!
                                    Love,
                                    Mom

"Mom." The boyfriend must have watched her write the note. I couldn't sleep. I kept seeing Buddy's body. It had floated up on a beach where there were all these people. They rolled him onto his back to get a good look at him. There were little black crabs crawling around in his eye sockets. The sharks had chewed up his gut. There was a bloody hole where his cock and balls belonged. The knife was in his right hand. There were letters carved in his chest: "Billy McIlvain." And he was smiling.

I hated her for not being there.

forty-four

I'm parked at the corner opposite the Howe residence. It's 8:40 AM. I've been here since dawn. I had to move the car for a street sweeper at 7:10. Howe left for "work" five minutes ago. Men here dress for work the way Philadelphians dress for the golf course. I'm wearing mirror sunglasses; a bushy brown mustache that looks quite real but itches; and a Denver Broncos T-shirt I got on clearance for two bucks. I saw the same thing in the Denver airport for $18.95. It's a beautiful day. Every day I've been here has been beautiful. Clear, sunny skies; cool at night. These people don't know how lucky they are.

On the way here, I bought two muffins and a doughnut. It was more than I wanted but I ate all of it, more from nerves than hunger. I washed it all down with a quart of coffee, which was cold by the time I finished it. I'm waiting for the rest of Howe's family to show themselves. I'm edgy and I have to piss. I followed Howe to work the last two mornings.

At 8:50, Deidre shoots out of the driveway in her blue

Volvo. She nearly gets away from me when I can't get
the rental to start. Finally, it kicks in and I catch up to
her and her brood at a stop sign two blocks east. I'm
relieved; I saw the whole day turning to shit before my
eyes.

First stop: Vacation Bible School at St. John's Episcopal
Church. Deidre leaves Andrew in the car and walks
Lizzie inside. The little girl is cute enough to eat: a blue
sundress and a red ribbon in her honey-brown hair.
Mom is in sandals, yellow Bermuda shorts, and a white
polo shirt. The faded deb. Her ass hangs halfway to her
knees. I debate ducking into a clump of evergreen
bushes to piss; I can't risk it. Deidre reappears almost
immediately. The front view reminds me of the rear: Sag
City. We're on our way again. Every dip and bump in
the road is agony. I'm scared my bladder is going to
rupture. It happened to a guy hitching a ride out of the
joint in a mail cart. He was under the knife for three
hours.

She drops Andrew next, at the home of another little
boy. I need to talk to Andrew. I consider letting go right
here. I'm wearing black chinos. It wouldn't show, but I
hate the smell. She stops next at a dry-cleaning place.
There are other people ahead of her. I get out, walk casually to the back of my car, and pop the trunk. I lean
over like I'm looking for something and pull the rip
cord. Victoria Falls.

At the supermarket, I give Deidre a three-minute head
start, then go inside. It's time we met. While I'm looking
for her, I toss some paper towels and cans of pork and
beans into my cart. I find her in Produce and watch her
pick over the romaine lettuce. She makes no effort to put

back the display the way she found it. Her next stop is the melon stand, the perfect place for our chance meeting.

"Excuse me," I say. I give her a big, dumb smile. "I have to pick up a few things for a party and I have no idea how you tell when these things are fresh. This is cantaloupe, isn't it?"

"Yes," she laughs.

"Can you help me? Are these fresh?"

"You mean ripe? Ready to eat?"

I laugh. "You see how much I know about this stuff!"

"I look for one that's yellowish," she says, "then check the webbing." She inspects the pile of melons and picks one out, a big one. She holds it cupped in both hands. "When the webbing's prominent, like this, that's a good sign. You can press, here, opposite the stem end. It should give a little, not too much. You don't want them overripe."

"Oh, no."

"How about the smell?" I ask, the eager pupil.

"I'd never thought about that," she says. She raises the melon to her nose. "This certainly has a good, ripe smell to it." I quickly lean over and put my nose close to hers. I cup my hands under hers. I want to rub my boner on her ass.

"Ummm," I say, "I see what you mean." As she pulls away, I step back quickly. I've offended her. Good. "Thanks for the lesson," I say. "My name's Ron." She dumps the melon like it grew hair and stalks off toward the celery. "Hey, thanks for your help!"

While I load about eight melons into my cart, I catch her looking and flash her a smile. I leave her behind in

Produce while I drift off to the meat department. Don't want to press it, yet. From Meat, I can see both ways out of Produce. Five minutes later, she emerges at the far end, near the front of the store. She looks around, doesn't spot me. I make it to the front of the store in time to see her turn into the personal-care section. I count to five and follow. Very casual. She's picking up toothpaste. Crest, Tartar Control. She notices me and looks away. I put four boxes of tampons in my cart and head toward her. She moves off. I pick up a tube of Crest, same as hers, and follow. Dog food. I enter the aisle from the opposite end and park my cart an inch from hers. She's struggling to load a big bag of Pedigree Low Calorie into the bottom of her cart. I take an identical bag and grunt suggestively as I mimic her actions. She mutters into my smile and wheels past me. No crack in the superior facade. I follow. Closer now. She goes to the bakery department. Hot dog rolls; me too. A baguette? Just what I had in mind. Paper goods, chicken parts, breakfast cereal. She moves faster and faster. I pick out the identical items she does, aisle after aisle. She does her best not to look at me, but she can't help it. I'm driving her nuts. In the condiment aisle, it gets to her. She knocks over a bottle of ketchup. It crashes; she looks at me. Raw fear and anger. I'm all smiles, finger-fucking a jar of mayonnaise. I lick my fingertips and laugh as poor Deidre abandons her cart, fleeing for parts unknown.

forty-five

I wanted so badly to tell Grace about Buddy that I convinced myself it didn't matter if she turned me in. Still, I could never bring myself to do it when the chances came, and each day that went by, it became more impossible.

Every night, all the lights came on the second my head hit the pillow. Some nights, I didn't get in bed until three or four in the morning because I couldn't stand to lie there shifting around, thinking about Buddy. If I did sleep, I had nightmares. I was really afraid. A couple of times, I had a premonition I was going to be arrested, so I stayed home from school because I didn't want to be embarrassed. I was constantly checking the papers and watching TV news, but there was never anything at all about Buddy. It was as if it hadn't happened.

When I thought I couldn't stand the worrying anymore, it started to get better. I'm not sure why; maybe I was just bored with it. Whatever the reason, I welcomed the end of my trouble with Buddy and the period of healing I thought had begun. But of course, the trouble wasn't over just because I said so. I wasn't the only player in the game. I was reminded of this one afternoon when I came in and found two of my bureau drawers open.

I knew the cleaning lady hadn't done it, because it wasn't her day, and I knew I hadn't done it because I never leave my drawers open, definitely not two of them. If Grace had been searching my things, she wouldn't have left the drawers open. I knew it wasn't a robbery because nothing was missing. If it was someone trying to put a scare in me, there was only one possibility: Willie. I thought the idea was nuts at first myself. I kept telling myself that Willie is not about to drive all the way from New Jersey to Haverford, break into our house, leave two stupid drawers open, and then leave. But I knew from the trial that he was pretty smart, and if he had figured out what happened with Buddy, coming into my room like that was a good warning. It let me know that he knew about Buddy and that he could get to me if he wanted. But even though I could understand why Willie would have done it, the theory seemed pretty farfetched.

Then, a couple days later, I came in and found the TV set on. Right in the middle of the afternoon. It was tuned to a sports channel. I never watched sports; neither did Grace. Furthermore, I had left the house last that morning and I knew for a fact that the TV was off. I asked Grace about it and she said she hadn't done it. Later on that week, on Friday, I saw Willie in the parking lot of my school. We'd been having finals. I guess I was fairly depressed because I had done so poorly, not that that was surprising, since I hadn't studied. Anyway, I was feeling lousy. A couple of geeks in my class had asked me if I wanted to get high with them. I said no. I was on my way to my car, and I saw this guy about six rows over waving at me. The sun was in my eyes, so I had to squint. For a second, I wasn't sure he was looking at me, but then I saw who it was. Big, shit-eating grin on his face, same honker nose. He was even wearing one of those stupid baseball hats with a company logo on it. In a second, I was ten years old again. I didn't know what to do. He wasn't trying to get closer to me. He was just standing there, waving. I couldn't see what he was driving. All the cars around him were just what I always saw in the Harriton lot, no old bombs or rusty pickups like you'd think of Willie driving. I started walking slowly toward my car; he didn't follow. He just stood there. At first the car wouldn't start and I figured he'd done something to it, but I had just flooded it from being nervous. I even checked around for a bomb or something. When it finally started, I drove around the lot to see if he was going to follow me. But there was no sign of him. I even drove by the place where he'd been standing. But he was gone, even the cars where he'd been standing were gone.

I drove to Wyncliff right away and asked the guard if he'd seen anyone like Willie. He said he hadn't. Instead of going in, I backed out and started driving around. I was scared and I had no idea what to do. I knew no one would believe Willie was trying to harass me unless I told them about Buddy and I wasn't about to do that.

Grace had told me she was bringing Marty Shoemaker home for dinner and she expected me to be there. I showed up a little after seven. I could tell they'd just gotten there: Marty was still sober and Grace was diddling in the kitchen. They both looked worn out. The late-day sun caught Grace's face in a way that filled every laugh line and wrinkle with black shadow. The pale pink dress she had on was pretty and, I'm sure, expensive, but it would probably have been as becoming to a wire coat hanger. Marty was slouched at the table, done in by another week of shredding secrets. The drink on the table in front of him looked like his usual vodka, but there was a chunk of lime in the bottom of it; for summer, I guess. He smiled when I walked in; Grace didn't. I had hoped that being home with her would make me feel more secure after seeing Willie, but somehow, I felt more alone.

"Where you been, Wild Bill?" Marty crowed. "One of them li'l cowgirls lasso you in the old hayloft?" Grace frowned and shook her head.

"I thought we agreed that you would be here at six," Grace said. Marty threw her a puzzled look. I went to the refrigerator for a soda. "We'll be eating in a few minutes, Billy."

"I just want something to drink," I said. She started stuffing cucumbers into her new food processor.

"Did you think Marty and I would just sit here all night waiting for you?"

"Sorry." I found a Frank's cherry soda and pulled the tab.

"I have to be able to feel that I can trust you, Billy," she scolded. She had to raise her voice to make herself heard above the machine. Grace had been off booze five years. I was proud of her and grateful, but there were moments when I thought a drink might do her some good.

"Hey, Wild Bill," Marty said. He beckoned me to join him. I took my usual seat as he lit a fresh Pall Mall. "School's out nex' week. That right?"

"Yeah."

"Mom tells me you don't have any plans yet for the summer, so I was wondering if you'd like to have a job on one of my trucks. Pay's four an hour. I need a man for vacation relief. You know, drive the routes when one of my regular guys is on vacation. Interested?"

He took a long pull on his drink while he waited for my answer. I wanted the job but I knew Grace would disapprove. I looked toward her. She was just shutting off the processor. She hadn't heard what he said. "I haven't said nothing to your mother," Marty went on. He winked at me. "I figured this could just be between us men. Give us a chance to know each other better."

I had a feeling he thought having me on the payroll might help him hold on to Grace. "If it's okay with Grace . . . ," I said.

"If what's okay?" she asked. She set a plate piled high with cucumber slices on the table and, next to it, a package of fancy ham Marty had picked up at some deli. "I probably should have put that ham on a plate. Oh well. If what's okay?"

"Marty offered me a job driving one of his trucks," I said, "for the summer."

"I wanted it to be a surprise," Marty said apologetically. She flashed him a look that changed from resentment to appreciation in the flick of an eyelash.

"That's sweet, Marty," she said. She gave his shoulder

a little pat as she sat down. "I wish he could, but unless our young man wants to end up doing that sort of work permanently, I think he ought to plan to spend this summer developing proper study habits and a will to succeed. . . ." I couldn't tell by looking at Grace whether she was making this crap up to put off Marty Shoemaker or if she meant it. "Chip Schaefer in our office is going to send one of his boys to the Sunapee Institute in New Hampshire this summer. It's a ten-week enrichment program. They practically guarantee a hundred-point improvement in the SAT. There's tennis, too, and finance. It sounds *won*-derful!" Marty shook his head and got up to make another drink. "We're about to eat, Marty. . . ."

"Are you serious, Grace?" I asked.

"Completely. I think it's made to order."

"Why didn't you say anything?"

"The brochures just came. I wanted to be certain that it's suitable. Look, we have the whole weekend to discuss it."

"I won't go," I said as Marty headed back toward us. I felt like yelling the words at her and pounding my fists on the table. "I won't go." The idea of her sending me to that stupid place made me so mad I could hardly believe it.

"Look at me, will you?" Grace laughed. "I've forgotten the plates and silver." As she rose, Marty turned his chair around so the back was against the table.

"I hate cucumbers," he grumbled when she was out of hearing range.

"So do I," I said. With a groan, Marty mounted his chair like some redneck rodeo rider easing onto a wild bull. Grace came back and passed out the plates and forks. Marty said he was going to "sit out" dinner. I ripped the paper off the ham and put about half of it on my plate.

"You must be hungry," Grace said.

"Starved."

"Won't you have some cucumbers with your meat?"

"They make me sick," I said. Marty tried to cover a laugh by clearing his throat. We sat in silence for a few minutes. Well, not quite. Marty was wheezing and slurping, and Grace's jaw clunked as she chewed and her knife made a god-awful squeaking sound on the plate. When I couldn't stand it anymore, I said, "Are you happy, Marty?"

"Happy? You mean right now?" He laughed self-consciously.

"I mean in general. Mr. Fullbright, my civics teacher, said he'd love to trade places with one of those guys that travel from one place to the next and live under bridges and stuff. He said you can never be happy unless you're really free."

"Tell you the truth, Bill, I've never thought much about it." He was squirming a little. Grace was uncomfortable, too. She hadn't shaken the habit of reaching for her glass when she got nervous, even if it was only iced tea. "Yeah, I guess I'm happy," Marty finally admitted. "The business is coming along. I've got my health. I could stand some improvement in my personal life." The last remark seemed to be for Grace's benefit, but she had tuned out. "Happiness is like a dream," Marty went on. "It's like the pot of gold at the end of the rainbow. You can run like hell after it and never catch up. It's always out there beyond where you can reach." He

made a series of grasping motions over the table to show
what he meant.

"But would you trade places with the guy who lives
under the bridge?"

"I guess that would depend on the bridge," Marty
laughed. "Near the clubhouse at Pebble Beach, I might
give it serious thought." Marty laughed too hard and
got a mouthful of cigarette smoke in his esophagus.
Soon, he was gagging uncontrollably.

"God, Billy," Grace scolded. "Are you all right,
Marty?" His face was crimson, his eyes filled with tears.

"S'okay. M'all right," he gagged. "S'not his fault. Get
me 'nother drink." He shoved the glass in front of her.

"How about you, Grace?" I said. "Are you happy?"

"Haven't you caused enough trouble for one night?"
she snapped, rising from her chair.

"Please, Grace. It's nothing to be ashamed of." At
Gaillard, she talked about her feelings practically nonstop. She wallowed in them.

"Nobody's happy," she muttered grudgingly, "not
completely. Marty's right. It's an ideal. I'm happier right
now than I've ever been, I'll tell you that." She held the
vodka bottle at arm's length over Marty's glass as if the
contents might contaminate her.

"I've gotta go," Marty said glumly as Grace set the
drink down in front of him. "The goddamn shredder on
one of my trucks froze up again. Third time in five
weeks. You believe that? They want me to see if I can
pull the goddamn shaft 'cause they can't get a man out
till nex' week. They sold me a goddamn service contract.
Now they're asking me to pull the shaft. You want service anymore, forget it. Now I got to run one of the other

trucks a double shift. I love it." He was totally bummed. The drink disappeared in four swallows. "They're no better at IBM. They're all shit." Grace was getting agitated. She lit a cigarette.

"Billy, why don't you go watch TV? Marty and I have things we need to discuss."

"Go ahead," I said.

"Don't be difficult, Billy. Leave the room."

I said, "Okay," and both of us looked at Marty. He was listing to starboard, sound asleep.

That was the last time I saw Marty Shoemaker. He was a jerk, I suppose, but a decent man basically. Of course, that wasn't nearly good enough for Grace.

forty-six

The grades on my final report card were terrible, although by some miracle, I didn't fail any subjects. Grace was furious. I heard another tirade about Sunapee Institute, and she swore she was going to talk to my teachers before summer vacation. She didn't do it though. She had to go to Trenton for three days of meetings about Wyeth Run, the fancy new development she was working on. They were having trouble borrowing money. It had her worried.

For the next two weeks, Grace worked virtually around the clock. They wanted her to redo all her plans for Wyeth Run and make everything cheaper without making the project itself seem cheaper. I hardly saw her. Then one day she came home about four o'clock and put on records. Johnny Mathis, I think. After that, she spent about an hour in the bathtub. She didn't say much to me, but let's say that when she gave me thirty bucks and told me to disappear until midnight, I wasn't surprised. I guess I must have snickered as she was giving me the money. Anyway, she told me to go to hell.

Instead, I went to my car and stayed there until he showed up. He drove a black BMW, one of the big ones, Jersey plates and a Hun School decal on the back window. He was good-looking in a slimy way—Grace's boss's brother, Jerry Bellarosa. I had met him and his wife and their kids at a Con-Land thing when Grace and I were living in Ravenswood.

When he went inside, I got an overwhelming urge to get wasted. I didn't want to spend the next five or six hours thinking about him with his dick in her and her telling him how good it feels and that he ought to lay off Wyeth Run. I drove around for a while trying to figure out how I was going to get high. I knew some kids at Harriton who dealt, but I'd never bought anything from them. They weren't home. Finally, I went to a Sherwin-Williams place and bought paint thinner. I'd heard you could get high with that, but I'd never tried.

I must have looked pretty strange sitting in the Super Fresh parking lot with my face in a paper bag, but that's what happened. I did get high. At least, I got dizzy and the front of my head started to burn. When I had a pretty good load on, I decided to see the sights. The first thing I did was back into somebody's Rambler. It hadn't been there when I drove in. Anyway, nobody noticed. When I got to the first traffic light, I realized that driving was going to be a problem. I didn't hit anybody, but I kept thinking that the car in front was backing into me. I honked and they gave me the finger.

The nearest place I could think of to throw up was the good old Llanfair train station. It was probably a three-minute drive, but it seemed to take half an hour. The road kept stretching out in front of me like it was made of rubber, and I kept wanting to stretch out on the front seat and go to sleep. When I finally got there, I had to sit still and take deep breaths because I was afraid if I got out of the car the way I felt, I'd pass out on the pavement. After a couple of minutes, acid started to climb up my throat. I knew I had to make my move, no matter what. I spotted a bunch of bushes near the tracks. I thought I could make it to them, but no such luck. I got about six steps, fell on my knees, and decorated the left front wheel of an old Buick.

A lot of times when you throw up, you feel better. Not this time. My head was still spinning as I staggered over to the platform. There were a couple of benches inside the little enclosed place they'd made for waiting. I stretched out on the nearest one and closed my eyes. Right away, the world started whizzing around underneath me. Then suddenly, I was floating off the bench. My eyes were closed but there were colors shooting all around. I squeezed my eyes tighter and saw dragons and huge, prehistoric birds. The sky was black, but all the monsters and shooting stars were neon colors. A train came and stopped the dream. I rolled my head over to look at it. The place vibrated like an earthquake. I could have sworn the cars were two stories high and about to topple over and squash me. It was a freight. I zoomed in on the wheels—the bright, flat part that rolls along the tracks. No matter how dirty the cars may be, the wheels and the tracks stay bright. They glowed orange from the sunset. Warm and clean. *Ka-clunk-ka-clunk-ka-clunk.* My life was turning to shit as I lived it. I remembered that Fourth of July long ago when I'd come to the station to kill time. The day of the *Ebony Witch*. The day Grandad died. One more time, my face got hot and the tears came. *Ka-clunk-ka-clunk-ka-clunk-ka-clunk*. The shelter filled with the hot, bitter fumes from the wheel oil. I used to count the cars when I was little. I made myself sit up. I swallowed hard. I could fuck up now in ways that would last my whole life. I couldn't make myself care. Nobody I knew was happy. The Soo Line. Chessie System. Burlington Northern. What was the point to any of it? I could kneel beside that train, lean forward, and it would all be over. The bright orange wheels would do their work and be clean before they got to the next station. But I was angry. And before I finished thinking, the caboose rolled by and a guy in one of the windows threw me a wave. There was no reason for him to do that. I waved back.

forty-seven

Wednesday afternoon, one-fifteen. I've left the Subaru a block and a half west of the Howes' on Maple. I have on my tan sport coat and brown tie, no sunglasses or mustache. My hair's slicked straight back. I'm carrying the Bible from my motel room. I keep smiling. There's a Methodist church a block east of the Howe place. In front, there's a bus stop and a bench. I can watch the house from there.

As I approach the corner, I see Elizabeth and Andrew arranging glasses and a pitcher on a card table near the sidewalk. A lemonade stand. No sign of Deidre. Still, I consider turning back. She must be nearby and I don't want to take a chance on her recognizing me after our little dance at the supermarket this morning. The kids start hailing me. "Lemonade! Ten cents a glass! Cookies. Best you could get!" It would be easy enough to turn north or south and avoid any sort of encounter. But it wouldn't be fun. I step off the curb and walk toward them. My throat is suddenly dry. On the front of the card table, there's a sign made of taped-together pieces of typing paper. "Lemminaid." The crayoned letters, I'd guess, are the work of Elizabeth.

"Well, well," I say, "you kids must have known I was thirsty!" I have a knack with children, though I don't expect to have any of my own. They look at me excitedly. I must be their first customer. I take out my change holder. "Fill 'er up," I say grandly. Andrew grabs for the plastic pitcher but Elizabeth is there first.

"You can do it next time," she announces. "Do you want a cookie?"

"Chocolate chip?" I ask.

"Oatmeal raisin," she says.

"We made it," the little boy boasts.

"How much?"

"Two for a quarter," she says.

"Make it two, then," I say. I find the encounter unexpectedly exciting. I can't help studying these two and wondering. He's missing a front tooth. She has as many freckles as Howdy Doody. Classic Anglo-Saxon good looks. I put two quarters on the table and nibble on one of the cookies while she gets my change from a jelly jar. The dough is undercooked. "Is this your house?" I say.

"Yes," Andrew assures me, "we live here. That's our mom."

My heart stops momentarily. But Andrew is pointing toward an empty chaise on a patio beside the house. He realizes his mistake.

"She went inside to answer the phone," Elizabeth reports.

"I'm sure she's gorgeous," I say, "just like both of you. Is your daddy home?"

"No," Andrew says, "he's at the office. It's a big meeting."

"Oh," I say, pretending to be impressed. "You must love your mommy and daddy very much." Elizabeth puts two dimes on the table in front of me. Her eyes are green.

"We do," she says, "because they love us."

"I know karate," Andrew announces.

"That's too much, honey," I tell her. "Do you have any nickels? You owe me fifteen cents." She cups her hand over her mouth in embarrassment. I hand her one of the dimes. She takes it and dumps out the contents of the change jar. "Just give me one nickel or five of those pennies."

A skeptical look crosses her angelic face. "Wait," she says, "I'll get my mom."

"Just forget it," I say. But it's too late, Lizzie is running toward the house. I put my cup down on the table.

"Would you like to take a little walk with me?" I ask Andrew. "Just down to the corner? I'm new here and it gets pretty lonely."

"I don't know...."

"I'll tell you a story, about a time when I was just your age...."

Suddenly, the front door of the house swings open and Elizabeth trots down the front steps. Deidre can't be far behind.

"Well," I say, "perhaps another time. Bye now." I walk away briskly. I don't want Mommy to see my face.

"Free refills," the little girl calls after me. "Don't you want any?"

"Refills!" Andrew yells.

I hear Mom's cheery voice behind me. They're giving her a blow-by-blow of the entire transaction. Suddenly, I feel sick to my stomach.

forty-eight

I had something important to tell Grace. I waited up for her, but by the time she finally came in, I'd fallen asleep. I woke up about three in the morning; I had to piss. After I'd done it, I noticed how quiet the place was. All I could hear was the blood in my ears; even the air conditioning and the fridge were off. I didn't flush so I wouldn't disturb her, which was silly considering that I went straight from the john to her room.

The carpet felt soft and cool under my bare feet. I was like an Indian stalking his prey. The springs in the doorknob made a little chinging sound as I turned it to let myself in. Her head and shoulders were just visible in the soft orange light from the clock on her night table. As I got closer, I could make out the rise of her hips and the shape of each of her long legs under the light summer covers. I got self-conscious about wearing only briefs. I sat on the bed beside her.

"Grace," I said in a low voice. She turned slowly toward the sound and murmured. Then she opened her eyes about a third of the way. Suddenly, her eyes popped out like a frog's and she made a kind of grunt-screaming noise as she pushed herself hard away from me, clutching the covers to her chest.

"Christ Almighty, Billy! What on earth are you doing in here?"

"There's something I've got to talk to you about, Grace. I waited up, but I—"

"You might have knocked, dammit. God, I wake up in the middle of the night and see a half-naked man sitting on my bed. . . . I don't even want to tell you what went through my mind."

"I'm sorry. I should have knocked." Her expression softened but she was still holding the sheets over her chest.

She sighed. "What do you want?" She took a drink from the glass of water on her night table.

"The stone on Grandad's grave has been wrecked." She gave me a really strange look, like she was waiting to see if I was joking or something, then she sighed again.

"I guess I don't understand why you find it necessary to give me heart failure in the middle of the night to tell me that."

"I think Willie Smyers did it."

"No, Billy, no. That's over. Please. Let it alone." She reached for her cigarettes.

"I didn't want to worry you, but I think he's been watching me, even coming in here. Remember when I found the TV on?" She lit a cigarette and put the pack and lighter back on the table. Then she just sat there for about thirty seconds with the heels of her hands covering her eye sockets. I didn't know whether she was worried or scared or whether she just didn't want to hear what I was saying. Finally, she looked at me again.

"I have had a killer day, Billy. We may lose the entire project and I'm out there doing everything humanly possible to save it. I am dead. I am totally exhausted and I just don't know how to deal with what you're telling me. In the first place, I doubt very much that it's true, that that man would vandalize your grandfather's headstone. It makes no sense. I'm not saying that you're lying, just that what you're saying makes no logical sense. Do you understand?"

"Sure." She turned away from me and took a drag on her cigarette. She did look tired; even in the light from the clock I could see that.

After a few seconds, she looked at me again. "I know that what happened to your grandfather had a devastating effect on you, and that life has been no bed of roses these last few years. Believe me, I'm sympathetic. It's been pretty rough for me, too. But things are getting better, Billy. . . ." I noticed her looking at my bare chest. "We've got income and a future. You're here all day with nothing to do. You're sixteen. Of course your mind makes up things. It's human nature. . . ." She had figured it all out in two minutes.

"What about the gravestone, Grace? It's cracked. One end of it is smashed. My imagination had nothing to do with that. You can go see it for yourself."

Another sigh. "It was probably the lawn mower. I'm sure they use those big tractor mowers. The driver was probably careless. It could have been a backhoe for that matter. Was there a fresh grave nearby? I'm sure the cemetery has insurance. . . ."

"Grace, I saw Willie Smyers in the parking lot at school last month, on a Friday. He was staring at me and waving."

"Why, Billy, why? The lawsuit is over. They got their money. What earthly reason would that man have to harass you? I have got to get some sleep." I turned away from her. I felt like I couldn't talk.

"I'm hurting, Grace," I said finally.

Again she sighed. This time, she looked at the ceiling. "Billy, I want the best for you," she said. "I know I'm not around as much as we'd both like. We don't spend time together the way we used to, and I regret that. I really do. But there's food on the table and we have a nice place to live. I'm only one woman, Billy. There's only so much I can do. At your age, it's not unreasonable for a parent to expect you to be more responsible for your own welfare." She stubbed out her cigarette. "I won't even mention Sunapee. There's probably still a chance we could get you in."

"This conversation isn't making sense to me," I said.

"I've got six meetings tomorrow, Billy. Two of them are in New Jersey. I have got to get some sleep. I'm sorry, but that's reality. I can't change it. I have a date to play golf Saturday afternoon, but I'll cancel it if you like. We'll have lunch somewhere and talk things over. I'm sorry, but that's the best I can do. Will that work for you?"

I said, "I bet if he was messing with you, you wouldn't wait till Saturday."

"Christ, Billy," she said. She pulled her legs up and

swung around so she could get out of the bed. Then she went into her john and slammed the door, not very hard, but hard enough to make her point. A few seconds later, I could hear her pee going into the toilet. "Are you trying to punish me, Billy?" she called out from the john. "Is that it? Are you trying to get even?"

I didn't answer her question, but I thought about it, that's for sure. And on the way out of her room, I slammed the door. Not hard, but hard enough to make my point.

When I got into bed, I waited for a few minutes to see if she'd come in to talk to me, but she didn't. We didn't spend Saturday afternoon together either.

forty-nine

I spent the next day working out in front of Grace's mirrors. I turned off the air conditioning because I wanted to sweat. I liked to see myself all shiny and dripping. I wanted to hurt. I kept adding weight to the bars. I turned up the sound system louder and louder. I pushed it till I couldn't stand up; then I took a half-hour bath in Grace's Jacuzzi and went to bed.

When I woke up in the morning, I felt like I'd been run over. Even my toes and my ears hurt, but I felt good about myself. I liked being able to take pain, any kind of pain, and not show it. That day I went to Willie's for the first time. I knew where he lived from the trial. Just like he knew where I lived.

I didn't mean to have anything to do with Willie, just to see where he lived and check out what he was driving, things like that. But then, I'd had the same intentions with Buddy. I dug out that fancy silver carving knife that belonged to Grandad's great-grandmother and taped it to my leg, just above the ankle. I'd seen them do it a hundred times in the movies, but when I was heading out the door, I noticed that my sock felt kind of funny. I looked down and saw that it was full of blood. It hurt like hell trying to pull the tape off. I don't know how I expected to get that knife out quickly if I needed it.

When I had my right leg fixed up with Band-Aids, I shaved my left leg where the tape had to go and made a sleeve thing out of cardboard and tape. That's what I taped to myself. The knife fit right inside it. On my way out, I went into the hall closet and dug out an old pair of binoculars that Ned had used to watch tennis.

Willie lived in a trailer park near a town called Villas on the Delsea Drive, maybe fifteen minutes south of where Buddy lived. I've been asked what I was thinking about as I drove down there that day: Was I scared or anything? It may seem funny, but I felt really good about it. I was a little bit scared, but I had this feeling in my gut that I was doing the right thing. As I say, "closing the circle."

Playland Mobile Home Village was on the east side of Delsea Drive, right on the road. If you looked down the streets on the west side, you could see Delaware Bay. There was a pregnant girl with two little kids standing next to a bus sign at the entrance to the park. She was a blonde, about twenty. They were standing next to a pile of bags. It was at least ninety; hazy, but bright. They watched me drive in, all three squinting from the glare. They looked so unhappy.

I had no idea how to find Willie's trailer. All I knew was 11 Palmetto Way. There must have been two hundred trailers parked in there, fifteen or twenty feet apart.

Some were huge and had awnings and little porches, even gardens and birdbaths. Others were tiny and made me think they'd be like living in a bucket. There were barking dogs everywhere and signs that said "5 mph."

As you got toward the back of the place, the neighborhood went downhill. The trailers were smaller and more beaten up. The cars were older and the dogs and kids looked scruffier. It reminded me of settlements you see on news stories about the Middle East. I knew I was on Willie's turf and it made me nervous. I told myself I was only going to drive by and see where he lived, but that didn't seem to help. Deep breaths didn't help much either. My heart was pounding and my hands were starting to sweat.

The north-south streets were alphabetical, so when I got to Olive Lane, I decided to drive down a couple more blocks and then swing over to Palmetto. The way the numbers were, I figured his trailer would be on my right as I went by so I'd be harder to see if he was outside.

It was the next-to-the-last trailer on Palmetto. Behind it was a big field where they grew gladiolus flowers. That day, there weren't any flowers, just little green spike things sticking out of the sand. The lot south of Willie's was empty. His trailer was one of the smallest I'd seen. It was white with a pale green stripe around the middle and rust stains at every opening and joint. Tall weeds were growing all around it. The number 11 on the door looked like it had been painted by a drunken monkey. The front steps were piled-up cinder blocks. It made me smile to see how Willie had been living while he waited to cash in.

The parking spot next to Willie's trailer was empty, but a guy in a wheelchair was getting his mail out of a box across the street so I kept on driving.

I had pizza at a grease trap on the main drag and got back to Playland in less than an hour. The pregnant girl and the two kids were still standing out there in the hot sun. The little girl was about five; the boy, maybe three. The pregnant girl had him by the arm. He was sobbing and trying to pull away. I stopped to watch them. I don't know why exactly. I guess because I knew what it's like to be as unhappy as they looked. The pregnant girl was crying, too. On impulse, I swung back up Delsea and bought three large lemonades at a 7-Eleven. I couldn't quite believe I was doing it, but it made me feel good and they looked like they could really stand to have someone be nice to them, even a stranger. I didn't get the chance, though. When I got back to Playland, they were gone.

Inside, on Palmetto Way, nothing had changed. Willie's parking space was still empty. I knew Willie had some kind of part-time job at a lumberyard, but I had no idea what hours. The wheelchair guy was still outside. I figured him for some kind of weirdo. He had long black hair and a big bushy beard. His T-shirt was black; his pants were black; his boots were black; his sunglasses were black. His trailer was black. There was even a big, black, jacked-up pickup truck with flame decals on the doors parked out front. All around his little yard there were flagpoles with flags on them I didn't recognize, except for the US and Vietnam. As I drove by, I heard Oriental music. This time, he was messing with a couple of nasty-looking dogs. He shot me the hairy eyeball and

I realized I'd worn out my welcome for the day.

I drove back to the highway, turned south, and then took a farm road east until I came to the road that ran along the far side of the gladiolus field from the trailer park. I went north on that road a few hundred yards and parked under a half-dead tree where there was a little bit of shade and I could get a pretty fair view of the side of Willie's trailer where the door was. There was a sign right in front of me: "D'Orazio's Gladiolus Farm—Commercial Growers—Just Ahead." That's how I knew what kind of flowers they were. Until I saw the sign, I thought it was asparagus.

It had gotten to be about two-thirty. There were big clouds building up over the bay. From where I was parked to Willie's trailer was probably a thousand feet, but I'm lousy at guessing distances. Anyway, when I looked through Ned's binoculars, the heat waves rising off the field made everything look ripply.

The time didn't go by very fast, but I wasn't really bored. Actually, it was fun, being on surveillance. Of course I didn't have the grumpy partner eating dough-nuts and drinking coffee and telling me I ought to get married and bitching because the judges let all the crooks off too easy. But I did have lots of lemonade. The only thing I really didn't like was using Ned's binoculars. I didn't like putting my eyes in the same place where his had been. Four years had passed since we'd heard from him.

To pass the time, I thought up ways to waste Willie. My favorite was rigging a second line from the propane tank into the trailer while he was out. Then when he was sleeping, I'd turn it on and after a while, throw a firebomb through a window. *Ka-booom!* Some fish in Delaware Bay could eat his dick for breakfast.

A little after five, I noticed movement and grabbed the binoculars. It was a car, a red Corvette. Brand-new, from the look of it. It pulled up right in front of Willie's door, and he got out. He looked like one of those golfers on TV: yellow slacks, white shoes, and a dark blue Hawaiian shirt. Then this bimbo gets out of the other side. Bleached hair, huge knockers under a pink tank top, and jeans that fit her like shrink wrap. He gave her a big kiss and started grabbing her ass; then they went inside. Willie was having himself a pretty good time with my money. And of course, he was just getting started. I sat there cursing and looking at the Corvette, getting angrier by the minute. Then I noticed something over the back end of the 'Vette that I hadn't seen before. It was the wheelchair guy sitting in his little yard with the flags and the black trailer and the black pickup. He had binoculars, too. And he was looking right at me.

fifty

After that first afternoon, I ran my little stakeout maybe eight times. I'd drive in past the gladiolus farm from the north and park just far enough down the road that I could see Willie come and go without showing myself to the guy in the wheelchair. A few times, I got up at dawn and drove down just to follow Willie to his job.

Weekday mornings, Willie always left the trailer at ten to eight. From eight to one, he worked at the Bayside Lumberyard, just north of Villas on Delsea Drive, where his job, as far as I could tell, was to strut around with a clipboard telling other guys what to put on the delivery trucks. At one o'clock, he usually went to Brown's Derby Bar ("Drown at Brown's"). His hours there were less regular, but he was usually back at the trailer somewhere between three and six. Sometimes with the blond bimbo. Sometimes with a redhead who didn't look much older than I was. He'd usually take his company back to Brown's by eight or nine o'clock and come straight home. Other than the 'Vette and a lot of bad-taste clothes, I couldn't see that my inheritance was affecting his life-style particularly. Really, it didn't look like much of a life.

On what turned out to be my last day on the stakeout, I got home about six-thirty. I was hot and tired and confused about what to do. I was also tired by then of driving between South Jersey and my place, especially during rush hour. Grace was sitting in the living room waiting for me. She was furious. She had on this kind of white sweater thing, low cut in the front so her boobs were practically falling out, and a tight skirt. I had never seen her looking so much like a floozie. She actually looked like one of Willie's whores. I was barely through the front door, when she threw aside the magazine she was reading and jumped off the couch.

"Give me your car keys," she said in a voice so bitchy it made me back away from her.

"What for?"

"If you want to drive again this summer, give me the goddamn car keys. Right now." I dropped them into the palm of her hand. She was wearing lots of jewelry and too much perfume. "You were supposed to be at my office at four-thirty this afternoon. Where the hell were you?"

"I didn't know. I'm sorry."

"I told you my car was being serviced today. You were supposed to pick me up and take me to the dealer. I waited over an hour for you. By then, it was too late to get the car and I had to take a cab home. That cost me thirty-two fifty, which is how much less allowance you're getting next month."

"I didn't know."

"I left you a note. I put it right on the refrigerator where we agreed you'd look."

"I'm sorry. Couldn't someone else have taken you?"

"That's not the point. *You* were supposed to take me."

"Grace, I'm sorry. I really am. I promise it won't happen again."

"Billy, I am tired of being disappointed in you. You act like you just don't care." She gave me one of her exasperated sighs. "I'm going out. A friend and I are having dinner. I may be late. Be in your room by ten and stay there. Is that clear?"

"Yes."

"You're grounded until Monday. Some people are coming tomorrow to clean the carpets. Let them in and be sure they don't leave here with anything they didn't bring with them. Do you think you can manage that?"

"I don't think you're being fair. I didn't do it on purpose."

"Don't push it, Billy." She looked like some over-the-hill Barbie doll with everything inside her going sour.

"Who's your date?"

"It's business. The company has three projects on paper right now. One of them is going on the shelf because of interest rates. If Wyeth Run goes now and sells out within forty-two months, I'll have over a million dollars coming to me in profit sharing and bonuses. Over a million dollars. If you'll forgive my saying so, I think that entitles me to a little understanding and support."

"Sure. I just wondered who your date is. Jerry Bellarosa?"

She picked her purse off the couch and started fishing

for her cigarettes and lighter. "I'm going to wait outside," she said.

I just wandered around the house when she left. I didn't look out to see who was picking her up. I didn't care. I was hurting too much. After I had been walking for a while, I went in my bedroom and got on my knees and asked God to kill me. Soon, my voice got louder and louder until I was screaming for God to kill me, and then I started hitting my head against the wall. Slowly at first and not too hard. Then harder and faster, until I could see blood on the Sheetrock. The more I did it, the less it seemed to hurt. I stopped when there was a four-inch crater in the wall and I could feel the blood running down beside my nose and taste it going into my mouth. I took about ten aspirins and went to bed.

The next day, I had a spectacular bruise. Yellow splotches and black-purple around the center. Toward the edges, it was more gray. In the very center, where I had broken the skin, there was a big lump and it was all scabby. It was so sore I couldn't touch it. People may have thought it was disgusting, but to me, it was beautiful.

After one look at my forehead, I could tell the carpet guy wanted to cut and run. I told him I'd been beaned with a line drive in a baseball game. I guess he thought that was okay. I decided to use the same line on Grace. I knew she'd be glad to hear I was playing baseball. The hole in the wall of my room was no problem; I moved a bookcase to cover it.

My head kept throbbing, and if I bent over or turned suddenly, it was a lot worse. I took four or five Bayers every couple of hours, which helped the pain a lot. It scared me to think about what I had done to myself. I couldn't understand it exactly.

The carpet guy was there less than two hours. He did a nice job, but the carpet was practically soaking when he was through. He put squares of heavy silver paper under the furniture so there wouldn't be rust stains, and turned the air conditioning way up so the carpet would dry faster.

It was too cold and damp to stay in the condo when he left, so I went out walking. I guess I was out a few hours. I walked over to the business district first, but everybody kept staring at my head so I went to the Merion Cricket Club and watched all the preppies and their snob mothers playing tennis. You could tell just by looking at them that they thought they were better than everyone else.

By the time I got home, the central air had dropped the temperature in the condo down to fifty. It was bizarre. Even the outside doorknob was cold and sweaty. I got goose bumps all over as soon as I went in. The windows were covered with condensation on the outside so the light inside was strangely bright and diffused. I didn't notice the footprints right away. I'd taken off my shoes as the guy had said to and was on my way to the kitchen to get something to eat. It was then that I saw the footprints ahead of me. You could see them very clearly because the carpet had just been cleaned and it showed everything. The second I saw them, I think my goose bumps got goose bumps. The prints were about size thirteen and they went straight into my bedroom, turned around, and went back to the front door. The ones coming in near the door had crumbs of sand or dirt in them. I must have followed them back and forth about ten times to see if they went anywhere else. It frightened and sickened me to look at them. I could hear Willie laughing inside my head. The more I looked at his footprints, the louder he laughed at me. Finally, I screamed, *"Shut up!"* and he did. I guess that does sound kind of nuts, but it worked. It made him stop laughing at me.

I lost my appetite. My head hurt and I was cold so I took more aspirin and got into bed. I dreamed that Grace and Willie were screwing. I was in bed with them and they were fucking and laughing and telling me to get out, but they didn't make me because they were having so much fun. Really, I wanted to get away from them, but I was all tangled up in the sheets and I couldn't get away. I felt like I was drowning. Then Grace started kissing me, all wet and hungry with her tongue going in my mouth, then she opened her eyes and saw it was me and started screaming at me to go to hell. Then she went back to Willie. They were both laughing. She had her back toward me, but she was looking right at me and laughing this incredibly dirty laugh.

I woke up covered with sweat, but I was still cold, and I had an erection. As I started to sit up in the bed, I swear I saw Willie standing in the corner by my desk. My heart jumped and I must have blinked, because when I looked again, he was gone. In that second, I knew I had to kill him.

fifty-one

I spent the weekend psyching myself for the Execution. By Sunday afternoon, I was wired. Grace had been out to brunch with some sleazoid real estate type, but she was back, screwing around with spreadsheets; still being an incredible bitch.

I don't think I had ever felt further from Grace than I did that Sunday. I wanted to ask her what she was working so hard *for*. I wanted to tell her what I was going to do. I felt excited and proud. I had let Willie mess me up for too long. With him gone, I could see myself going to a good college and making friends. I could see that without having Willie to worry about, I would be free.

I tried to go to sleep about seven-thirty, even though it was still light. I was so excited I couldn't stand waiting anymore. I couldn't sleep either; I started doing sit-ups and push-ups in my bedroom. I could hear Grace tapping away on her new "musical" calculator. She loved it: every key played a different note. She had no idea what was going on.

As I lay in bed, I remembered a night after I'd told her about Willie wrecking Grandad's headstone. I drove to her office. She was working late. I found her car and stuck an ice pick through one of the tires and put a note under the left wiper blade. It said she was being watched and called her a whore and a home wrecker. I put a big W at the bottom so she would think it came from Willie. I thought it might make her believe me; I wanted it to bring us together. She was pretty shaken up for a couple of days, but she never said a word to me about it. It blew me away. Then I realized my mistake: She *couldn't* tell me about it because she was ashamed. What my note accused her of was true.

I dozed off. About one-thirty Monday morning, I woke up again. Wide awake. My light was still on. There was a time when Grace would have checked on me and shut it off, but no more. I got out of bed intending to turn off the light, but instead, I went to her room. I stood at the foot of her bed for maybe twenty minutes. I listened to her breathing, and looked at the shape of her under the sheets. I wanted to touch her, but I didn't. She seemed so vulnerable in sleep. So innocent.

fifty-two

Monday. I dressed all in black. Black boots, baggy black paratrooper pants, and a black turtleneck. Hot for August, but intimidating. I even put a can of black shoe polish in my pocket so I could darken my face for camouflage, and to look more frightening. I carefully sharpened the nine-inch blade of the silver carving knife and rigged it up under my left pants leg, just like before. I wrote her a note that I was going to check out Princeton as a possible college and spend the rest of the day at the shore.

It was almost four o'clock in the afternoon when I left. I couldn't make my move before seven-thirty. From Thirtieth Street Station south, the expressway was stop and go. Once I got into New Jersey, I could see masses of tall thunderheads over Delaware Bay, fifty-thousand-foot tops. The sunlight hitting them from behind made their edges bright orange, like fire. All the clouds in between were pink and yellow. Periodically, I saw flashes of lightning.

I got to Villas about six-thirty. The entire field of glad-
ioli was in bloom. Every color from deep purple to hot
pink. Not only was it beautiful, but the stalks were tall
enough so they'd conceal my trek across the field to Willie's trailer. I took it as a good omen.

Willie's 'Vette was there, but I couldn't tell whether
he had anyone with him or not. I was set and ready. I
got the knife out and put it on the seat beside me. I tried
not to think about anything that would upset me. The
sky darkened overhead as the thunderheads moved on-
shore from the bay. The wind swirled in miniature tor-
nadoes over the gladiolus field. I smelled rain coming.
Suddenly, drops as big as grapes started hitting everywhere. Then the thunder and lightning arrived. It got a
lot darker. I tried to keep the car windows cracked open
so I could breathe, but I couldn't because the wind was
blowing in every direction and it was raining too hard.
The car started to shake. It was the hardest rain I can
remember. I couldn't see anything outside the car. I
thought of Dorothy in Kansas and how nice it would be
to end up someplace better when the storm was over.
The clouds blackened the sky till it was dark as night.
Rainwater poured onto my left foot through the vent
system. It started to hail. For an instant, I thought I
might panic. I cracked open the door beside me just to
be sure I wasn't about to float away. In that one second,
my neck and shoulders got drenched. Two minutes later,
it quit. I had never seen such a storm. The inside of the
car steamed up because the temperature outside must
have dropped twenty degrees in ten minutes. I opened
all the windows. Willie's 'Vette was still there. Puddles
pockmarked the road and fields as far as I could see.

Hailstones had piled up under the sign for the gladiolus farm.

It was nearly eight-thirty. The sun had set. There were goose bumps all over my forearms. The night bugs were clearing their throats. There was clear sky at the far edge of the bay. The air smelled wonderful, clean and fresh; full of nature, healthy and fertile. I had just started to reorganize myself when I saw Willie coming down his front steps with the blonde. Through the binoculars, I could tell he was loaded as usual, not really smashed, but the smile was too big and the movements kind of exaggerated. The woman was more out of it, laughing and hanging on his shoulder. I could tell he didn't give a shit about her. She knew the drill: into the 'Vette and back to Brown's. They never stayed over. In the space of ten seconds, Willie and the blonde were gone, and all of a sudden, it was time for me to start moving. I'm not sure why, but I wasn't ready for it to happen just like that. One minute, you're looking at this guy and waiting to see what he's going to do, and the next, you're supposed to get out of the car and start over there with a knife to kill him. It seemed like there should be something in between. But there was nothing. Willie and the floozie were gone and it was time for me to go. Ready or not. I tried not to think about it. I just got out of the car and started over there.

I felt really conspicuous, like I was in the middle of a three-ring circus. I tried to use the flower stalks for cover, but a lot of them had been knocked over in the storm. The sandy muck under my feet was covered with shredded petals and pea-size hail. It was actually pretty, like confetti. My feet got soaked. I could feel the knife in its sheath pressing against my leg. It gave me confidence. I kept going. The closer I got to the edge of the field, where the trailer was, the lower I tried to hunker down. Finally, when I was about six feet from the edge of the field, I squatted to check things out. It didn't take long for the gnats and mosquitoes to find me. From where I was, you couldn't really see anything but Willie's trailer and the little bit of yard he had behind it. It was about twenty-five feet to the front door. I figured I'd run to the near end of the trailer and then stay hard against the side until I got to the steps. That way, the wheelchair guy had almost no chance of seeing me. I was breathing hard and my chest was thumping. I checked up, down, and sideways about ten times. I stood and started to run at the same time; I slipped and damn near fell on my ass. Then, halfway there, I stumbled on some metal thing hiding in the weeds and practically broke my ankle. For what seemed like a long time, I stood panting with my back pushed against the trailer. "Forget this shit," I told myself. "You're going to screw up and ruin the rest of your life as bad as the first part." Then I heard a car on the gravel. Instead of running away, I went for the door. It was unlocked. He never locked it when he took them back. I went inside. The car or whatever just kept going. I was in Willie Smyers's trailer by myself and staring into a mirror. I had forgotten to paint my face black, but I was there.

The place smelled like wet dogs. There was a little air conditioner buzzing away, but it was losing out to the humidity. The mirror was on the far wall from where I was standing. It was round, cracked, and said "Babette's" in pink script across the top. There was some kind of gross belt or loop of something that looked like hair hanging on it. I checked to be sure I'd closed the door tight when I came in. I figured I had twenty minutes tops before he'd be back. Part of me wanted to run like hell away from there, but I kept thinking about what Willie had done to Grandad and what he was trying to do to me.

There was an old sofa across the end of the room where you came in. It was green and looked like a thousand gypsies had spent the night on it. In some places, the stuffing was hanging out. His fat recliner was brown and in about the same condition as the sofa. There was a coffee table with a stack of old newspapers on it and a bottle of booze and two glasses; also, a big red plastic ashtray half full of butts. The TV set was the biggest you could get at the time. There was also a flashy new stereo with all the bells and whistles. Courtesy of Grandad and me, I'm sure. The carpet was that shag crap, probably orange but so filthy it was hard to tell.

I took a few deep ones to settle myself. I can't say it worked, but it was better than nothing. Off to my left was the kitchen, with all the clutter and dirty dishes you'd expect. The little table was piled with paperback books and dirty magazines. Actually, not all the magazines were dirty, but most were. There was also *Time* and *National Geographic*, which surprised me. The books were about all kinds of stuff like wars and history and famous people. At the far end of the trailer, I could see the bedroom. I didn't go down there, but it looked like he had a water bed. I remember it had a fancy black leather headboard and shiny black sheets. Willie's Pleasure Palace.

I took a peek out the little window over the kitchen sink. It was a straight shot over to the wheelchair guy's place. Nothing was happening. It was getting dark. Time to get ready. I bent over and pulled up my left pants leg to get the knife. That's when I felt his gun against the bare skin above my belt. I jumped and banged my head against the counter.

"You're as crazy as I am, shitface," he said.

I straightened up, but kept my back to him. For the moment, I was too afraid to worry about the sharp pain where I'd smashed my head.

"Flashback seen you, two, three weeks ago when you first come snooping around. He told me. He don't miss shit around here. I been waiting for you to show up. Kind of shy, ain't you?"

I wanted to say something, but I didn't know what. I started to turn around.

"Don't move. I ain't that pretty that you got to see me just yet. You know, I never figured out what I was going to do with you when you showed up. I suppose I could just put one through your spine. That way, if you live, you can spend the rest of your life in a chair, like Flashback. He got his from a bullet, too. In Nam. Guy's a real freak."

I heard Willie open the door of his little refrigerator. A second later, he yanked the pull tab on a beer. "Let me go," I said. "There's about ten guys—"

He gave me a chop on the right side of my neck that dropped me to my knees. "Don't lie to me, shit-for-brains. Get this straight: You're a freebie. You busted in here. No way I'm gonna get locked up for blowing you away." He kicked me in the ass. "Stand up!" He started feeling me. At first, I thought it was a grope; then I realized he was patting me down like the cops do. He found the knife. "Pretty cute," he said. "You learn that off TV?"

"You can keep the knife, okay? It's silver. Just let me out of here." My voice was high and shaky. He grabbed my left shoulder and turned me around. He had the knife and a beer in his left hand and a revolver in his right. I could hardly see his face, it was so dark. He smelled of beer breath and bad cologne. "What about it? Can I go?" He stood so close I felt the heat of his body.

"You're scared shitless, aren't you, kid?"

"No." He stomped on my left foot. The pain made me yell.

"You're gonna have to tell me the truth unless you want me to waste you right now."

"I'm scared," I said. "Okay?"

He didn't answer me. Through the window near the sofa, I could see house lights, far away. I could hardly breathe. He reached around me and put the knife on the counter. It struck me as a sloppy thing to do. I wondered if he was drunker than he seemed.

"You want a beer, or don't they let you drink?"

"Are you serious?"

"Yeah, I'm serious. You and me have some talking to do and I don't like to drink by myself."

I didn't say anything. In the light from the refrigerator, Willie looked about seventy years old. I don't think he'd shaved in a week. He had on a yellow sport coat and a dark brown shirt with the top three buttons open. I guess he thought it was sexy. His pants were tan. The zipper flap was folded back under his belt and there was a big stain on his right thigh.

He handed me a Pabst with the same hand that was holding the gun. It was like he wanted me to jump him. He flicked a wall switch and an overhead came on in the kitchen. There was a piece of glass with painted flowers hanging under the bulb. I can still see the dead flies and moths.

"Go in there," he said. "Sit."

We went into the living room. I sat on the end of the sofa nearest the front door. It felt like my ass was on the floor. He sat opposite me in an orange plastic chair with black metal legs. He didn't look very comfortable. He reached over and pulled the chain on a floor lamp. The walls in the room were covered with fake wood paneling. Behind him, above the TV, there were these two pictures: in one, a bunch of dogs were playing poker, and in the other, a puppy with huge eyes was peeing on a guy's shoe. They didn't go with Willie, not at all.

"Flashback thinks the Cong is after him," Willie said. "Two summers ago, he tried to hire a couple kids to rig booby traps around his place. He's always seein' stuff. Mostly he imagines it, but every once in a while, he comes up with something. When he tells me there's some kid in a white Nova spookin' me from across the field, I figure he's jazzin', but damned if I didn't see you for myself. Flashie lent me this gun and said he'd keep watching. Tonight he calls and says you're back and he's got a feeling you're gonna make your move. I drove Dawn over my cousin's trailer in the next block and hot-foot it back here. I come in the patio door by the bed-room. I'm hidin' in the toilet and tryin' to get my breath when you come in. I figured you could hear me panting for sure.''

He waited for a response. I shook my head.

"So what are you after, the 'Vette or the TV? Or both?" He laughed and drank the rest of his beer. "Come on, spit it out before I call the cops. You're one of them kids delivered the TV, right?" My chest got tight, but there was no way I could let myself wimp out.

"I'm Billy McIlvain," I said. "You killed my grandfather six years ago and stole my inheritance." Willie's face went sour. He started to raise the empty beer can to his lips but stopped halfway and crushed it. I sat taller and tensed my legs to make a run for the door. Willie started fiddling with the gun. I said, "At least ten people know I'm here."

"Bullshit." He straightened himself and leaned forward. "Christ," he sighed. He looked at my beer. I hadn't touched it. He shook his head. "What did you think you were gonna do, kill me?" I looked down. "You're no killer. Pass that beer over here." I handed it to him. "What the fuck am I supposed to do with you, for chrissakes?

"Those fucking lawyers took damn near everything me and Buddy sued for. Did you know that? I swear our lawyers split their cut with the insurance company lawyers. Everybody loses except the fucking shysters, that's always the way."

Nobody said anything for a couple of minutes. I wondered if Willie had passed out with his eyes open because he didn't even drink. He just sat there staring at me. I could only try to guess what was in his head.

"I don't want to hurt you, kid," he said finally. "You

been hurt a lot already. The shysters told us your old man run away and your old lady's a lush. I know that's rough—"

"Don't talk about my mother, you fucking piece of shit."

"Look, I'm just trying to say I know how that can be. As far as your grandfather, I ain't proud of what happened that night and that's no secret."

"Then why did you steal the money?"

"Look, there's two sides to every story. . . . If I could bring back the old man, I would."

"Fuck off," I said. I almost yelled it. "You got a 'Vette and that fucking TV, and you're just getting started." Suddenly, I was angrier than I was scared. "You ruined my life. Go ahead and blow me away. I don't really care." I started to get up. He stood and pointed the gun in my face.

"Sit the fuck down. Right now." I did. "You want this fucking beer or not? I'm getting one. You might as well."

"I don't believe you," I said.

"I gotta figure out what to do about you," he said. "That don't mean I can't drink a beer at the same time. You, too. Might help your disposition." He put the beer back on the table in front of me and went to get a fresh one for himself.

"I knew it was you," he said when he'd come back and had a couple of chugs. "Pennsylvania license plate. Like I said, Flashie don't miss much. Then watching me like you did. No punk wanting to rip off the TV is going to go to that kind of trouble. I wanted to see how you'd go if I made out like I didn't recognize you. I gotta hand it to you for sayin' who you was straight out. How old are you?"

"Sixteen."

"You was ten that night. That's what I remember. Buddy and me was scared shitless despite of how it might of looked. Oh yeah, at first, we was just pissed and wanting to give you and gramps a hard time, but we were drunk and things got nuts. I guess we was showing off for Marie. After, when we had a chance to think about what we done, like I said, we was scared out of our minds. We knew you was rich and high class and they'd just throw the book at us, especially after you told how Marie sucked you off and all. We knew we couldn't escape. We figured our best chance was to blame it on the old man. After all, he was dead and there wasn't no bringing him back by us going to jail, was there?

"The lawsuit part, that was the lawyers' idea. I mean we fed them the same bull about how it happened as we told the cops, so they says, 'This Chesterton's president of a bank. He's loaded. You guys may not realize it, but what happened done you a lot of harm if you think about it.' Believe it or not, I did have blackouts, a couple anyway. And Buddy, well, he was already fucked up, so who's to say wasting the old man didn't put him over the line? After a while, we started to believe all the shit we was slingin', at least part of the time."

"You want me to *forgive* you?" I said. I couldn't believe it. "You're out of your fucking mind. I came here to kill you. I dream about killing you. If you've got the balls to kill me, just do it. Cut the crap and blow me away."

He shook his head. "I'm sorry we killed your grandad, kid. I am. There's days I can't stand to look at myself for it, even now. I have nightmares about it. So does Buddy. Shit, he's disappeared. Dropped off the map four days before the checks come. His family's worried sick. You think the cops give a shit? Forget it. Three months he's been gone."

"I'm really sorry things have been so rough, you know? How about explaining why you've been spying on me and busting into my home?"

"That's nuts. I don't even know where you live."

"You smashed my grandfather's headstone, you miserable fucker." For the first time, Willie looked worried. I was glad to see that I'd finally come up with something he didn't have an answer for. He started fidgeting with the gun again. "Go ahead, kill me, you pussy," I yelled. I grabbed the beer off the table and ripped the pull tab while he just stared at me with this weird look on his face. The beer was so cold it made my head hurt, right across the eyes. It wouldn't stop. "I just want you to know," I said after I gulped down more beer, "I think you're totally full of shit."

He started shaking his head again. "I thought maybe if you was willing to talk, we could talk . . . I decided to say I'm sorry. That's all. Trying to get some peace of mind. At first, I just figured I'd let you come in here and blow you away for breakin' in. Then I talked it over with Dawn a couple times and she says, 'Try sayin' you're sorry. Maybe the kid'll understand. Maybe now he's growin' up he can accept that. It's worth a try.' "

"You should have a telethon," I said. "You're breaking my heart."

"Believe what you want," he said, "even all that crap about the headstone and all. Why the fuck would I do all that stuff you were saying? I want to forget that night ever happened. If I do you, I'll never have any peace the rest of my life."

I was getting confused. I tried blaming it on the beer, and the pain in my head, but I was actually starting to believe him. And if I believed him, it seemed like it would change just about everything I'd been thinking for the past six years of my life. It seemed like it would change my life completely. Nothing was making any sense to me. I hated myself for being so confused. I asked him if I could have another beer.

He left the room and came back with two bottles of Colt 45 and two shot glasses. We were having a party. I'd spent hours and hours fantasizing about killing Willie Smyers, and here I was sitting in his living room and he was bringing us drinks. I couldn't figure out what the hell exactly was happening. I couldn't believe that he could just say a little bullshit like that and I'd be willing to sit there and drink with him. I actually felt like I knew him in a way, like an uncle or someone you don't see very often but you know them because they're part of your family. After I got past thinking how weird it was, I realized I *wanted* to drink with him. I fucking *wanted* to drink with *Willie Smyers*. I felt connected to him, like I felt connected to Grace. Sometimes you do something just because it's the last thing you ever expected to do.

He poured each of us a shot from the bottle of Four Roses on the table. He was wheezing. Some of the booze slopped out of his shot glass and dripped onto the shag as he went back to his chair. When he'd sat down, he raised his drink to me. "I'm sorry, kid," he said. "I really mean it. If I could do anything to bring the old man back, I would, and Buddy feels the same." Then he gave me a hard look I couldn't read and drank his shot. I took a swig of beer.

"I don't know why the fuck I'm sitting here with you," I said.

"You and me fought in the same war, Bill. On different sides, that's all. We both got hurt. You seen pictures of them guys from World War Two in the paper, haven't you? Germans and American guys on some battlefield in Germany, old and fat, having a beer together. We're the same. It was just a smaller war, that's all."

"Fuck off," I said. I was beginning to get a buzz from the beer. I didn't want Willie to know it.

"You plannin' on going to college, kid? Be a lawyer or something?"

"You're scared of me, aren't you?" I said. "You want to forget you killed my grandfather so you can enjoy his money, and here I am wanting to mess you up. You're not ready for that, are you? You don't think you can get away with killing me, at least not without a whole lot of hassle, so you're trying to suck up to me so I'll get out of your life, right?"

He pulled a mashed-up pack of cigarettes out of his jacket pocket and lit one with a pale blue Bic. "You're just like I was back when Buddy and me met up with you and your grandpop. There wasn't a fuckin' thing I didn't know back then. Six years can change a man. Yeah, I want you out of my life. I want that night to be over. Every fucking day for six years has been that fucking night. I wish to God none of it happened. I wish to

God I never went along with them lawyers and sued. But I did and now, here you are like you said, and I wonder just how much more rotten I'm supposed to feel and for how much longer. I'm twenty-eight years old and I feel like I'm sixty."

I remember, when he said he was twenty-eight, for a second, I thought he was joking. I'm not sure how old I thought he was, but a lot older than twenty-eight. When I was ten, I thought he was man-aged: thirty or something. I guess I had just added years to that as the time went by. It blew me away to realize he wasn't that much older than I was. It scared me. He was a man on the downhill side of his life if ever I had seen one.

"I want to show you something," he said. He got up and went into the kitchen.

While he was out of the room, I drank the shot. I didn't want him to see me do it, but I had been staring at it and wanting it. It burned going down. For a second, I felt sick and light-headed, but then it got better. I felt all warm and high in my face. My head didn't hurt anymore.

I straightened myself as he came back into the room. He stopped in front of me. I thought I saw him notice the empty shot glass, but I'm not sure. He was carrying the gun. I hadn't even noticed that he didn't have it when we were sitting there before. He pulled back the trigger with his thumb and extended his arm to aim the gun at me. I can still hear the crisp, clicking sound as the hammer ratcheted into the cocked position. My throat went dry and I felt like my temperature jumped thirty degrees. I thought, "He just wanted to get me drunk so there wouldn't be a fight. Now he's going to blow me away. I'm totally fucked. Dead."

He just stood there smiling and kind of swaying back and forth. He had the cigarette in his mouth. The smoke was curling up along one side of his face and making him squint. "I could blow your brains all over the back of that chair right now, kid," he said, "and there ain't a fucking thing you could do about it. I could bury you in the salt marsh and ditch your car in the bay and no one would ever be able to pin nothing on me. Ain't that right?"

I tried to answer him, but the first time, my throat was so tight nothing came out. The next time I said, "Yeah, I guess so." I could tell he knew I was scared out of my mind.

Then he surprised the hell out of me. He uncocked the trigger and handed me the gun. "That ain't on safety, kid," he said, "be careful."

I just shook my head and looked at him.

"Shoot to kill," he said. Then he stepped back and spread his arms out like they do in the movies. He nearly fell into his chair. He said, "I figure, let's get it over with right now. I don't want to have to go on feeling like shit for what I done that night, and I bet you don't want to have to go on thinking about whether you're gonna kill me and how to do it. So let's get it over with. I say you're no killer. There's a big difference between hating someone and thinking you want to kill them and really doing it. I couldn't do it, I know that. Not just cold-blooded blow somebody away. This way, it's over for both of us whether you pop me or not." He picked up the Four Roses bottle and took a couple of swigs.

I drank the last of my beer. The gun was warm and heavy in my hand.

"Go ahead, look inside," he said. "There's real bullets in there. Look at them. Just push that little slide thingie on the side there and the barrel flops out. Then you can tilt the gun back and the bullets come out. Blanks don't have no points on them."

I turned the gun toward my face. I could see the tapered points of the bullets in the chambers. I stood and pointed it at him. He took a step back and swallowed hard.

"You've got to pull back the trigger first," he said. "It don't cock itself." He took another long drink. "Now I'm scared," he said.

I cocked the gun and extended my arm toward him. I aimed for his face. He just stood there smiling this stupid smile, and rocking a little from the booze.

I lined the sight up just below the bottom of his nose. Steady as iron. I thought I wanted Willie Smyers dead more than anything; I imagined the flash from the barrel of the pistol as I fired, the explosion of gore as the bullet blew his head apart and he went smashing into the stupid dog pictures behind him. I could see the pathetic, dead expression on what was left of his face.

But I couldn't do it. He was right about that. He was right about something else, too: It was over.

"Fuck you, Willie," I said. I tossed the gun onto the sofa. It hit a book or something that was lying there and went off. I think it sounded probably ten times louder than it was. Both of us jumped back and nearly shit bricks from the shock of it. Then we laughed, and I went out into the night, unsure exactly what had gone on in there and why things had turned out as they did.

Halfway across the gladiolus field, I realized I had forgotten the silver carving knife. I didn't go back for it. I had a feeling Willie's trailer was as good a place as any for it to be.

fifty-three

I must have gone over it a thousand times driving home. I had a million different emotions, but mostly, I did feel better. I had to admit that all the stuff I'd been blaming on Willie, like the phone calls and the headstone, could have been done by someone else. Maybe that was him in the parking lot at school that day, and maybe not. I couldn't swear to it either way. I could swear that when he had a perfect chance to kill me, he didn't do it. Not only that, he'd given me the same chance to kill him. I don't know, there was a kind of trust there. That meant something to me. It was like we had a truce or something, and if he ever did start harassing me again or I found out he was lying about something, I could always go back and waste him.

I asked myself, "Am I being disloyal to Grandad? Should I have killed Willie for him?" I knew Grandad would have wanted what was best for me, like he did that night, like he always did; and I knew he wouldn't want me to live with having murdered someone else.

Besides, Willie had suffered. I believed that. All you had to do was look at him and you could see it.

As for Buddy, he had actually killed Grandad. I felt entitled to his life. At least.

I was still buzzing when I got back to the Main Line. Not from the booze; that had worn off. I was just pumped up from what had happened. At the same time, I felt totally exhausted. It was a strange combination.

It was a little after midnight when I pulled into Wyncliff Place. All I wanted to do was head for the rack. I needed the privacy to think. More and more, I had this huge feeling that something incredibly good had happened, but I needed more time to study it. I had to be sure. I had to try to figure out just what it meant.

I couldn't believe it when I saw that Grace had company. Jerry Bellarosa's BMW was parked diagonally across my slot and the one next to it. I found a place in the visitors' lot and parked there. After all we'd been through, the little Nova was finally starting to feel like *my* car. I was even starting to like it.

I found myself hoping that Grace and her boyfriend were in her bedroom screwing. I really, really didn't want to have to deal with them. I thought about going out again, but somehow what had happened had made me feel stronger. I made up my mind I was going to go in there and go to bed, and if Grace didn't like it, that was tough shit.

I could hear music playing inside as I stood at the front door getting out my key. It was Frank Sinatra or Tony Bennett, one of those guys that turn on women Grace's age. I should have knocked. Things got rearranged pretty fast, but Grace and lover boy were going at it hot and heavy on the couch. The top of Grace's dress was all pulled down so her boobs were hanging out, and Bellarosa had his hand inside the bottom part groping her crotch. It looked like she was tonguing out his ear. I wanted to puke. She jerked away from him and yanked her dress up the second she saw me.

"Christ Jesus, Billy," she said. "Couldn't you have knocked? Am I to have no privacy in my own home?" Bellarosa did a double take and stood up like I was Grace's father or something. His shirt was all open in the front. There were only a couple of lights on, but I could see that one of his nipples was all red and bothered-looking like she'd been sucking it. He didn't have any hair on his chest. Right away, he started buttoning his shirt.

"Sorry," I said. "Look, I just want to go to bed, okay?" There was a champagne bottle on the coffee table, and two glasses. I flashed back to the night Paul Schuyler's mother brought me home and we found Grace stone drunk on the floor. One glass of champagne, or the whole bottle, I had the same feelings of disgust and betrayal. I tried not to make eye contact with either one of them as I crossed the room.

She spoke as soon as I was out of sight. "I'm sorry, honey," she said. "I had no idea he'd come barging in here. . . ."

"I should leave," he said. I wanted to go into my room and try to forget what I'd seen but I couldn't. I stood there with my hand on the doorknob and listened like I was frozen or something. Like that, I felt totally shitty again.

"No!" she said. "At least now we know there won't

be any more interruptions." She laughed. "Let me freshen your drink. Come on, it's early. We're celebrating!"

"I'm gonna take off," he said. I smelled fresh cigarette smoke.

"No. . . ."

"You probably ought to say something to him. That was quite a scene he walked in on."

"Why should he spoil our evening? At least stay for a nightcap; we'll have one more toast to Wyeth Run."

"Give me a rain check. Now that you're not so uptight about having a glass of wine with the boss, we'll have lots of celebrations."

"I want you . . . ," she said in her little-girl voice.

"Look, Bev's taking the kids into New York to visit her sister Saturday. I'm all yours if you're interested. We'll check out that new bed-and-breakfast Len mentioned up by Chadd's Ford. Billy can have the place to himself. A handsome kid like that's not likely to be lonely if Mom takes a night off." Their laughter sounded mean and dirty. I went into my room and locked the door. I couldn't stand to hear any more. I felt like I was going to explode.

From inside my room, I couldn't make out the words of their conversation. After a few minutes, I heard the front door close. Then it got very quiet, almost spooky. I wanted to think she'd gone to bed, but I couldn't make myself believe it. All of a sudden, I got really tense and pumped up. My head started to hurt. I stood by my door listening. I was thinking of the night she tried to kill herself. I don't know why exactly. After all, she said she was celebrating. I heard something in the kitchen. I'm not sure what. I was dripping sweat and panting like something had sucked all the air out of the room. She put on a record. Tom Jones. More sex music for "The New Grace." She had it up really loud, like she was telling me to go fuck myself. I couldn't breathe. I opened the door just a crack. I could smell her, cigarettes and perfume, but more. Her. Not a smell *like* anything. It was Grace, a smell I'd known all my life.

I went out into the hall. Her bedroom was to my right, the living room and kitchen were to my left. I had no sense of where she was. She was everywhere. I was in her territory. I realized I was afraid, like a little kid who's done something wrong and is scared of the parent. But I didn't want to hide, that was the funny thing. I felt repelled and drawn to her at the same time.

I went along the hall toward the kitchen, slow and soft like I didn't belong there. I looked carefully around the last corner. There was a cigarette burning in an ashtray on the kitchen counter. The smoke was curling into the ceiling light above it. Beyond the kitchen was the living room, where she and Bellarosa had had their party. It was dark in there. Next to Grace's cigarette was a full glass of champagne. I could see bubbles rising through the pale liquid.

I thought again of the night she tried to kill herself. I remembered the bloodstained sink and the blood smeared over the white tile. I remembered her, leaning over the blood like some pale ghost of herself. I remembered the blood dripping out of her wrists, and the fine gashes she had made in herself, and the sweet pink flesh the parted skin exposed.

Her voice ran like ice water down my back. "Does it make you feel superior to spy on me?"

I spun around. She was at the far end of the hall, in the doorway to her bedroom. The light was behind her so it was hard to see her face. Her hair was all messy. She'd been wearing it up, but it was kind of half falling down around her ears.

"I just wondered where you were," I said.

"Bull. Jerry is one of the dearest, kindest men I've ever known, if you must know. He and I were celebrating. . . ." She started walking toward me, swaying a little. Not really drunk, but under the influence. In her bare feet, the top of her head was even with my nose. She hadn't changed out of the dress she'd worn for the boyfriend, a strapless thing made of shiny, light blue material. "I have nothing to explain or apologize for. He has the same kind of shitty marriage I did. Thank God, he and I can bring each other a little comfort."

"Forget it," I said.

"No, I won't forget it, buster. This was a very special night for me. The board decided to go full steam ahead with Wyeth Run. . ." She was directly in front of me. The light from the kitchen made her squint. Her lipstick was smeared. She looked fifty, at least. ". . . and I did the whole goddamn thing myself. Fighting. Working. Staying up all night with bids and contracts. I made it happen. And it was hell. Hell. And you have as much to gain as I do. More, and you didn't have to do a damn thing."

"Look, I said I'm sorry. Okay? Believe me, I'm no happier about what happened than you are. It won't happen again."

"You're damn right it won't. ..." She let out a huge sigh and brushed past me. The sigh made me yawn. She picked up the glass of champagne and turned toward me. I stayed at the end of the hallway, as far from her as I could. She raised the glass at me like a toast and drank. "Tonight was the first I've had anything to drink in more than five years, in case you were wondering. We may as well have it all out right now, don't you think?"

"That's up to you."

"I've come a long way, baby. I've been under incredible stress and tension. ..." I didn't want to hear anything she was saying. "God knows, I'm entitled to kick up my heels a little after what I've been through. Tell me, do you disagree with that?" She was so smug, so proud and sure of herself.

"I guess not," I said. "Can I go?"

"Just tell me one thing," she said. She was at the refrigerator. She got out the bottle of champagne and poured herself another drink. It overflowed onto the counter. "First of all, don't think I don't smell the beer on your breath." She took a drink. The glass was dripping. Some of the overflow dribbled onto her bare chest. She didn't seem to notice. "You may not believe it, but I know a thing or two about boys your age, and all I can say is I hope you're using condoms. You may think it's none of my business but if you get some girl pregnant, *then* it'll be my business and it'll be too late. Did you ever think of that?"

"You're out of your mind," I said. I wanted to yell and scream and tell her what a fucking whore I thought she was. I wanted to kick something.

"What?"

"You don't know what you're talking about. That's all."

"So what am I supposed to think you're doing out late at night, gone for entire days without ever a word of explanation? And, please, don't tell me you were playing baseball. Give me credit for having a little intelligence."

"I'm going to bed," I said. I turned to go. I was afraid of what was happening.

"Don't turn your back on me," she yelled.

I turned to look at her. She looked like shit. She looked worse than shit. "There's something else I intend to clear up with you right now. . . ." She refilled her glass. "Come with me."

She led me down the hall to her bedroom. I looked around to see what she had on her mind. "Look," she ordered. On the floor near one of the folding, mirrored doors to her closet was one of my weights, a dumbbell, twenty-five pounds.

"Sorry," I said. I picked it up.

"I have practically killed myself these last few years trying to support you and I think the least I'm entitled to is a little consideration . . . a little privacy. Tonight, I came in here to my own bedroom to change clothes and I tripped and practically broke my neck on this god-damn thing. You are not to come in here. Is that clear? For any reason, at any time. Do I make myself clear, mister? This is *my* space."

"O-*kay*," I said. There was this lump in my throat all of a sudden like I wanted to cry or something. I thought if I didn't get out of there in the next second, I was going to go nuts. I started toward my room.

"Sometimes I wonder why I bother," she said. "Really..." She grabbed my shirt as I was going by. "Just wait a goddamn minute," she said. The motion made her spill what was left of her champagne. "I'm not through with you." As she squatted and wiped at the champagne with her hand, the ash fell from her cigarette onto the wet spot and made a smudge. She tried to steady herself to stand up, but somehow she lost her balance and fell over on her side.

I was starting to get really hot inside, like there was lava in my veins. She looked up at me. Her face was all twisted and ugly. Marie had looked just like that when Grandad yanked her off me after he saw that she was sucking my cock. For a second, Grace just sat there on the floor, gross and pathetic, staring at me with that hateful expression. Then she said, "Go to hell," and time stopped.

Everything went black for a second and my body got full of electricity. I opened my eyes and Grace was a snarling bitch of a dog with a dripping red cunt and slobber drooling out of her mouth. I was terrified, but I knew I was seeing the truth. I couldn't move or breathe. Everything was frozen. I was being crushed.

Suddenly, I could move and breathe again and Grace was Grace. I yelled, "You fucking whore, it was *you!* My whole life, it's been *you!*"

She looked at me with burning eyes and said "*shit!*" like she was going to let me have it.

She tried to stand. I smelled the sour stink of champagne on her breath. When she was halfway up, she brushed against me and it was like she'd puked on me or something.

I shoved her away, pretty hard, I guess, because she fell over. Right there, I lost it. Without thinking, I heaved the dumbbell at her. It glanced off her forehead and landed in her lap. She howled like a dog and started backing away from me on her ass.

For a second, I wasn't sure what was happening or what I should do next. Then she started to scream for help, and I got really angry at her. I don't know why exactly. It really bothered me that she was screaming for help.

I picked up the weight. I didn't just want to stop her screaming; I wanted to hurt her. I threw it as hard as I could. It hit her on the shoulder and smashed into the mirror glass behind her. The whole panel shattered. Some of the glass fell on her shoulder and into her lap. Her face was all bloody from the first time I hit her. She kept sobbing and screaming for help. I couldn't believe what I was doing. It was like I was watching someone else. She started to move away from me, scrambling across the floor like a crab.

"Stop!" I yelled at her. I kept yelling it, *"Stop! Stop! Stop!"* She kept crawling and sobbing. She was halfway out of her dress.

"I've done everything for you," she sobbed. "It's all been for you."

I couldn't stand listening to her. I wanted to destroy her.

"I love you," she said.

I hated her for saying it. I hated her for everything.

She kept repeating it. I followed her. I felt helpless. She got to her bedside table and pulled the telephone onto the floor. I got on top of her and started choking her to shut her up. I felt like my hands were in shit. Her face was covered with blood from where the dumbbell hit her. Even with my hands around her throat, she kept saying, "I love you."

"I *hate* you," I said. "I fucking *hate* you!" I yelled at her to shut up.

She let go of the phone. Blood was streaming out of her nose. I got up and went to the other side of the room. I was crying. I turned to face the wall. I could hear her gagging.

I heard her behind me starting to say it again: "I love you. I love you." It was like she was saying, "You've got cancer. You've got cancer." She just kept saying it. I hated it more than I could stand. I knew she was just saying it to stop me from hurting her.

I went over there, trying as hard as I could not to look at her, and yanked the phone out of the wall. Then I went into the kitchen. I drank some of her champagne out of the bottle and washed the blood off my hands. I could still hear her coughing and sobbing. I hated myself for what I had done, but I hated her more. I was shaking all over. I'd cry for a minute and stop to think, and then I'd start crying again. I guess I'd been wanting to hate her for a long time.

I went into the bedroom. She was gone. I panicked for a second. I looked everywhere: in the closet, under the bed, out the window, places I knew she couldn't be. There was nothing left of her but bloodstains on the carpet and the side of her bed. Then I went to the door of her bathroom. There was no light on inside, but it was locked.

I sat on the edge of her bed. Soon I could hear her

breathing on the other side of the door. I got up and went to my room and got the barbell. I had 180 pounds on it. I came back and stood there with it in front of the door. I could hear her breathing.

I started swinging the barbell back and forth in the direction of the door, like I'd seen them do in movies with a battering ram. Her breathing got louder and faster, like she was doing it right inside my ears. I swung the weight in time to it. Faster and faster. I heard her heart beating. Then I saw the knob move. I swung the bar in a bigger and bigger arc until it was as high as my shoulders. Then I rammed it into the door next to the knob. As hard as I could. The weight smashed into the knob and the end of the bar went right through the door panel. The impact pushed the latch through the frame. She screamed as the door swung open.

She was up against the wall beside the tub, holding these little scissors, ready to stab me. She just kept moaning and sobbing, and yelling for help. She never tried to talk to me. It was like I was a total stranger or something. I don't know; it made me even madder.

I dropped the barbell on the floor. That scared her. The whole room shook. I flipped on the light. It was one of those movie star things with all the bulbs around the mirror. She took a couple of little swings at me with the scissors. I ducked away from the point and grabbed her wrist and took them from her. They were only a couple of inches long. I was looking at them in my hand as she tried to get by me.

I grabbed her by the hair and pulled her back. The tile floor was wet from her blood. We both slipped and went down. I hit my head on the side of the tub, but it was nothing. She squirmed desperately, like an animal, to get away from me. She was a stranger. She acted like she didn't know me. I started stabbing her in the chest over and over. I held her by the hair at the back of her head and just kept stabbing her, while she sobbed away. I must have done it a hundred times before it seemed like enough. She kept twisting to get free, even with all the holes in her. I was so angry I grabbed her head with both hands and slammed it against the tub. Then she was quiet.

It was completely quiet. It was like the Llanfair house after they took her to the hospital the night she tried to waste herself. It was just the two of us. I rested her head in my lap and just sat there like that for a long time. Somehow, even though she wasn't moving or even breathing that I could see, I knew she was still alive.

I wasn't scared anymore. I tried to think of some good memory of her. I looked at her limp face. My mother. Grace. I cried, but I didn't cry for her. I cried for the emptiness in my heart. I cried for all the hope I'd had for her, and us, and the life that we were never meant to have. I cried for how I'd thought things were supposed to be, and I cried because it was a lie.

When I started feeling tired, I got up carefully so her head wouldn't fall on the tile. When I was standing, I leaned over and picked her up in my arms. She weighed about 120. That was all. I lowered her body into the tub with her head away from the faucet so the water wouldn't splash her face. When I had let the water warm up, I closed the stopper and filled the tub. It took a while. When the water reached her nose, she twitched a little. I held her head down until there were no more bubbles. Then I closed the shower curtain. It was pink with huge red roses on it.

It took me a while to clean the place up, but I didn't think the mess was anyone's business. By the time I finally finished, it was getting light out. You could see a little piece of Montgomery Avenue through the living-room window. People were already going to work. It was a Tuesday.

Four more days until the weekend. Four more days till her date with the boss. I lay back on the couch and watched it get lighter outside. I felt a lot more peaceful than you would ever think. Even so, it took me a while to clear my head before I started to feel drowsy. Around 8:30, there was a man right outside the window running a lawn mower; I figured I'd never get to sleep, but I did. I dozed off right after that.

The phone rang a lot that afternoon; even more on Wednesday. I knew it was just a matter of time before someone came to check on her. It didn't bother me. I had no desire to run away.

I went through everything. Every speck of everything in that condo that belonged to Grace and me. I knew it might be a long time before I'd see any of it again, if ever. I wanted to remember.

One thing surprised me. In the very bottom of her purse, carefully wrapped in plastic, I found the note I'd written to go with the Christmas present I gave her after she tried to stop drinking the first time.

Dear Mom,
    Merry Xmas to a great, wonderful, beautiful,

kind, lóveing Mom. Your the best Mom in the whole world. I really love you and I know how hard its been for you to stop drinking alchol. I hope this is the best Christmas ever for you. You deserve it!

Its been a hard time for us this year, but I know we can do okay as long as we're togther. I will love you always and be your best friend.

I hope you like this candy. I wish I could give you a million dollars to show how much I love you. I read on the box that it isn't that much candy so I bought you some Hershey Kisses to go with it. I hope you like it. Happy New Year!

Love forever,
Billy

The purse was nearly new, so it wasn't as if she had just put the note in there six years earlier and forgotten about it. Besides that, she switched purses during the year. I assumed she'd moved it from purse to purse, each time she changed. Maybe twenty times in six years. It was hard for me to think about it. Sometimes, I wish I'd never found the stupid thing, but I've kept it with me, and a picture of her. It makes me sad, but it's all I have to remember her by.

I assumed that Jerry Bellarosa, the boyfriend, would show up at the condo Saturday; Sunday for sure. But nobody came until the following Tuesday. She'd been gone a week by then. It was some jumpy little lawyer from her office. He said he had to see Grace right away about Wyeth Run. He made out like it would be the end of the world if he didn't get to see her. I took him into the bathroom. I couldn't resist.

fifty-four

It's 11:45 here in Denver; 1:45 AM in Philadelphia. The Eve of Atonement. Why shouldn't I be tense?

There was a big thunderstorm earlier. A good omen, I think. It hailed. Hailstones the size of jumbo olives. The sound on the motel roof was frightening. I reach under the sheets and think of Cinnamon. I blame myself for the way it turned out. She's used to men who take control, men who'd have fucked her senseless while I was playing pussy with her roommate. I'm ashamed. My penis begins to respond to gentle strokes and the memory of Cinn's cunt rubbing my back. . . . Thoughts intrude of those "live girls" at the "bookstore" just north of here. The place has haunted me since I arrived. Like a dare. They have them in New Jersey. I never have the guts to go inside. But this one, so close, so far from home, on this of all nights. I am erect. I drink from the bottle of bourbon beside my bed. I imagine the writhing beauties waiting for me. Living images from magazines . . . red-lipped bimbos flaunting their cunts and tits and asses in settings from barnyards to yachts. The innocent blonde, bare-assed and bareback on a golden stallion; the sultry redhead sunning her gleaming flesh on a seaside boulder as the surf lashes her waiting crotch with white foam. I always resist the temptation to use them quickly. The eye must wander slowly, caressing each pore and pubic hair. . . . It takes me only a minute to dress and comb my hair. I drink again from the bottle.

The bookstore is lit up like McDonald's. It's a cinderblock building, same size as a 7-Eleven. No windows. There are three cars and two pickups in the gravel lot. I park the rental in shadows where I can see the door. My throat dries. I'm afraid. Of what? I take another drink, then get out of the car. How bad could it be? What chance in the world is there that anyone I know will be inside?

The door is red metal. A sign warns teenagers to stay out. My heart is pounding again. I tell myself it's only sex, not a bank robbery. No effect. My hand slips on the knob as I turn it.

The inside is a downer. No "girls" in sight, just a tiny reception area, brightly lit. There's a seedy-looking creep with stringy red hair sitting at a small counter covered with green carpet. Signs point in different directions to the bookstore and "entertainment" areas. The creep tells me it's five dollars either way. He's fiddling with a pack of generic menthol cigarettes. I'm turned off, but there's no way out. I give him five for entertainment. He tells me room 2. I need a belt of the bourbon.

There are three doors on each side of a narrow hallway. I find 2 and go in. There's a stool in a darkened space about four by six. Beyond is a larger, lighted, area.

In the middle of it is an easy chair, upholstered in black vinyl. The two areas are separated by a clear partition.

I sit down. There's a roll of toilet paper hanging from a wire bracket on the wall beside me. As a pneumatic closer shuts the door behind me, I notice an acrid smell. Foreign, yet familiar at the same time. I realize it's the stink of other men's jit, and I gag. The floor under my feet is sticky. In the dim light, I see shreds of toilet paper near my feet. I nearly vomit. I decide to leave. I'm half-way to my feet when a door opens in the back of the lighted chamber and a young woman in a night thing steps in. The light hurts her eyes. She squints for me in the darkness beyond the glass.

"Are you there, hon?" she asks. She's about the same age as Cinnamon, but harder looking. Stringy black hair. Olive skin. Round face. Five-five or-six. Ten pounds overweight. Big boobs bulging under the pale pink gown. Black panty hose, no shoes or slippers. Does the smell of jit turn you on?

I sit back down. I'll find out what five bucks bought me. "I'm here," I say.

"That's great," she says. She turns it around a few times so I get all the angles, then leans, with her hips cocked, against the chair. "Well," she laughs, "you here to party, or what?"

"Just do it."

She looks puzzled. "Ahh, you been in one of these places before?"

"No. No, not really."

She shows me that there's a drawer between the two rooms, and demonstrates it. I need to feed it money, she says, or the lights go out. Two bucks a minute. She slumps into the chair and starts rubbing her thighs. "Hmmmm," she says. "I'm hot to party, sweetheart, how about it?"

I miss the booze and the music. I can't understand why there's no music. I slip a five in the drawer and shove it toward her. She leaves the chair and goes to the drawer like a zoo animal at feeding time.

She frowns. "We'll hardly get started for this, hon." She raises her gown and shoves the five into her G-string. "How about five more, then you and me can have a good time?" I sigh and send her five more. She puts it with the first and starts a timer above the window. Soon she's slowly gyrating near the glass. Hips grinding. Hands rubbing her crotch. I'm getting hard again. "How's it going out there?" she asks. "I hope you're having as good a time as me. I can almost feel you inside me. Hmmm, you're so big! God!" I want her to take her clothes off.

"Take your clothes off," I say.

The lights go out. If that was five minutes, I'm a hundred-and-six years old.

"Oh, hon," she moans, "don't let it stop. Have you got a twenty? I just want to be with you." My hands are shaking. I'm hard and I don't want it to stop either. I find a twenty in the dim glow of the safety light above the hall door and feed the drawer.

"There," I say, "there's twenty." She turns on the light and examines the bill, all business. She blows me a kiss and stuffs it in her crotch with the other money. I wish she'd get back to it. She sets the timer.

"Take off your clothes," I say. "Show me your tits." She pulls the gown over her head. The bra matches her

G-string and gown. Soft silk cups, like the G-string but upside down. Her tits bulge out in all directions. "Get closer. Take off the bra." I drop my zipper, but it isn't enough. Soon, everything's down around my ankles. I'm standing and rocking. She's moaning and rubbing her nipples on the glass. I kiss the glass. She reaches up and rubs her whole body against it. "Do you love me, baby?" she asks.

"I do. I'm fucking you." I step back and pull hard on my dick.

"I'm Charelle," she says. "Remember me." She reaches for her G-string, to pull it down.

"No! No!" I yell. "Leave it alone!" She keeps pulling. I turn away. "Stop it, Goddammit, stop it! *Stop it!*"

I've never seen a cunt in life. Hers can't be the first. It can't.

fifty-five

TARGET/SUBJECT: *Charles Spencer Howe. Married. Wife: Deidre. Children: Andrew, age 5; Elizabeth, age 7. Occupation: Trustee, The Eli Gentry Foundation, Boulder, CO. Initial Contact: alumnae magazine, Sarah Lawrence College. Verdict: GUILTY. Sentence: EXECUTION.*

William C. McIlvain, age thirty-three.
Excerpt from my Private Computer Journal.
File Name: *Nemesis*

fifty-six

The earliest I've seen Howe leave the house is 8:34. It's 8:03, Thursday. I'm on their front walk. I tell myself over and over to be calm. I am in control. They have no reason to be suspicious. I have covered myself in every conceivable way. I swallow hard and ring the bell. Almost immediately, there's commotion on the other side: the dog barks; the kids fight over who will answer. Elizabeth wins. The door swings open. The sight of me disappoints her. I resist the urge to step into their front hall.

"Federal Express," I say, "for Mr. Charles Spencer Howe. Your daddy?" She screams for him. Both kids are in pajamas. Andrew has a quizzical look. Despite the uniform, clear glasses, and a lower voice, I wonder if he remembers me from the lemonade stand. The old dog remembers me; he's wagging his tail. Deidre comes, still in her robe.

"Sorry to disturb you, Mrs. Howe," I say, dropping the voice a bit further. "I have a secured delivery here for Mr. Howe. I'm afraid he has to sign." I bought the pouch, uniform, and a dozen envelopes from a prison contact for $300.

She frowns. All she sees is the uniform. "I'm afraid he's still dressing. Do you mind waiting a minute? I'll tell him to hurry."

"No problem," I say. She starts to close the door in my face.

"I'm sorry," she says. "Would you care to wait in the hall?" She opens the screen door. Our eyes never meet.

"Thanks," I say. I'm in. I position myself in front of the control panel for the security system. She scurries up the steps to fetch him. The children hang around me. In the pouch is a SIG-Sauer 9mm semiautomatic pistol, silenced. Every muscle in my body is tense. The anticipation is crushing. I hear them talking. He's speculating about who sent the package. I quietly close the front door behind me. "Old habit," I tell the kids. "My mother told me never to leave it open. No telling who might come in."

"What did you bring my daddy?" Andrew asks.

"Something very important. . . ." He's at the top of the steps, coming down. Still tying the tie, all dressed up for the big meeting. Deidre has stayed upstairs.

"Sorry to keep you," he says. I slip my hand into the pouch. This is it. I'm shaking. We're face to face.

"You don't recognize me," I say.

"What?"

"Take both of the children by the hand," I tell him. It doesn't register. I take the pistol out of the pouch and point it at him. The little girl starts to cry. "Take both of your children by the hand. Right now." He does. "Call your wife. No warnings. Tell her to get down here."

"Deidre," he yells. "Come down. Right away. I'm afraid we have a problem." Andrew is bug-eyed, sniveling.

"One minute!" she says. I nod.

"We keep very little cash in the house," he tells me, "but you're welcome to it. Anything. Just don't harm us, please."

I stand close to him so that she won't be able to see the gun as she comes down the stairs. "Do you have a closet that locks? For the children," I explain.

"That coat closet," he says. His voice is suddenly high and uneven, hardly a trace of the accent. "There's a key in the door."

"Put the boy in there, *now*."

"I want my mommy," Andrew screams. Elizabeth is sobbing. I point the gun at her.

"Put him in the fucking closet, Howe, or I'll shoot them both right here."

"What about . . . ?"

"Not her," I say, "not yet." He flashes me a look and drags his sobbing son to the closet. In the corner of my eye, I catch movement at the top of the stairs.

"Oh my God, Charlie, what is he doing?" She ducks out of sight.

"Get down here. *Now!*" I tell her.

"No!" she wails.

Howe is locking the closet. There's panic in his eyes. Lizzie sobs for her mommy. "Deidre, you've got to," Howe pleads.

I gesture toward the stairs with the gun barrel. "Up," I tell him. "Now." My head is pounding. "Faster." We

run up the stairs. Elizabeth stumbles; Howe drags her to
her feet. The old dog follows, barking now.

Deidre is hysterical. "No. No. My God, no!" She's in
the doorway to their bedroom, backing away, repelled
by me and drawn to her screaming daughter at the same
time.

"Hold it," I say. But she just keeps sobbing and backing into the room. Howe says something to her. Her eyes
are wild.

"No, Charlie. My God. Who is this man? What do you
want?"

"Stop right there," I tell her. She lunges for the alarm
system. "*Bitch!*" I fire three rounds into her above the
waist. She slumps to the floor, whimpering. The system
is still flashing standby. "Stupid bitch." I turn the gun
on him. The dog snarls. I shoot it in the head. It col-
lapses.

The little girl clings to Daddy and sobs convulsively,
"*Mommy . . . Mommy . . . Mommy . . .*" Tears spill from
Howe's eyes. He drops to his knees and crawls to Dei-
dre.

"It came to me one night when I was in prison," I tell
him. "I was about twenty-five. You were selling penny
stocks in Reno and Deidre was just a fantasy fuck. The
shadow on the road. In fifteen years, I'd never thought
of it. Can you believe that? The shadow. They knew we
were coming. The night it hit me, it was like a miracle.
The fucking shadow, Ned. One of them covered up the
stop sign when he saw Grandad's car coming. He must
have signaled the driver with a light or something. Once
I figured that out, it all came together."

"Let me call a doctor. Please."

"I'm your *son*. Isn't there anything you want to *say* to me after twenty-three years?" I catch myself yelling and bring it down. "Haven't you ever been sorry for any of it?"

"At least let me put my daughter in another room where she doesn't have to see . . . this," he sobs.

"That's how Willie knew about Grace's drinking. You told him. You put them up to it for the money. And when there wasn't any money, you told them to sue. A few months after I remembered the shadow, I saw the picture. You and Deidre. God delivered you to me just like that."

"I won't turn you in," he begs. "We'll swear it was an accident."

"Forget 'We,'" I say. "She's dead; I know the look. Willie's disappeared. I can't find him. I found out he moved two weeks after the night I was there. Tell me where he is and I won't kill your kids, Ned. *Tell me!*" He grabs my legs and begs.

"In the name of God, I'm *not* this man!"

"Green eyes, Ned," I say, allowing myself a taunt, "just like mine. Freckles, too." He looks up at me with weak and pleading eyes. "Where did Elizabeth get those pretty green eyes?"

"I implore you. . . ." The little girl looks at me strangely through her tears, as if, on some level, she knows.

I step away from him. Too much sniveling. "You make me sick, Ned," I say. I step back and fire one round into his precious Lizzie's freckled face. Baby doll drops in a heap to the floor. Ned throws himself over her, a pair of cats snuggling on a sofa. I relish the silence. I hadn't realized how her crying grated my nerves.

"No! No! No!" he sobs, pounding the floor. *"I can't stand this."*

"You brought it on yourself, you miserable fuck." I am numb. I have lived this a thousand times in my mind. "Get on the bed, or the boy is next, I swear it."

He looks at me like something from hell, but he obeys.

"Take off your clothes." I get some panty hose from Deidre's dresser. "Don't worry," I tell him, "I'm not gay." He's quiet now, submissive. The guilt of all the years has caught up with him.

When he's naked, I tie him to the bed, face up, spread-eagled. He stares at the ceiling and cries silently. I want to speak to him. To talk. There is so much to say. There is nothing to say. We are strangers. We have always been strangers. He won't even look at me.

I take the butcher knife from my pouch and plunge it into his crotch. That gets his attention. He screams. As he writhes to break free of the ligatures, blood gushes from the flesh above his dick and floods over the sheets. Using both hands, I work the knife around his dick and balls. I'm hard. There's nothing sexy about cutting off your father's reproductive organs, but somehow, I have an erection. I can't help laughing at the irony of it.

His organs are hardly recognizable for what they are, severed from his body. I put the gun barrel against the side of his head. "Say 'ahh,' Ned. *Say it.*" The sound he makes would hardly qualify as a proper *ahh*, but it serves the purpose. I stuff the gory mass of his genitals into his mouth. "Chew," I command, "for little Drew's sake, Daddy." He vomits without swallowing, but I've made my point. I fire a single round into the side of his head. The Black Curse rises from my soul.

I step back and look at the death around me. The scene is vile, but the cancer is vanquished. The patient has used his only option for survival. As firstborn, it was my right.

I look at Deidre, wishing I had witnessed the precise moment of her death. She reminds me of Grace. I hadn't noticed it before, but the resemblance is definitely there. They say we keep marrying the same person over and over again. I wouldn't know.

Deidre's luscious red lips are freshly glossed, ready for the day's amusements. They speak to me in their own silent, sensual language. An impulse. An opportunity. We are alone. I drag her to the side of the bed and prop her against it. I spread the front of her robe, loosen my pants, and plant my feet on either side of her. Her mouth falls open as I push her head onto the top of the mattress; she's looking up at me. Waiting. Yearning. I kiss her, then stab my needy cock between her lips. Onto her tongue. So warm and moist, still. Ancient sensation. Bliss. I close my eyes and fuck. It's sublime. "Suck me, Deidre. Fuck me. I love you. . . ."

Everything we do is meant to be.

There was a cluster of five tiny moles on Ned's back, right below the left shoulder. They reminded me of a star when I was little. I look. They aren't there. I check the other side. Their absence is meaningless. Such things are easily removed by lasers.

It takes me nearly an hour to clean up. I remove all connecting traces of myself, everywhere, including Deidre's mouth. . . . The best people gargle with Drano.

In my Federal Express pouch is a nylon backpack. I put the gun, knife, and uniform in it and put on one of Ned's jogging outfits.

I hear Andrew whimpering as I prepare to leave. I've left him plenty of food. He will grow up alone, the way I did. He will become strong like I am. He's my brother. And if he ever comes for me, I will welcome the sweet mercy of his revenge.

When the sidewalk is clear, I slip out the back door, just another Boulderite, albeit a pale and slightly flabby one, out for a morning run. It's a beautiful day. I feel clean and full of hope. The malignancy is excised. The circle is closed.

fifty-seven

I've left the Subaru in a Park-and-Ride lot about ten
blocks away. Nobody notices me get in and drive off.
At a Safeway near the entrance to the Boulder Turnpike,
I put the nylon backpack in a black plastic trash bag and
heave it into a dumpster.

I not only save forty dollars by flying back Thursday
but win a seat assignment next to a pair of empties on
the shady side of the plane. I wonder when they'll find
Ned and the others. A week went by before anyone took
the trouble to look for Grace. Are any of us as connected
to the world as we like to think? I treat myself to three
of those tiny bottles of Jack Daniels. I know I shouldn't
feel smug about pulling it off, but I do.

Thanks to Jack D., I'm half asleep when the captain
announces that we're over St. Louis. I'll catch it next
time. I'm going to ask Cinnamon for a date when I get
back. Dinner, a movie, anything she wants. It's time for
our relationship to move forward. I feel tremendous energy for our future.

The stewardess offers me coffee, but I want to sleep. I want to dream. I close my eyes and breathe deeply. Before long, I'm in the warm, friendly place where I feel safe.

I'm fishing with Grandad, the way we have a million times before.

fifty-eight

TARGET/SUBJECT: *Norman Edward Sturt. Divorced. Ex-Wife: Carol. Children: James, age 19; Rebecca, age 17; Robert, age 11. Employment:* Director of Athletics/ Varsity Tennis Coach, St. Anne's Academy, Seattle, WA. Born: Manchester, England. Initial Contact: Court & Racquet *magazine, July 1993.*

It's Ned. This time I'm certain.